The COLOR *of a* SILVER LINING

JULIANNE MACLEAN

Cover Design: The Killion Group, Inc.
Interior Formatting: Author E.M.S.

CHAPTER
One

Bev

Halifax, Nova Scotia

On the day the tall ship *Dalila* went down, taking all its passengers—including me, my sister, and my five-year-old daughter Louise—into the cold waters of the Atlantic, I had just turned thirty years old. I was a single mother and had started to notice a few wrinkles I'd never had before, and the odd gray hair in my curly blond locks.

As for *Dalila,* she was a magnificent, recently refurbished 153-foot, three-masted square-rigger. She was commissioned in 1936 and worked as a support vessel for fisheries in New England and appeared in several movies for the big screen in the 1980s and '90s. In recent years, she'd become a tourist attraction at Halifax Harbour, Nova Scotia, taking landlubbers on day trips around Sambro Island to view the oldest surviving lighthouse in North America.

It was my sister Claire who convinced me to get onboard that day, because it was something we'd talked about for years. She insisted that my thirtieth birthday deserved a special celebration, something I could tick off my bucket list, and a voyage aboard *Dalila* had been sitting on that list for a while. What sealed the deal was the fact that my daughter had become fascinated with sailing ships after watching *Pirates of the Caribbean*, and she was desperate to go "on a big pirate boat."

So off we went—just the three of us: Claire, Louise, and me—while Claire's husband Scott stayed home to take their four-year-old daughter, Serena, to a birthday party.

As it turned out, it was a good thing they didn't join us. It meant there were two less loved ones to worry about when the wave hit.

~⊘~

The sky was blue and the forecast clear when we stepped onto the gangway in downtown Halifax that morning. It had never even entered our minds that it might be a bad day to go sailing.

In addition to sixteen crew members, there were twenty-five passengers booked for the voyage. Claire, Louise and I were first in line on the wharf, so while other passengers were still arriving, we explored the ship, craning our necks to look at the tops of the masts, which seemed to reach halfway to the sky. We walked around the main deck, marveling at the complex rigging and the sheer volume of rope everywhere we looked.

Louise had always been a mindful, sensible child—surprisingly mature for her age—and she was well-behaved. As always, she kept to a walk when she might have preferred to break into a run toward the bowsprit.

After we'd seen everything on the top deck, we

ventured below to the main hold—an impressive, wide-open space with a gleaming oak floor and knotty antique planks forming the hull.

"Feels like we're inside a giant wooden barrel," Claire said as she fingered the wrought iron hardware holding the planks together.

"That's not a disturbing thought at all." I raised an eyebrow at her while Louise danced around on the expansive deck.

Claire and I turned to watch her do a few pirouettes and pliés, which she'd learned in ballet class. Her blond curls bounced as she moved, and the smile on her face melted my heart. She curtsied and we gave a round of applause.

Continuing our exploration toward the forward deck, we found the galley—an ultra-modern kitchen with the newest technologies—and back toward the stern, through a narrow passageway, we came upon a number of small private cabins for the crew. The captain's quarters were located aft and spanned the full width of the stern.

"It's very luxurious, isn't it?" Claire said quietly as she peered in at the varnished oak furnishings, shiny brass fittings and crimson upholstery.

Louise was about to run in and climb onto the bed, but I held her back. "I don't think we're supposed to do that, sweetheart," I whispered gently.

She gave no argument, then followed Claire and me back to the companionway that took us up to the top deck. By that point, other passengers were exploring below deck as well.

A short while later, it was time to depart.

"Everyone is welcome to take a turn at the helm today," our captain explained as we motored away from the wharf. He was a handsome older gentleman, very distinguished looking in a navy blazer, white trousers, white shoes and a smart-looking captain's cap. "Our crew members are expert sailors and if you're interested, they'll be happy to show you how to set sails, assist with maneuvers, and once we're beyond the mouth of the harbor, I'll talk to you all about navigation, weather observations as well as plenty more. Now…" He spread his arms wide. "Are you all ready to see this gorgeous girl leave the harbor under full sail?"

We all cheered and clapped as the crew set to work.

"It's going to be such a fun day," I said to Louise, hugging her close and kissing the top of her sweet head. She wiggled with excitement on the bench, and Claire and I shared a happy glance.

We learned later that the crew could never have predicted the extreme wind gusts that would slam into the *Dalila* shortly after we circled Sambro Island, nor could they have done anything to save the boat. What happened was a meteorological phenomenon called a "micro-burst," which is an abrupt downdraft during a thunderstorm. The wind shoots straight down from the clouds and bounces off the ground or water. Typically, it affects less than a two-and-a half mile geographical area, and wind speeds can reach hurricane force in a matter of seconds. It's very precise. If you're near the bullseye of a micro-burst, it's almost like getting struck by lightning.

First came the rain, but that wasn't a surprise to any of us, as we'd seen bad weather approaching from the horizon. The crew donned their foul weather gear, and as soon as the rain was upon us, the captain ordered us all to the main hold below to stay dry, while assuring us that he and his crew had sailed in far worse weather than this.

Down we went to the place where Louise had danced pirouettes a few hours earlier, and where they had served us a delicious hot lunch just before we reached the island. There were no portholes in that section of the ship so we couldn't see out, but we felt the intensifying movements of the ship through roughening seas.

There was a sudden crash of thunder that seemed frighteningly close, and Louise started to cry.

"It's okay, baby, don't worry." I scooped her into my arms and steadied myself against the center bulkhead. "It's just a thunderstorm. And the captain knows what he's doing."

The ship pitched and rolled, and one of the other passengers—an older lady in her sixties—began to complain to her husband that they should have simply taken the ferry back and forth to Dartmouth like she wanted, rather than get on a sailing ship headed for open water. It would have been far cheaper, she said, and they would be on dry land by now. They continued to argue about it.

I was beginning to think the ferry boat sounded pretty good at that point, because I'd never been a risk taker when it came to wild adventures. I was a nurse in the city hospital, so I'd seen enough broken bones and concussions to steer me away from unnecessary risks to the only body I had. Yet here we were, on an old-fashioned square-rigger, riding violent ocean waves in the middle of a thunderstorm.

"The captain seemed confident," Claire said to me,

rather uncertainly, as she grabbed hold of the center post and braced her legs farther apart. "I'm sure he'll get us out of this. Right?"

"Of course," I replied, swallowing hard over a sudden surge of seasickness in my belly.

All the passengers grew quiet, even Louise, who remained very brave in my arms and didn't cry. I suppose we were all too petrified to speak. It went on like that for a while, with the floor pitching and rolling beneath us while we fought to hold on to whatever was fastened to the floor or walls.

Then suddenly there was great roar from topside, as if it had come from a supernatural beast in the sky, and water came sloshing down the companionway.

The ship heeled sharply to starboard and we were all thrown against the hull. I tried to hang onto Louise, but I didn't want to crush her as I slammed into the wooden planks and iron fittings, so I let her go and she flew out of my arms, catapulting into another couple and landing on top of them.

When I gathered my senses and looked up, I realized that the ship was on her side.

"*Louise!*"

"*Mommy!*"

Everyone started screaming. I climbed over a man to reach my daughter, while Claire followed beside me.

"Are you two okay?" she asked us.

"Yes, are you?"

"We have to get out of here!" someone shouted in a panic, and everyone began scrambling to clamber out of the hold.

Water was pouring in through the main hatch, and some

of the passengers pushed and shoved to be first up the companionway steps, which was no easy task when the ship was lying on her side and heaving on enormous swells.

A man held up his hands. "Everyone stay calm! One at a time!"

He assisted some of the older passengers up the sloped floor and helped me lift Louise past the rushing water. Two crew members appeared at the open hatch and reached their arms down to us.

"Give us your hands! We'll pull you up!"

Above, they were being battered by wind and rain and I could only imagine what they must have gone through in the past five minutes while trying to keep the ship afloat. As I stared up at them in awe, it all seemed like a terrible nightmare. It had been sunny and clear when we stepped aboard that morning. How could this be happening?

"Give her to me!" a crew member shouted, reaching his hands down to Louise. The wind blew his hair in all directions while he beckoned her forward. I didn't want to send my child out there. I didn't want to go out there myself, but I knew we had to.

"Maybe we should stay here!" an older lady shouted from behind me. "It looks too dangerous!"

"If you stay down there, you'll drown!" the crew member replied. "The ship is sinking. We have to get you in lifeboats. Hurry! Give me the little girl!"

Out of nowhere, crew members appeared behind us, wading through the frigid seawater that was quickly filling the hold. They must have entered from some other passageway near the stern.

They began handing out lifejackets to those who weren't wearing them, and shouting instructions to get us all out in an orderly fashion. I was grateful to see them, and grateful for their competence.

They began the evacuation while ice-cold water sloshed around at our feet. Within moments it was at our knees. Then we were waist-deep.

"*Mommy, no!*" Louise screamed as I handed her up to the crew members above, who took her by the arms and lifted her out. For a blistering second, I couldn't see her. My heart raced as I hurried to follow, to stay with her.

Someone tried to push in front of me. A man. I shoved him back, glared at him and shouted. "That's my daughter! Wait your turn!"

I scrambled up the sideways ladder, through the hatch to the outdoors, where the wind hit me like a speeding truck. A crew member grabbed my arm but I immediately lost my footing and slid down the vertical deck toward the churning, raging sea. The sails floated on the water. There were ropes and lines everywhere along the bulwark.

I don't know what happened after that. I think I must have hit my head and fallen into the ocean, because I woke up coughing and sputtering in an inflatable yellow life raft. A young, female crew member was leaning over me, frowning with concern. "Are you all right?"

She was drenched and so was I. There were three other people in the boat with us, but I didn't know them.

"Where's my daughter!" I screamed, sitting up, my panicked gaze darting around as the wind and rain struck my cheeks. "Louise!"

"She must be in one of the other rafts!" the girl shouted, sitting up to blow a whistle.

I tried to look for another boat somewhere, but we were being tossed about on giant swells and it was near impossible to make out anything. Then I spotted *Dalila* on her side, her great sheets of billowing canvas filling with water.

My heart nearly pounded out of my chest, and white hot-terror flooded my bloodstream. "Louise!" I shouted again. "Louise!"

I crawled to the side of the raft to look over the side, scanning the whitecapped sea and searching for my daughter. Then I saw another yellow raft near the stern of the ship. It was full of passengers.

"Louise!" I screamed at the boat. "Claire! Anyone! Is my daughter with you?"

"They can't hear you over the noise of the waves," the girl shouted. "Please sit down or we'll lose you over the side again."

"But did they get everyone into the lifeboat?"

"I don't know."

I fell onto my behind, buried my face in my hands, drew my knees to my chest, and began to pray. "Please, God, let my baby girl be okay. Let her be safe. Please don't take her away from me."

"My God." The woman beside me spoke the words in a low, horrorstruck voice.

I looked up to see *Dalila* rolling over so that her masts were pointing straight down. All we could see was the bottom of her hull. She bobbed there for a few seconds, then her stern went down and she sank beneath the surface. A second later, she was gone.

I put my hands together and prayed that everyone had gotten out. The woman beside me did the same.

Then I heard something. Someone was calling my name.

I scrambled to the edge of the raft and looked over the

side. Panic and terror rushed into me, and I pointed at someone in the water, bobbing up and down on the enormous breakers. "There! I see someone!"

The female crew member in command of our little lifeboat dove over the side and swam toward the struggling survivor. Only then did I hear it again—the sound of my name over the din.

I realized it was my sister Claire in the water.

I called out to her as loud as I could. "Hold on!"

Her head disappeared beneath the surface and I almost dove in myself, but the crew member reached her and pulled her back up. She began to swim toward us, dragging Claire to our lifeboat. Only then, when they were close, did I realize that my sister was holding onto Louise, who did not appear to be conscious.

CHAPTER

Two

Bev

One, two, three.... *Come on baby, wake up.*

I'd been pumping my daughter's chest for more than five minutes in the life raft, with the assistance of the female crew member who was taking care of rescue breaths, but Louise wasn't responding. I fought to stay focused and clear-headed and remember my training, while the mother in me wanted to collapse in grief and just hold my baby in my arms, rock her, beg and plead with her to open her eyes, tell her everything was going to be okay. But I couldn't do that. I had to keep fighting to save her. Chest compressions—*one, two, three, four, five...*

"What's your name?" I asked the crew member, trying to keep my mind focused as I sat back on my heels.

"It's Susan," she replied, between breaths.

"I'm Bev." I shook out my arms to prepare for more compressions, but nothing was making a difference. Louise wasn't breathing and she had no pulse. Her tiny body was as cold as ice.

But I couldn't give up. I'd never give up.

Suddenly I heard the beat of helicopter blades in the sky

overhead and realized only then that the force of the wind had slowed in the last few minutes. The rain was falling more softly. I glanced up and saw a red Coast Guard chopper with divers at the open door, ready to jump.

Down they came, splashing into the churning water nearby with a rescue basket. One diver swam toward the other raft while the second came our way. Another chopper arrived with two more divers.

Meanwhile, I was still performing CPR on my daughter, and I had no intention of stopping.

When the diver reached our raft, he grabbed onto the side and pulled the snorkel mouthpiece out of his mouth. He saw what I was doing. "Let's get her out of here!"

"She's not breathing!" Susan shouted. "She needs to get to a hospital!"

That was obvious.

The diver shoved the basket up over the side and into the raft, but I didn't want to put Louise in it because I'd have to stop CPR.

"Do you have a defibrillator in the chopper?" I asked, still doing chest compressions.

"Yes! We've got an AED. Let's get her up there!"

Claire helped steady the basket in the center of the raft while I lifted Louise's tiny, cold body and placed her inside. It was a challenge because the swells were still enormous and we were rising fast over the crests, then sliding down into the troughs.

The diver made sure Louise was secure, then he signaled to the chopper pilot to quickly hoist her up. As she rose out of the raft, I fell to my hands and knees, finally breaking down into an agonizing fit of sobs as I watched her go.

"Please, save her!" I cried as I looked up, even though I

knew they couldn't hear me over the noise of the chopper and the waves.

Claire wrapped her arms around me while I wept uncontrollably, never taking my eyes off Louise until she was safe inside the helicopter.

$\sim\!\mathcal{O}$

The chopper hovered there for a moment, then the basket was lowered again.

"Why aren't they going?" I asked the diver who was still in the water, hanging onto the side of our raft. "She needs to get to a hospital! They could come back for the rest of us." I was incredulous and nearly hysterical.

"We've got a paramedic up there," he replied. "Your daughter's in good hands. Let's get you up."

The basket dropped into the water. The diver swam to fetch it and bring it back.

Everyone agreed that I should be next because Louise needed me, and I didn't argue. I got in as quickly as I could. When the basket lifted me up, I realized I was shaking uncontrollably from both the cold and the unimaginable trauma of the past ten minutes. With teeth chattering, I clutched the metal cage with numb, aching fingers, praying continuously that Louise would be okay, because I couldn't lose her. I loved her more than life itself. If she died, I was certain I'd die too. I'd never get over it. I'd never stop crying or blaming myself for losing sight of her, for not being able to save her.

The noise from the chopper engine and spinning blades was deafening as I was hauled up to the giant red machine hovering above. I looked down at the two yellow life rafts below, where others were being plucked out of the frothing ocean. A fishing boat arrived just then and approached the second lifeboat. They threw a ladder over the side.

I looked up again. With every inch that brought me closer to the helicopter, I was more desperate to reach Louise.

At last, I felt the pull of the cable as the basket was dragged inside.

"How is she? How's my daughter?" I asked, my gaze darting wildly around the interior of the chopper.

She was on a gurney, tucked under a blanket, strapped in.

"*Mommy!*"

A rush of relief flooded my body. I burst into tears and fought like a wild creature to get out of the basket and reach her.

"Louise, I'm here!" I scrambled on hands and knees across the floor and buried my face in her tiny neck, where I wept uncontrollably. *Thank God...*

I was vaguely aware of the paramedic wrapping a blanket around me.

"Your nose is cold," my daughter said in the sweetest voice imaginable, though she seemed weak and groggy.

My tears turned to laughter, and I drew back to look down at her angelic face. I pushed her wet curls away from her forehead and kissed her cheeks.

"It was chilly down there," I replied, rubbing my nose against hers, "but we'll both be warm soon. Everything's going to be okay now, sweetheart. You're safe."

I gazed down at her for a joyous moment. My love for her was bursting out of me. I felt so incredibly blessed. I never knew such a release of pain and fear.

"Is Auntie Claire okay?" she asked, weakly.

"Yes, she's fine. They're bringing her up soon. But how are you feeling? Are you okay?"

"I'm tired. Are *you* okay?"

I laughed. "Yes, I'm great."

I turned to the paramedic who was waiting for the next arrival. "Thank you so much for bringing her back!" I shouted to him over the noise of the chopper. "There are no words to say how grateful I am!"

He handed me a headset to put on, then spoke to me through the microphone. "I saw you doing CPR down there. You were the one who brought her back, not me. She was conscious when I pulled her in here."

My surprised gaze swept back to Louise on the gurney, and the paramedic approached to put a headset on her as well.

"You woke up in the basket?" I asked her. "That must have been scary." My poor, darling girl wouldn't have known what was happening to her. She would have been confused and disoriented.

Louise blinked a few times. "I wasn't scared. Grampy was with me."

The chopper lifted slightly on a gust of wind.

I inclined my head at her, puzzled. "What do you mean...Grampy? Who are you talking about?"

My father had passed away when I was ten years old, so Louise had never met him. As for her paternal grandfather, I was a single mother and Louise's father and I weren't together. In fact, I knew very little about him. We'd only spent a weekend together. He didn't even know about Louise, and I had absolutely no idea if his parents were still alive.

"Grampy," she repeated, as if I should understand. "Your daddy. He's in heaven now."

Heat pooled in my belly, and my heart began to pound. "Is that where you were just now?" I asked, gently. "In heaven?"

She nodded, and I cleared my throat.

"What did…" I paused and swallowed uncomfortably. "What did your grampy look like?"

Louise wet her lips. "He had brown hair and a mustache and happy eyes that smiled at me. He told me not to be afraid. But I wasn't afraid. I was just sad."

Not entirely sure what to say, I glanced over my shoulder at the paramedic to see if he was listening through the headsets. He must have been, because he raised his eyebrows at me.

"Why were you sad?" I asked, turning back to Louise.

"Because I didn't want to come back. I wanted to stay there."

"Why?"

She shrugged. "I liked it. I flew over the clouds, and it wasn't rainy up there. The sunlight was pretty. But they all said I had to come back."

I felt breathless and shaky. "Who's *they*? Who said that?"

Just then, the basket clanged against the side of the chopper with a fierce gust of wind. Claire was inside, shivering in the wind. The paramedic pulled her in.

"My God, she's okay!" Claire said. "Louise!"

My sister climbed out of the basket and crawled toward us. I threw my arms around her and we embraced tightly, each of us crying our eyes out.

"Thank God she's all right!" Claire shouted over all the noise. "I was so worried."

"Me too, but you saved her in the water. You didn't let her go."

Only then did I realize I had no idea what had happened to Louise, exactly. They had been out of my sight for those crucial moments before *Dalila* sank into the depths.

"How did you end up in the water in the first place?" I asked Claire, still shouting. The paramedic handed her a headset as well. "The last thing I remember, we'd handed Louise up through the hatch…"

Claire nodded as she adjusted the microphone around her mouth. "Yes, and you climbed out of the hold next, but you fell into the water right away. One of the crew members went in after you—it must have been Susan—and another one had Louise in his arms. I'd just climbed out behind you when another big wave hit us and swept us all overboard. I was scared but I just kept screaming your name and Louise's name, and then I saw her in the water, in the middle of the sails and rigging. I swam to get her, then I tried to swim for one of the lifeboats, but I got disoriented. The waves were so huge. I couldn't get anywhere. I just started yelling for help. That's when Susan came for us."

I listened to this with shock and horror, unable to bear the fact that my sister and daughter had endured such a terrible ordeal.

And I had questions—important ones—but I couldn't ask them while Louise was listening through the headsets, so I decided to wait until we landed and Claire and I could talk privately.

The other woman from the lifeboat was brought into the chopper just then—we found out that her name was Margaret—and we all consoled each other.

~ C

The chopper pilot took us directly to the hospital where Margaret was reunited with her husband John, who had ended up in the other lifeboat. They wept as they held each other, because neither had known the other was alive.

Meanwhile, Claire called her husband Scott to let him know that we were all okay, and I called our mother. They were relieved to hear our voices because, by this time, the disaster had made local news headlines. Evidently, *Dalila's* captain and six passengers were still missing and a massive rescue operation was underway. Claire and I hadn't known about that until Scott informed us. We were grief-stricken by the news, and doubly grateful to be alive.

It wasn't long before a pediatrician arrived to examine Louise in the ER. He wore a tie with Elmo on it.

"I heard that you were very brave today," he said in a friendly voice as he listened to her chest with the stethoscope.

She smiled and nodded at the compliment.

"It must have been scary in such a bad storm."

Louise merely nodded again.

He draped the stethoscope around his neck and spoke gently to her. "Can you tell me everything that happened to you?"

She looked at me for encouragement and I squeezed her hand. "It's okay, sweetheart. The doctor needs to know if you hurt yourself. Go ahead, tell him what you remember."

Louise wet her lips and looked up at the doctor. "The boat sank and I fell in the water. I tried to swim because I'm a good swimmer, but I was scared."

He nodded sympathetically. "Did you hit your head or anything?"

"I don't know."

"And how long were you in the water? Do you remember?"

She shook her head.

"It must have been very cold."

"Yes."

He looked in her ear with the otoscope. "Did you swallow a lot of water?"

She nodded again. "Yes, and I couldn't breathe. I was kicking my arms and legs, but the waves were big. They kept splashing me in the face."

I had to fight to stay strong as I listened to her describe the details, because the image of my daughter thrashing about in the water, all alone and panicking, was not an easy one to swallow. I hated myself for losing sight of her, for not being able to protect her.

"Then I drowned," she said plainly, "and I died and went to heaven."

The doctor simply nodded at this, as if it were the most natural thing in the world for her to say.

"But your mommy brought you back to life because she's an excellent nurse. You're a very lucky girl." He moved to the foot of the bed. "Can you wiggle your toes for me? Very good." Returning to her side, he asked, "How are you feeling now? Overall."

"My chest hurts a little," she shyly replied, and pointed at her heart. "Right here."

He raised her hospital gown and examined some bruising where I had been doing chest compressions for over five minutes. He felt around the area, asked her to tell him if it hurt when he put pressure on it. Then he glanced across at me. "You were quite a hero today."

"No, really, I was just a mom."

"You saved your daughter's life."

A lump formed in my throat and I had to lower my gaze.

He tested Louise for strength, sensations, and reflexes and asked her questions to determine if she had suffered any neurological damage because of a lack of oxygen to her brain. There was no evidence of that, which was a relief to say the least, and I suspected that the cold water had slowed down her body systems, which helped bring her back.

When he finished examining her, he turned to me and said that he saw no reason to admit her. He then told me what to watch out for at home, and if there were any issues at all, to come back and have her checked out right away.

He said good-bye to Louise and pushed past the privacy curtain, but I still had questions, which I didn't want to ask in front of Louise. I told her to wait there, that I would be right back.

I caught up with the doctor by the nurses' station. "Dr. Patterson. Can I ask you something?"

"Sure." He turned to face me.

I glanced uncertainly at the women behind the desk and felt suddenly self-conscious, so I pulled him aside, down the corridor, and spoke in a hushed tone.

"Do you see many children who say they died and went to heaven?"

He considered that for a moment. "No, I can't say that I do."

"But you didn't seem to find it strange at all—that she would say something like that."

He studied my face. "No, I just thought it was something you must have said to her. I assumed you're religious."

I shook my head. "No. I mean, yes, we go to church, but I didn't tell her anything. I certainly didn't tell her that she died."

His eyebrows pulled together with concern. "Did she say anything else about it? That she saw a light, or anything like that?"

"Not a light, exactly," I replied, "but I haven't questioned her very much. She did mention clouds and sunlight, so maybe she did see that, I don't know. What I find most strange is that she told me she saw her grandfather, but she's never known him because he died long before she was born." I paused and took a breath, trying to make sense of it. "The way she described him... It was like she knew him intimately. Affectionately. She called him Grampy."

Dr. Patterson simply stared at me. I suspected he didn't have the slightest clue what to say.

I shivered a little and rubbed my upper arms. "You've never encountered anything like this before? With a child who died or flatlined?"

"No, but I've certainly heard plenty of stories about near-death experiences. I just never met anyone who actually had one."

A couple of nurses walked by, and I waited until they passed. "So... Do you think that's what it was? Do you think she experienced the afterlife?"

Hearing myself say the words felt completely crazy.

He quickly held up a hand. "Now, now, I don't know anything about that. I don't really subscribe to those beliefs."

"How would you explain it then?" I quickly countered, although I wasn't trying to argue with him. I wasn't even sure I subscribed to those beliefs myself. I just wanted to know what he thought.

He shrugged a shoulder. "I think that when we die, there are all sorts of electrical impulses in the brain that can cause hallucinations."

Suddenly, I *did* find myself wanting to argue with him...

"But isn't there evidence that some people see and hear things on the operating table when they flatline? I've heard stories where people say they floated up to the ceiling and witnessed everything that was happening while they were clinically dead."

He scratched the back of his neck, as if he were uncomfortable with the direction this conversation was taking. "Maybe, but as far as I know, there's no scientific proof of any afterlife, but it's not my field. If you like, I could ask for a psych consult."

Psych?

No. Absolutely not. I had no desire to go that route with my daughter. Not at this stage.

"Um..." I pretended to think about it. "No, thank you. Let's just leave it for now. Maybe she was imagining it, or dreaming. I don't know. I'll keep an eye on her and let you know if she needs to be seen. Thank you."

I turned away from him and hurried back to Louise.

Three

Emma

Victoria, British Columbia

There was a time I believed I would love him forever. But Carter and I were young when we met. I was barely fifteen, in the ninth grade, and caught up in the passionate madness of adolescent hormones. Not to totally discount what we felt for each other. Puppy love is just as real as grown-up love. But everything's so dramatic when you're that age. Emotions are heightened. That's why Romeo and Juliet died tragically. If they had been in their thirties when everything happened to them, I doubt Romeo would have taken the poison, and Juliet most certainly wouldn't have stabbed herself in the stomach. They would have known that life has ups and downs, and we must go on, and even if the heart can't mend completely, there will be joy in other places, somewhere further down the road. I understood that now.

At the time I came to realize this, I was thirty years old, and though my heart had been broken, I knew it was time to patch up the wounds I'd suffered lately and get on with living.

Which was why I needed Carter to sign the divorce papers.

~⊘~

Carter and I had arranged to meet at our house in Victoria, on the southern tip of Vancouver Island, where he continued to live after we separated. We had purchased the house together the summer before we got married, with the help of his parents, who gave us the down-payment as a wedding gift.

I loved that house, even though it fell squarely into the category of "starter home" and needed work to this day. When we bought it, it was dated and rundown, but we preferred to call it cozy and "lived in." What made it special was its magical backyard with an expansive stretch of green grass, a patch of forest with a wooden bridge across a babbling brook, and best of all, hidden in the trees, surrounded by carpets of lush green moss, was a child's playhouse that looked like something out of *Hansel and Gretel*. It was a miniature Tudor Revival structure painted pink and blue, with mature English ivy spilling out of tiny window boxes. When we were shopping for our first home, it was the playhouse that had sealed the deal. It was also one of the reasons why I couldn't continue to live there with Carter. I couldn't bear to look at it.

When I met him that afternoon, I parked on the street, not in the driveway where I could peer into the backyard. A light spring rain was falling.

I got out of my car and walked up the front steps,

pausing for a few seconds at the door because I wasn't sure if I should ring the doorbell or just walk in. This used to be my home, after all—for five happy years. Well…four of them were happy. But it was Carter's home now. I lived elsewhere.

I decided to ring the doorbell.

He took his time answering, which irked me because he knew I was coming. I'd even dressed up for the occasion, in my belted three-quarter length trench coat and slacks with heeled boots. I wanted to look confident and well put together.

At last, the door opened and Carter stood there on the threshold, regarding me with that cranky, displeased expression on his face, as if he already found this whole experience inconvenient and tedious. He didn't say hello, and that started things off on the wrong foot, because his crankiness was contagious. My back went up and I steeled myself for a battle.

All of this was unfortunate because I'd hoped we could be civil and start fresh that day. I wanted to move on to this next phase of our lives on friendly terms. But Carter didn't seem to want that. Clearly, he wasn't finished punishing me. I wondered if he ever would be.

I held up the envelope. "I have the papers."

With a wide sweep of his arm, he stepped back and gestured for me to enter.

I walked in and halted in the foyer, because it still smelled exactly the same, and so very familiar. A single whiff sent a wave of homesickness into my core, which I fought to suppress because the last thing I wanted was to feel wistful. There was no point in that, because neither of us could ever go back. This house would never be what it once was to us. It would always stand under a dark cloud.

Suddenly, I wondered why I had agreed to meet here. I should have suggested a coffee shop or something.

"Where do you want to do this?" I asked. "The kitchen table?"

"Sure." Carter led me into the kitchen without offering to take my coat.

I glanced into the living room as we passed by. It was tidy and neat, which was unexpected because Carter had always been terrible about leaving old newspapers lying around on the floor after he'd read them, or dirty dishes on the coffee table.

We reached the kitchen and I noticed the counter was clean as well, the sink and dish rack empty.

Maybe, like me, he'd wanted to appear "well put together." Or maybe he truly was in a better place, now that I was gone.

Sliding the papers out of the envelope, I wasted no time setting them on the tabletop. I turned to grab a pen from the jar on the desk where Carter kept his laptop. He practically ran his whole business from there—a landscaping and home maintenance company—though he had office space in the basement.

I returned to the papers, flipped through to the page that required our signatures, and signed my name. Dated it. Then I leaned back and held the pen out to him. "Your turn."

He stared at me for a moment. "So that's it. It's that easy for you? You can just sign away the past ten years of your life without the slightest hesitation?"

Were we really going to do this? Was he truly going to seize this last opportunity to put me down, to make me feel guilty?

"It's not as if I'm blindsiding you with this," I told him. "We've been separated for two years. And you were the one who asked me to leave, remember? You said, 'I think you should move out.' Those were your exact words, and clearly you *still* think I'm devoid of feeling and you still hate me. So here we are. Getting divorced. As it should be. Please sign these papers so we can move on."

It all came barreling toward me then—the passionate love we'd felt for each other when we were young and thought it would last forever. Our wedding day. Our honeymoon in the Poconos. Finding out I was pregnant. And then that horrible, tragic day three years ago...

The way Carter looked at me now—with disdain and disappointment—brought it all back and nearly knocked me off my feet. I resented him for it because I'd been doing so well lately. When I came here this afternoon, I'd promised myself I wouldn't think about any of those things. But somehow, I couldn't help it. Setting foot in this house and seeing that look in Carter's eye made me want to crawl back into that dark hole.

See? I wanted to say. *This is why we need to sign these papers. Because I don't want to feel like this anymore.*

It's the day after Samuel was pronounced dead at the hospital. I'm sitting at our kitchen table, staring out the window at the blue plastic backyard swimming pool, which no one has thought to remove. My body feels cold and numb and I don't want to get up from my chair. I don't know how long I've been sitting here, but eventually my mother convinces me to go and lie down in the bedroom because she and Carter are making phone calls, taking care of funeral

arrangements. I can't help them because I can't bear to look at tiny coffins today.

Carter hasn't spoken to me since he shouted at me and shook me in the hospital—so hard he almost gave me whiplash. His father had to restrain him before someone called security.

People have been dropping by the house all day with casseroles and pies. They're genuinely sympathetic, but they offer awkward condolences to me because they know it was all my fault and they don't know the right thing to say.

That's because there is no right thing. There are no words to console me. I just want everyone to leave me alone so I can curl up and die. Time moves slow as mud.

⸻

"I don't hate you," Carter said to me. "I never hated you."

I held the pen out to him again, willing him to take it. "I don't think that's true, but I don't want to debate it. All you need to do is sign on the dotted line so that we can get on with our lives."

He stared at me with those intense blue eyes. It was difficult to believe they'd ever looked at me with desire, or laughter. Those eyes had always disarmed me, usually in a good way. Half the time we ended up in bed, even when I was trying to stay angry with him about something silly, like forgetting to take out the garbage for the hundredth time. But today, I saw only angst and disapproval in those eyes, and it had the opposite effect on me. Up went my armor.

I kept my gaze fixed on his, holding the pen out. There was no way I was going to be the first one to look away.

"What's the hurry anyway?" Carter asked.

I wished he would go to the fridge and get a beer or something. Anything to get him to take a step back.

"If you really want to know…" I held out my hand to show him my ring. "I just got engaged."

Carter let out a breath as if I'd punched him in the stomach. Then his steely eyes lifted and he spoke with that tone I hated—as if I were an idiot. "You're joking. Please tell me you're joking."

"No, I'm not joking, and why should you be so surprised? You've been with Melissa for four months. Clearly, *you've* moved on. Am I not allowed to move on, too? Am I not allowed to be happy?"

He shook his head with condescension and turned away from me. He moved to stand at the window with his arms folded at his chest, staring at the falling rain.

While he looked out at the backyard, I looked down at my shoes and squeezed the pen in my fist.

Finally, he turned. "Who is the guy?"

To my surprise, Carter didn't ask the question in a threatening way—as if he wanted to get in his truck, speed away from the curb and warn Luke to stay away from me— which is exactly what he would have done in high school, because Carter had always been the jealous type. But we weren't in high school anymore. Today, in this moment, he was behaving more like a big brother who wanted to make sure I was with someone who would treat me right.

I let out a breath and felt some of the tension release from my shoulders. "His name is Luke Hawkins," I replied. "He works in corporate finance and he's a really good guy."

Carter frowned and shook his head as if to clear it. "Wait a second. Is this the same Luke you went home with after Lori's birthday party? The guy you met in the bar?"

I squeezed the pen again. "How do you know about that?"

"Because Lori has a big mouth," he replied. "She always has. You know that."

Yes, I did know that about my cousin.

I clenched my teeth and exhaled sharply. "Fine. Whatever. Lori shouldn't have told you that, but it doesn't matter, because as you can see, it wasn't just a one-night stand. Luke called me afterward and we got together and we've been together ever since."

Carter raised an eyebrow. "Sounds like a *real* gentleman."

I shot him a look with daggers in it. "He is. So let's just leave it alone, okay? It's my life, and I have no doubts about him. None whatsoever. He's an amazing person."

Carter frowned. "Amazing? It's been what…five months? Six, tops? Emma. Seriously. How well can you possibly know him? Isn't it a bit soon to be making decisions about spending the rest of your life with him?"

I was so tired of this. Why wouldn't he just sign the papers and let me go?

"It might seem that way to you," I replied, "but we're not kids anymore. We're grownups, and when you know, you know. Luke and I are meant to be together. I know we are. And life's short. I can't just sit around torturing myself about things I'll never be able to change. And you know what I'm talking about. I want to have a life, Carter. A family. It's what I always wanted."

He stared at me for a moment, then strode to the fridge. He opened it up, withdrew a beer and twisted off the cap. "I see. So, you've met your soul mate and he's going to help you move on and forget everything."

I felt a muscle twitch at my jaw. "I hate it when you do that. You know I'll never forget. You should know that better than anyone. Which makes me wonder if you would actually *prefer* to see me continue to hate myself until the day I die. Because you don't think I deserve to be happy."

He gave me that look again, as if I were an idiot. I wanted to pound my fists on his chest.

"Will you please just sign the papers?" I asked.

He kept his eyes fixed on mine while he tipped the bottle of beer up and sipped it. Then he set it down on the counter behind him and kept me in suspense.

"If that's what you really want." At last, he pushed away from the counter, but he stared at me long and hard. "Is it?"

I wasn't going to waver. Not now. Not ever. "Yes, it's what I want." I held out the pen again.

Carter took it from my hand, bent forward over the table, and finally signed his name.

Everyone kept telling me it would get easier in time, that there would come a day when Carter and I would feel ready to have another child. That day never came. How could it, when my husband blamed me for what happened? He'd said unthinkable things to me in the hospital, after the doctor came out of the trauma room and spoke the words no parent ever wants to hear: "I'm sorry. We did everything we could."

Somehow, Carter and I had made it through the funeral, but when it was all over and our relatives went home, we barely spoke to each other. We walked around the house like a couple of zombies, and I knew he was doing everything possible to keep from strangling me. That's how angry he was with me.

But Carter had it easy. And still, to this day, he's never realized how lucky he was not to see what I saw: our darling four-year-old son face down in the blue plastic paddling pool.

I still don't know how or why it happened. I'd gone inside, just for a few seconds, to use the washroom. Everything after that is a blur.

For a whole year afterwards, I was grief-stricken and depressed, and Carter had no sympathy. He looked at me only with contempt. It was a vicious cycle. The more he looked at me that way, the more self-loathing I felt. I must have spent six months in sweatpants. I took a leave of absence from work at the head office of a grocery store chain where I worked in the payroll department. I remember getting in the shower only when my hair was so greasy, I couldn't bear to look at myself.

But even then, my clean, blow-dried hair didn't help with that. I still couldn't look in the mirror.

In the end, the straw that broke the camel's back came in the form of Carter's arrival home drunk one night, a year after Samuel's death, stinking of whisky and cigars, which had become more and more common as the months passed. He wanted to get frisky, but there was nothing playful or romantic about it. It was as if he were challenging me to say no. I sensed that he wanted to hurt me, emotionally.

I shoved him away, ran out of the room and slammed the door in his face. He followed and said horrible things I'll never forget—because they were all true.

When morning came, I thought he might have forgotten what happened because he'd been drunk, but then he walked into the kitchen and made himself an omelet without speaking a single word to me.

When he finished eating, he suggested I move out.

It was probably a good thing, because heaven only knew what we might have done to each other if we'd stayed together. I understood how he felt about me, and to be honest, I couldn't blame him. I felt that way about myself. I don't know if I could have forgiven him if *he* had been the one responsible for Samuel's death. It would have been very difficult to get over that.

With the signed divorced papers in the back seat of my car, I turned into Luke's driveway and made my way to his beautiful home, which was set deep in the property, making it extremely private. The house itself overlooked the Strait of Juan De Fuca and the Olympic Mountains on the opposite side. It had mature gardens, rolling lawns and wide flagstone patios, as well as an ocean's edge infinity pool and hot tub.

I hadn't mentioned to Carter that Luke was wealthy. Before we met, Luke had been a stock broker in Toronto for ten years. Then he retired at the age of thirty-three with a few million dollars in his back pocket. He chose beautiful Oak Bay to retire to because he'd grown up in Victoria, but he continued to do consulting work which paid extremely well.

He was handsome with dark features—brown eyes and thick, wavy hair—and an athletic build, not because he went to the gym constantly. He was simply the outdoorsy type and spent a lot of hours kayaking, hiking and running.

I didn't tell Carter any of that because he would think I'd been wooed by Luke's money, which was not true. For the longest time, I'd had no idea he was rich, because on the night we met, we went home to my place—a small one-bedroom apartment in Victoria, not far from the bar where Lori had held her party.

Luke wasn't actually a guest. He was there after a business dinner, to loosen his tie and have a drink. We started talking when we wound up sitting next to each other at the bar, fighting to get served.

I'll admit, I'd had too much to drink that night, so I was less inhibited than I would normally be, and I was tired of sitting home in my sweatpants, feeling ugly. I'd come out that night with renewed purpose, fiercely determined to have a good time. So, when this incredibly classy, good-looking guy asked me to dance, I didn't say no, and we hit it off.

The next thing I knew, I was dragging him back by his silk tie to my place. The following morning, he took me to breakfast in his modest Honda Civic. We went to a cheap neighborhood diner that served the most incredible hash browns.

Luke called me a few days later, took me out to dinner and a movie, then out to dinner a few more times. He didn't invite me back to his place until our fifth date. By that time, I was already head over heels in love—or maybe it was just infatuation at that point, because we'd only known each other briefly. But he was, hands down, not just the best-looking man I'd ever dated, but the *nicest* man I'd met since I left Carter, and I felt comfortable enough to tell him what had happened to my son. I let it all come spilling out on the morning Luke took me to breakfast after our "one night stand," which turned out to be so much more. Luke showed exactly the kind of compassion I needed and never received from Carter. Luke didn't judge me or make me feel like a terrible person. Nor did he blame me. It created an intimacy between us, from the very start.

Later, when I saw his house for the first time, I nearly swallowed my gum.

~ C

"Hey," Luke said, rising from the sofa in the family room as I walked through the door. Toby and Max, his two rescue dogs from the local shelter, trotted to greet me. I gave each of them a pat and said hello.

Luke met me in the front hall and kissed me on the cheek. "How did it go?"

I handed him the large manila envelope. "He signed them."

While I removed my trench coat and hung it on the coat tree, Luke set the envelope on the hall table. The dogs continued to wag their tails.

I turned to Luke, felt something inside me come apart, and stepped into his arms.

"Oh," he said in a tender voice, gathering me into his embrace and kissing the top of my head, "I'm sorry, babe. I know how hard that was. But everything will be better now."

His calm, loving nature was exactly what I needed. Somehow, he understood that I couldn't jump for joy, nor did I want to pop the cork on a bottle of champagne— because a life I'd once cherished was over now. The marriage I'd believed in with all my young, innocent heart had failed spectacularly. It had gone up in flames the day Sammy died, and it was now a charred wreckage. There was nothing left in its place but hard feelings and resentment.

Besides that, what I'd endured that afternoon had drained me emotionally. I'd had to lock horns with my soon-to-be ex-husband and push hard to get him to sign his name on the dotted line, which made no sense because he'd made it abundantly clear thousands of times that he couldn't stand the sight of me.

I'd also set foot in the house where I once rocked Sammy to sleep in his cradle. Where I breastfed him, and changed his diapers. I hadn't even been able to look at the playhouse out back. I wondered suddenly if Carter had decided to get rid of it. I wouldn't blame him if he had. It would be difficult to look at every day.

Luke took my hand and led me to the family room—a cozy space with antique lights, a Persian carpet on wide plank floors, cherry wainscoting, bookshelves, and a charming wood-burning fireplace in a stone hearth. The dogs followed us and curled up on their beds in front of the windows that overlooked the stone patio and water beyond, where a group of sea kayakers were paddling by, oblivious to the rain.

We sat down on the brown leather sofa and faced each other, still holding hands. Luke wove his fingers through mine. "Do you want to talk about it?"

I shifted my position and lay my head on his shoulder. He put his arm around me while the rain fell softly on the patio stones outside the glass doors.

"I don't know. It was weird."

"Weird, how?"

I stared at the coffee table. "It was just really tense.

There was nothing but contempt in his eyes, and he spoke to me like I was stupid and unfeeling for wanting to get married again. *That* definitely caught him by surprise. And then he gave me a hard time about signing the papers, which is the weird part because he doesn't love me anymore. He doesn't want to be married to me. He hates me. He just wants to keep punishing me, I guess, and he knows that if I move on, he won't have that power over me."

"At least he signed the papers," Luke said, after a pause.

"Yeah. But he was a jerk about it because whenever he sees an opportunity to tighten the screws—to remind me about what happened—he takes it, because he doesn't want me to be happy. It's his way of being vengeful. I think he enjoys it."

Luke stroked my arm lightly with his thumb. "Well, *I* want you to be happy, because you're a good person, Emma. I hope you know that. What happened was an accident, and it could just as easily have happened to Carter. He shouldn't feel so superior, because it could happen to anyone."

I closed my eyes and allowed Luke's consoling words to wash over me. I tried to absorb them, but still, there was a part of me that couldn't fully accept what he said.

I knew I'd probably never be entirely free of my guilt. And there would always be a hole in my heart, but at least, with the passing of time, I'd come to believe that I might be happy again, in other ways and in other places.

I lifted my cheek from Luke's shoulder. "You're a godsend. I don't know where I'd be right now if I hadn't met you. I think my life would still be very…" I took a moment to think of the right word. "Bleak."

Luke twirled a lock of my hair around his forefinger and

gave me a look of encouragement. Or maybe he was seeking assurance. I wasn't sure. "But it's not bleak now, right?"

I smiled and tipped my face up for a kiss. "Not in the least."

He pulled me close and our kiss was passionate, full of fire.

Later, when the rain stopped, we took the dogs down to the rocky shoreline to let them run around without leashes. The water was calm, reflecting the sky and mountains in the distance, and the air was fresh and fragrant. It seemed as if my day had gone from the very depths of misery to the heights of pure bliss.

What a gift it was to feel content.

I decided I would never take contentment for granted again. I would make the most of it while it lasted.

As we picked our way over the rugged coastline rocks while the water lapped gently below, we talked about wedding plans. We hadn't set a date yet, but Luke thought New Year's Eve might make it extra special.

As far as I was concerned, I would have been happy to elope to Vegas on a whim because I'd already had the big white wedding with bridesmaids and speeches and a DJ who played until one o'clock in the morning. Luke, however, had never been married and I didn't want to deprive him of a proper celebration. Besides, I loved the idea of starting a new life on the first day of a new year. It felt like a good omen.

So, on that day, on the rocks, gazing out at the sea, I agreed to a New Year's Eve wedding wherever Luke wanted. Money would be no object, he said, so he was confident he'd be able to find a good venue.

CHAPTER

Four

Bev

Halifax, Nova Scotia

It was early evening when we finally left the hospital. Louise was exhausted, so I carried her to Scott's SUV, buckled her into her booster seat, then rode in back with her, toward home, where Claire and I lived across the street from each other. It was a quiet residential neighborhood in the south end of Halifax, where towering oaks provided shade in the summer and filled our world with color in the fall. Claire had been the original owner of my house—a charming little bungalow with hardwood floors and a private backyard. She'd bought it with her first husband, Wes, but when he died, she married Scott who lived across the street. At first, she rented her little bungalow to me, but I bought it from her a year ago, which worked out beautifully because I was a single mom with an only child, and they, too, had only one child. Serena was born a year after Louise, and it was nice that they had each other. They were more like sisters than cousins.

It was a quick drive home, as we lived only about ten blocks from the hospital. I kept looking at Louise, checking on her, because she seemed overwhelmingly tired, which concerned me. It made sense, logically, considering what she'd been through that day, but something about her seemed different.

"Are you feeling okay?" I asked, laying my hand on her small wrist.

She nodded her head.

"You've been very quiet," I said, gently and quietly. "Does your head hurt? Or your chest?"

Louise glanced out the window, watching the houses pass by. "No. I'm just sad."

My stomach turned over with unease. "Do you want to talk about it?"

"No."

She seemed so tired, I didn't want to press. By the time we pulled into the driveway, she was starting to fall asleep. I got out of the vehicle, unbuckled her and carried her inside where our dog Leo—a ten-year-old golden retriever— greeted us with a swishing tail and a wet nose.

Louise buried her face in my neck.

My mother was waiting for us as well, with a big pot of soup on the stove.

She hugged us all, and while Claire went home to change her clothes, I carried Louise to her room, helped her into her pajamas and went with her to the bathroom to brush her teeth. I tucked her into bed with her blue bunny, Mr. Rabbit, and she closed her eyes and fell asleep right away.

Trying not to be too concerned, because it was normal for her to be tired after such an intense physical trauma, I switched off the light and went to change my clothes also. When I returned to the kitchen, Scott, Claire, and my mom were gathered there. Claire was sipping a glass of white wine while Scott was setting the table. Leo was lying on the floor by the fridge.

"Where's Serena?" I asked, wanting to tell them about Louise's near-death experience, but not wanting to bring it up in front of their daughter.

"Watching television," Claire replied. "She had a sandwich at the hospital so she'll probably fall asleep on your sofa. How's Louise?"

"Fine, but she's tired. I doubt she'll wake up again before the morning."

Claire poured me a glass of wine without me having to ask.

"Thank you," I replied as she handed it to me. "If there was ever a night that called for alcohol, this has to be it."

"Cheers," she said, holding up her glass and clinking it against mine.

"To our survival today."

We all fell silent as we thought of the passengers who hadn't been as lucky.

"Is there any news on the rescue effort?" Claire asked Scott.

He pulled out a chair at the table and sat down. "They've recovered most of the bodies from the wreck. All six were still in the main hold, trapped there, I guess, and the captain was caught in the rigging, just outside."

Feeling nauseous, I sat down as well. "That's awful."

Scott continued to explain what he knew. "Out of the five people in the hold, there were three crew members and two passengers—an older couple by the name of Jennings."

I turned to Claire. "I wonder if it was the woman who didn't want to leave the ship. She thought it looked too dangerous outside."

"I wonder," Claire replied.

We all sat down in somber silence while Mom served up bowls of hot chicken soup with warm rolls, although I didn't feel much like eating. I had to force myself.

"Thanks, Mom," I said, nonetheless. "It was really good of you to come over and cook for us."

"I'm just glad I was able to do *something*," she replied, squeezing my hand. "And I'm so grateful you're all okay."

I finished buttering my roll and thought about how I was going to tell them about what happened to Louise. It wasn't an easy subject to bring up, and I found myself wondering if I'd dreamed it.

I cleared my throat and set down my knife. "So. I need to tell all of you what Louise said to me after she woke up, when we were in the helicopter. It kind of freaked me out."

My mother set down her soup spoon and regarded me with concern. "What is it?"

I perched my elbows on the table and clasped my hands together. "You all know that she was…" I paused because it was difficult to speak the words aloud, let alone comprehend them. "She was clinically dead for at least five minutes while I was doing CPR."

"Yes," Claire replied.

"Well…" I swallowed before continuing. "She said she went somewhere. To heaven."

Claire's eyebrows pulled together with surprise. "She said *what?*"

I tried to remember exactly what she did say. It was all such a blur.

I turned my attention to my mother. "She said she wasn't scared because she was with her Grampy."

All the color drained from my mother's face and she placed her hand over her heart. "Oh, Bev. You don't think…"

"I…I'm not sure," I replied shakily, "but when I asked who Grampy was, she said he was my daddy. And that he was in heaven now."

Mom sucked in a breath and began to weep quietly. I rose from my chair and wrapped my arms around her while Claire leaned across the table to squeeze her hand.

When Mom wiped her tears away, she glanced up at me. "What else did she say?"

I sat down and spoke gently. "I asked her what he looked like and she said that he had a mustache and happy eyes."

"Your father had a mustache since you girls were born, and he certainly did have the most loving eyes I ever knew. What else did she say?"

I cleared my throat. "She mentioned that she didn't want to come back here because she liked it there. And when we were driving home just now, she said she was sad. I think it's because she was thinking about where she had been."

Everyone fell silent, staring at me in shock.

"That's unbelievable," Scott said after a few seconds. "Did she tell you *why* she felt that way? What it was like?"

"I didn't get much more from her in the helicopter because that's when you were brought up," I said to Claire, "and I didn't really get a chance to talk to her about it again while we were in the hospital. I didn't want to upset her or make too big a deal of it, or make her feel like she was a freak. But it was just so hard to believe."

"No kidding," Claire replied, slowly stirring her soup. Her eyes lifted. "Did you tell the doctor?"

I gave her a look. "Yes, but he didn't believe it was anything. He says he's not a believer in that kind of thing. He suggested a psychiatrist."

"Psychiatrist!" Mom shouted. "Goodness gracious. She doesn't need that."

I held up a hand. "Don't worry, I declined the offer." I turned my gaze toward Claire and Scott. "I'm just not sure what to make of it. Do you guys think she dreamed it?"

They considered it for a moment.

"Maybe," Claire replied. "Or maybe not. They say there's no proof of an afterlife, but people from all different religions have had those kinds of experiences. How do you explain that?"

"I don't know." I sat quietly for a moment, looking down at the table. "When you found her in the water," I said, "was she already drowned? I'm just trying to get a sense of how long she was..." I paused again. "*Gone.*"

Claire nodded, and seemed to have difficulty thinking about it. She closed her eyes for a few seconds, and when she opened them and spoke, her voice was shaky. "It all happened so fast when the wave hit. We all got swept into the water and I went down deep. When I fought my way back up to the surface and found her, she was floating, unconscious. But it couldn't have been more than a minute or two after the wave hit. It's a good thing she was wearing a lifejacket. And I'm glad we didn't get tangled up in all the sails and ropes, like the captain did."

"What happened then?" I asked. "Did she regain consciousness when she was with you?"

"No. I dragged her away from the ship, trying to get to

one of the lifeboats, but the waves kept pushing us the wrong way. I knew she wasn't breathing, but I couldn't do anything. I was just trying to keep us both afloat."

Claire began to cry and Scott and I both reached for her hands. "You were amazing. She wouldn't be alive right now if it weren't for you."

Claire wiped her eyes and regained her composure. "It was a team effort."

The phone rang just then. I leaped out of my chair to answer it before it rang again and woke Louise or Serena. "Hello?"

"Hello, is this Bev Hutchinson?"

"Yes."

There was a brief pause on the other end. "Hi, Ms. Hutchinson. This is Gloria Steeves from *Evening News at Six.* Would you have a few minutes to talk to me?"

Gloria Steeves. She was a TV reporter who usually covered the biggest news stories of the day, and her witty, off-the-cuff remarks on lighthearted stories made her a popular MC at all sorts of city events.

"I assume you want to talk to me about the accident?" I said.

"Yes, if you don't mind. But first, how are you doing? Are you okay?"

"As well as can be expected."

"I'm so sorry for what you went through. It's a terrible thing. We're all reeling from it."

"Thank you." Feeling suddenly nervous, I looked back at the table and mouthed the word *Reporter.*

Claire raised an eyebrow, and my mother whispered, "You should just hang up."

But I didn't want to be rude, nor did I begrudge the fact

that people wanted to know what happened, so I decided to stay on the line.

"What do you want to know?" I asked.

I heard papers flipping. "Well, if you could tell me everything you remember happening, that would be wonderful. And do you mind if I record our conversation?"

"I suppose it's fine," I replied, "as long as you don't broadcast it. I'd rather not hear my voice on TV."

"No problem," she said. "I'll just report on what you tell me. No one will hear this but me."

"Okay… Well then…" I described everything, exactly as it happened, from the moment the rain began to fall to when we heard the loud crash from above, and then to when the ship turned over onto her side. I told her how professional and helpful the crew had been, and how they came below to get us organized and safely out of the hold, into lifeboats.

"From what I understand," Gloria replied, "you lost your daughter in the water. Is that correct?"

My stomach lurched because I hated the sound of those words: *You lost your daughter.*

"Yes, that's correct," I reluctantly replied. "A big wave swept me over the side and I must have hit my head because I was unconscious for a while. But my sister found my daughter and they made it to the lifeboat."

"Thank goodness for that. You must be very grateful for your sister."

"Yes, I am."

Gloria was quiet for a few seconds. "But your daughter was unconscious as well, wasn't she? And you had to perform CPR on her?"

How did this woman know all this? I supposed she

must have already spoken to Susan or Margaret. "Yes. I'm a nurse."

"That was lucky for your daughter."

"Yes. We all feel very fortunate tonight. Not everyone was so lucky."

Something in me seemed to be shutting down, emotionally. I didn't want to talk about this anymore.

But Gloria pressed on. "Is it true that your daughter said she went to heaven during that time?"

My whole body jolted. "Excuse me, how do you know about that?"

"We've been speaking to a number of people that were involved today."

"What people?" I asked, incredulous, because I'd hardly told anyone.

I doubted it was Dr. Patterson, because he would know better than to break doctor/patient confidentiality. Maybe it was the paramedic. Or even the pilot, who might have been listening to our conversation through the headsets.

Before I could think about how to handle the situation, I ended the call and slammed the phone into the charger.

"What's going on?" Claire asked, concerned.

I covered my face with both hands. "It was Gloria Steeves from the six o'clock news. She knew what Louise said about going to heaven. I don't know how she found out."

"But that's private," Claire replied, exasperated.

"Evidently not. I don't know who told her."

Scott rose to his feet and began to clear away the dishes. "You might want to call a lawyer, Bev, just to make sure your privacy is respected. And you don't have to talk to reporters if you don't want to."

"I should have declined to comment," I replied. "What was I thinking?"

My mother approached me. "It's not your fault. You couldn't have known she was going to ask that."

I couldn't take it anymore. I needed to be with Louise, to hold her in my arms and reassure myself that she was okay. "Would you guys mind if I said goodnight? Please, don't worry about the dishes. Leave everything and I'll clean it up in the morning. Stay as long as you like, but lock the door behind you when you go."

"Of course," Claire replied with a worried look on her face. "But call me if you need anything."

"I will."

Making my way down the hall, I tiptoed into Louise's room and slid into bed beside her. Her eyes fluttered open. In a sleepy voice, she said, "Hi Mommy."

She rolled to face me and wrapped her tiny arms around my neck. I held her close as tears spilled from my eyes, across my temple, into my hair and onto the pillow. I felt such intense love for her, my heart was bursting with it—and such gratitude that she had come back from wherever she had gone.

A place she liked, where she could fly above the clouds.

Where she felt safe and happy.

I thought of my father then. I was only ten when he went to trim the hedge while Claire and I played in the yard, dancing through the cool spray of the sprinkler. I don't remember much about it. Maybe I blocked out the images, but I'm told he slipped and fell into the ditch and impaled himself on the clippers. Mom called an ambulance, but my father died before he reached the hospital. He was thirty-six years old, and he had a mustache at the time. I remember how it tickled my forehead when he kissed me goodnight.

In that moment, with my daughter in my arms, I felt my childhood love for him, which had never waned over the years. Even though I was only ten when he was taken from us, I never forgot how he loved us. I remembered his laughter, and how I felt so safe whenever he walked in the door. He taught me how to ride a bicycle, how to swim, and he never refused to help me with my homework.

I wished I could thank him—not just for all that, but for what he did for me today. For sending Louise home to me.

Did that mean I believed what Louise had said? Did I believe she went to heaven?

I still wasn't sure, and I wanted, more than anything, to hear more about what she experienced.

Tomorrow, I would suggest that we take Leo for a walk in the park where we might talk, alone.

CHAPTER

Five

Bev

While Louise was in her room getting dressed the following morning, and Leo was curled up on the kitchen floor, I stood at the counter with my phone, scrolling through a series of news items about our sailing disaster. There was a great deal to absorb because all the bodies had been recovered and next of kin had been notified, so many of the news sites were releasing video segments paying homage to those who were lost. They were digging into the private life of the captain and calling him a hero for doing everything possible to save all the souls on board.

On top of that, the science of the extraordinary weather system was explained by meteorological experts all over North America. The authorities were still investigating, but everyone seemed to agree that what caused the ship to founder was a rare weather phenomenon that no sailing vessel could have possibly survived: a sudden and violent downdraft from the clouds. They also agreed it was not likely a case of negligence on the part of the captain or crew.

Eventually, I couldn't bear to look at it because I'd met all the passengers who had died. I'd spoken to them, laughed with them, spent time with them at lunch. It ripped my heart out to imagine what their families must be going through today.

Then suddenly, I experienced a flash memory—as if I were back on the sinking ship, overcome with panic, climbing out of the hold and onto the slippery deck, searching for Louise as the roar of the waves and salty spray filled me with terror…

Stop it, Bev. Don't think about it.

Setting my phone on the counter behind me, I shut my eyes and tried to calm my racing heart. I inhaled a deep breath and counted to ten, but could still taste the salt water in my mouth. An image of Louise's tiny limp body as we pulled her into the rolling and plunging lifeboat caused a terrible commotion in me. I feared I might be sick. Resting a hand on my belly, I braced both my feet on the steady floor and pushed the memory away.

She came running into the kitchen just then, and my eyes flew open. I thanked God she wasn't one of the bodies that had been recovered from the bottom of the ocean.

We're both still here…

"Ready to go?" I cheerfully asked, because I didn't want to pass my anxieties on to her.

Besides, I wanted this to be a good day. I'd never been so thankful to see a sunrise. All I wanted to do was love my daughter.

"Yes!" She got down on her knees and patted Leo's thick golden coat. "Are you ready? Where's your leash?"

Leo's ears perked up at that, and we went to the front closet to fetch it.

~*e*~

Point Pleasant Park—made up of 190 acres of woodland with groomed walking trails—was a five-minute drive from our home. We pulled into the Tower Road parking lot and let Leo out of the back of the car. Louise and I then walked him to the wide shaded path where Louise always liked to run ahead. I kept reminding her to slow down and wait for us. Eventually, she walked beside me.

"Obviously, you're feeling better," I said to her. "As energetic as ever."

"I feel okay."

I noticed she was constantly gazing up at the treetops.

"What are you seeing up there?" I asked, wanting to steer the conversation toward the things she'd told me in the helicopter.

"Just the sky," she replied.

We continued walking, and Leo stopped to lift a leg and pee.

"Are you thinking about what happened yesterday?" I asked Louise.

Still looking up, she nodded her head.

"Which part, specifically?"

She gave it some thought. "How it's different here, and what it's like there."

My belly erupted into a swarm of nervous butterflies because this was a weighty subject and I was a bit afraid of what she knew and believed, and how it might change her life. It was all a mystery to me. How could I be a good mother when I knew nothing and she knew everything?

Or maybe something had happened to her brain—something neurological that I should be worried about. "Can you describe it to me?"

"Well…" She looked around at all the trees in the forest and the ground beneath her feet. "It was kind of the same, but nicer."

"Nicer, how?"

"More colorful. The water was *really* bright blue and the trees were *really* green, and there weren't any trees like those ones." She pointed at some skeletons of dead trees that stood without leaves or branches.

"What else was different about it?" I asked. "And how did you even get there? Do you remember?"

She nodded. "When I couldn't breathe in the water, I floated out of my body. Then I crossed a bridge."

"What kind of bridge?"

She bit her lip, as if she had to search for the right way to describe it. "It was made of stone. And curved like this." She made a motion with her hand.

"When did you fly over the clouds?"

"Just before I got to the bridge."

"And what was on the other side of the bridge?"

She skipped a few times, then slowed to a walk again. "Grampy was there waiting, and there were others too. They were nice. I liked them."

I cleared my throat and tried to think of the next question I should ask, which wasn't easy because I had so many of them. "Did the nice people talk to you?"

She considered that for a moment. "They didn't really talk with their mouths. But I could hear them in my head."

"I see. And what did they say?"

"First, they said welcome and they hugged me, and then they took me to some pretty buildings, but we didn't go inside."

"What did the buildings look like?"

She walked along, looking down at her sneakers. "They were shiny and white, and really *huge*!" She raised her arms up over her head and spread them in a giant arc to show me how big.

"Wow!" I replied. "That *does* sound huge."

"Yes, and there were other buildings that were really tall with shiny glass. One pretty white building had white steps and there were other kids there, and some dogs."

"Dogs? There were dogs in heaven?"

"Uh huh. They were wagging their tails, and they were really happy to see me. I liked it."

"No wonder. It sounds like a great place."

"It was." She looked down at the ground again.

Leo stopped suddenly, and sat down. Only then did I realize that Louise's chin was quivering.

"What's the matter, sweetheart?" I dropped to one knee and took hold of her hand. "Can you tell me what's wrong?"

She stepped into my arms. I hugged her and rubbed her back.

"I miss it. I didn't want to leave."

"Then why *did* you?" I asked, knowing it was a dangerous question. I certainly didn't want her to feel it would have been okay with me if she'd remained there, even if she liked it better. Nothing could have been further from the truth.

"Grampy said I was supposed to be with you. He said you needed me."

"Well, he was right. I do need you. I would have been very sad and lonely if you didn't come back."

"He said I'd stop missing heaven after a while. He said I'd forget how nice it was, and that it would feel like a dream, but I don't want to forget."

"Then maybe you won't. Maybe when we go home, you can draw pictures of it to help you remember."

She wiped her tears from her cheeks and nodded. "Grampy said I would come back later. After I'm old."

I smiled gently. "Grampy usually knows what he's talking about."

It felt odd to speak about my late father in the present tense...and yet, it didn't seem all that strange...

"Grampy knew everything, and he wanted me to tell you that he's proud of you and he can't wait to see you again, and that he loves you, Gramma and Auntie Claire."

All at once, my heart squeezed in my chest and I was overcome with emotion. I pulled Louise into my arms and held her tight. "I'm so glad you came back to tell me that. Thank you. Thank you for coming back."

I cried as I held her and couldn't stop the tears from flowing. It was a great flood of feeling, brought on not only by the things she'd just said about my father, but by the trauma of the previous day when I'd almost lost her.

She let me hug her for a long time. Then I drew back, cupped her sweet face in my hands and looked into her eyes.

"It wasn't up to me," she told me.

At first, I had no idea what she was talking about. I frowned with confusion.

"Something pulled me back," she said. "It was like a vacuum cleaner that sucked me away from there. Really fast."

Nothing about this was easy to believe, yet I found myself believing her, nonetheless. "A vacuum cleaner? That was the sensation you felt?"

"Uh huh. It didn't hurt, but I didn't like it."

All I could do was blink at her, in stunned silence.

She turned from me then and started running toward the grassy clearing where we sometimes watched *Shakespeare by the Sea* theatrical performances on sunny weekend afternoons. Whenever there was nothing going on in that secluded section of the park, we freed Leo from his leash to let him run, and we climbed all over the antiquated military ruins.

I climbed to the top with Louise and watched her play happily with Leo while boats came and went from the harbor in the distance.

All the while, I wondered if her experience had been real. Or had it just been a vivid dream?

How would I ever know?

When Louise and I pulled onto our street, there was a white news van and a number of unfamiliar cars parked in front of our house. I wished I'd had the presence of mind to hit the brakes, turn around and go somewhere else, but foolishly, I pulled into my driveway with the notion that there was something going on in our neighborhood that had nothing to do with us.

"Are you Bev Hutchinson?" a woman in a red blazer asked from the sidewalk as I got out of my car and opened the back door to help Louise out of her booster seat.

The woman started up my driveway, while a cameraman

and reporter with a microphone spilled out of the news van across the street.

"Is this your daughter?" she asked.

Feeling immediately threatened, I held up a hand. "Please stop. This is private property."

She didn't back off. "Can I just ask you a few questions about your daughter's experience?"

She was halfway up my driveway while the TV crew stood anxiously on the sidewalk, filming me.

"I don't have any comment. Please leave us alone."

In a panic, I unbuckled Louise, picked her up to carry her on my hip, and I let Leo out as well. He trotted to the front door while I hurried to follow, ignoring questions from the reporters who were lined up on the sidewalk, shouting at me.

As soon as we entered the house, I shut the door, locked it behind us, and set Louise down.

"Mommy, who were they?" she asked, her cheeks flushed with color.

I moved to the front window to close the blinds, then discreetly peered between the slats. "They're reporters, honey."

"What did they want?"

"They just want to ask us some questions about the accident yesterday."

She watched me while I continued to keep an eye on things out front. At least the reporters were staying back. They weren't on my property.

"Why wouldn't you talk to them?" Louise asked, moving closer.

I faced her and pasted on a carefree smile. "Because I already spoke to one on the phone last night."

"But why don't you want to speak to *those* ones?" She pointed toward the front yard, while I fumbled for an answer.

"Because they shouldn't have come to our house. It's not very polite."

"Would it be polite if they called you on the phone?"

"Yes, that would be better."

The phone rang just then, and my heart turned over with dread. I strode to the kitchen to answer it. "Hello?"

"Hi, may I speak with Bev Hutchinson?"

My heart began to race. "This is her."

The woman on the other end of the line introduced herself as a producer from CNN in New York, and she wanted to know if I'd be willing to talk to Jack Peterson. Live. On the air.

My knees nearly buckled because Jack Peterson was a celebrity host of his own prime time news program. For a few seconds, I was star struck. Was CNN really calling me? How did they get my number?

"About what?" I asked, even though I already knew the answer to that question.

"We'd like to talk to you about your daughter and what she experienced while you were performing CPR on her. We'd also like to ask her a few questions as well, if you'd be willing to let her appear on air?"

Suddenly, the spell was broken. It didn't matter that it was CNN or Jack Peterson. What I needed to do was protect my daughter from all this media attention. What happened to her was private.

"I'm sorry," I said, "I can't allow her to be interviewed, and I don't want to be on television. Please don't call here again."

As soon as I hung up the phone, my cell phone started ringing.

"My God, what is it with these people?" I hurried to retrieve it from my purse and was relieved to see that it was Claire. I quickly swiped the screen. "Hello?"

"Hi, Bev. Have you been watching the news? They're talking about you on every station. They even have video of you and Louise getting out of the helicopter."

"What? No way." I ran into the living room, picked up the remote control and turned on the television.

Sure enough, there we were, getting out of the Coast Guard chopper.

"I'll call you back," I said to Claire, and set down my phone.

The video showed paramedics wheeling Louise's gurney to a waiting ambulance while Claire and I followed. Thankfully, you couldn't see my face, and my hair was flat and wet, so you'd never know I had frizzy blond hair.

They cut to a priest being interviewed via satellite, talking about heaven and the pearly gates, and referring to members of his congregation that he'd counseled after near-death experiences.

"Mommy, what's happening?"

I jumped when I realized Louise was standing beside me. With wide eyes, she watched the priest on the screen. I quickly shut off the TV.

"It's nothing, sweetheart. Just more news about the accident." I reached for her hand. "Let's get a snack in the kitchen."

I led her out of the room, thankful that they hadn't mentioned our names, because it was very important that I protect our privacy.

Emma

Oak Bay, British Columbia

After a long day at work, I drove to Luke's house, poured a glass of wine for myself, and collapsed on his sofa to wait for him to come home. I switched on the television. It was my usual habit after work to go straight to a news station, just to see if anything major had happened in the world. Once I felt caught up on the current events of the day, I'd scroll through the channel guide until I found a sitcom like *Hot in Cleveland* or *Two and a Half Men*, just to give myself a little time to decompress.

On the news stations that night, they were still covering the ship that sank off the coast of Nova Scotia the day before. I was about to change the channel when the anchorwoman mentioned a five-year-old child who had drowned, but was brought back to life by her mother who knew CPR.

I began to chew hard on my lower lip.

I should have known CPR. I should have been a better mother, like that woman.

The news anchor turned to her guest panelists and said, "The girl is claiming she died and went to heaven, which has stirred up a lot of controversy in the past twenty-four hours. Everyone is talking about this, in every language, all around the world. Tell me, why do you think the world is so fascinated with this story?"

The remote control dropped out of my hand and I sat forward to listen.

"Fear of death isn't anything new," the first panelist replied, "and stories like this touch a nerve for a lot of people who are afraid of dying. Not to mention all the people in the world who have lost loved ones. Their pain is very deep, and if this little girl is providing some proof of an afterlife, where we're all reunited with loved ones in a happier place, it's very comforting to know that. It's exactly what those who are grieving want to hear—that their loved one still exists, and that they'll be reunited with them one day."

"But do you believe it's true?" the anchorwoman pressed. "Do you believe that this little girl actually went to heaven? Or do you think she's just trying to get attention?"

"I certainly would love to talk to her about it," the second panelist replied, and everyone agreed, laughing, that it would be an interesting interview. He then went on to comment that every society and culture from ancient times to the present has held some belief in the afterlife, and near-death experiences are often similar across different religions, so we can't just assume it's all a bunch of mumbo jumbo.

"But how can we prove it?" the anchorwoman asked. "Do you think we'll ever find the scientific evidence that we need, as a race, in order to believe in life after death? Or will it always be…just a matter of faith?"

They continued to debate the subject, while I sat in pure captivation, waiting for more information about what the little girl had actually experienced.

If she went to heaven, what was it like? Did she meet family members who died earlier? If so, did they take care of her?

I wished I could see a picture of the girl and her mother. I craved more information, and I wanted desperately to know whether or not it was real.

~⊘~

Luke arrived home an hour later and found me in the kitchen making supper. He kissed me on the cheek and asked how my day was, then poured himself a glass of wine.

"How can I help?" he asked, looking around the kitchen.

This was one of the things I loved about Luke. He enjoyed cooking and he never minded doing household chores, even though he could afford a chef and a maid.

"I have everything taken care of. I'm just waiting for the salmon to come out of the oven. You could set the table?"

He reached past me for a couple of plates in the cupboard, kissed me on the cheek again, then gathered cutlery from the drawer and went to the dining room.

A moment later, he returned to find me sipping my wine, staring absentmindedly into space.

"Hey…" He moved closer and rubbed my shoulder. "Everything okay?"

I shook myself out of my stupor and met his gaze. "I'm sorry. I saw something on CNN when I came home from work today, and I can't get it out of my head."

"What was it?"

I turned to lean against the countertop. "You know that ship that went down on the East Coast yesterday, because of the microburst?"

"Yes. That was terrible."

"Well, did you hear about the little girl who drowned? Apparently, her mother was a nurse and she did CPR on her in the lifeboat and brought her back to life. Now the girl's saying she went to heaven and back."

Luke watched me for a moment. "Yes. I did hear about that." He paused. "I think I know where this is going. Are you okay?"

A lump formed in my throat, but I swallowed over it because I didn't want to cry. I wanted to stay strong and talk about this.

"I wish I had known CPR," I said. "If I had, then maybe..." I stopped myself right there and redirected my focus. "I might want to sign up for a course. For the future."

He squeezed my shoulder. "That's a great idea. I could use a refresher. We could take a class together."

"That would be nice—to do it together." The timer on the oven started beeping, so I moved to check on the salmon. "This looks ready."

A few minutes later, we sat down at the table to eat, but I didn't have much of an appetite.

"You're still preoccupied," Luke mentioned as he cut into his potatoes.

I gave him an apologetic smile. "I'm sorry. I just can't stop thinking about that little girl. I wish they could get her on television so we could hear what she actually experienced. Apparently, it's all hearsay right now. The mother won't even go on record. She's trying to protect their privacy."

"I can't blame her," Luke replied. "The kid's only five."

"I know." I ate a few bites, then found myself pushing my food around on my plate. After a moment, I looked up. "What do *you* think about it? Do you believe we go to heaven when we die? Or do you think there's nothing else? That when we're gone, we're gone, and it's just death."

His shoulders rose and fell with a deep breath. "I wish I could say a definitive yes or no, but honestly, Emma, I don't know. I can't say that I believe in it one hundred percent because there's no real proof, but at the same time, I can't say I don't, because who knows what might be possible? I think it's arrogant for any man to assume that he knows *everything*."

I leaned forward over my plate. "Have you ever seen anything that would lead you to believe there's something more out there? Like a ghost or... Oh, I don't even know what."

Luke reached for his wine and took a sip. "No, but other people say they have. Are they all lying or having hallucinations? Who knows? But I do find it interesting whenever I hear stories about people having out-of-body experiences during operations, when they describe floating up to the ceiling and watching what was happening from above, even though they were flatlining and clinically dead. It makes me curious."

"It makes me curious, too," I replied. I took a sip of my wine. "I wish I could contact the mother of that little girl and ask her about what she experienced."

Luke watched me for a moment with concern. "I don't know if that would be a good idea."

"Why not?"

He hesitated. "Because all this is making you think

about Samuel and where he might be right now. Am I correct?"

I knew my voice would shake if I spoke, so I simply nodded.

"I just don't want this to set you back," Luke said. "I want you to be happy."

"I am happy." I raised Luke's hand to my lips and kissed the back of it. "I'm happy that I met you."

"Me, too." He smiled.

I rose out of my chair and kissed him across the table.

~C

The following day at work, I found it difficult to concentrate at my desk in my cubicle. I kept googling news sites about the *Dalila* tragedy. I was searching for new information about the little girl who said she went to heaven, but her mother continued to keep her hidden from the press. It was frustrating, to say the least, but I couldn't blame her. I'd probably do the same thing in her shoes, but oh, how I wanted to talk to her. I wished I knew their names so I could find the mother on Facebook and send her a message. I wanted to tell her what happened to my son, and ask if she truly believed her daughter's alleged trip to heaven.

I wanted to know if it was real, and I didn't want to rely on faith alone.

Unfortunately, as the day progressed, there was no new information released about the child, but my searches led me down other paths, to websites and blogs with stories about people who had experienced NDEs in all sorts of different circumstances. It was fascinating reading. I couldn't get enough of it and I was lucky it was a slow day at work because I didn't get much done.

After work, I went home to Luke's house and wondered why I had bothered to keep my little apartment in Victoria all this time. It seemed pointless to be paying rent there when I was practically living with Luke already, but I hadn't wanted to make the effort to get out of the lease. I had decided to just ride it out, but there were only a few weeks left now anyway.

When I walked in the door, Toby and Max were excited to see me. They greeted me with wagging tails and followed me into the kitchen where I poured kibble into their food bowls and refreshed their water.

While they gobbled down their dinner, I slid the patio door open and stepped outside to gaze across the water at the majestic Olympic Mountain range in the distance. I looked up at the clear blue sky and wondered... If heaven existed, what was it like?

I turned to go back inside, went to Luke's computer in the family room and logged into my bookstore account, where I searched for books about heaven and near-death experiences. There were too many to count, but I settled on a few that looked interesting. One was called *The Color of Heaven*, and it was written by a woman who had drowned after her car crashed into a frozen lake. She was clinically dead for forty minutes before they rescued her and brought her back to life in the hospital.

Another was called *Proof of Heaven*. It was written by a neurologist who'd had meningitis and claimed he experienced the afterlife. I ordered both titles as e-books and downloaded them to my tablet so I could start reading immediately.

When Luke came home with Thai food from our favorite take-out restaurant, he found me on the back patio, reading under the canopy with Max and Toby sleeping in the shade beneath the table. There were seagulls in the sky, calling out to each other.

I told him about the books I'd bought, and he was fascinated by what I'd read so far. He asked if he could read them too, and I was more than happy to share them with him.

I am just home from the hospital after giving birth to Samuel. Carter has gone out to give a quote on a landscaping job, so I'm home alone in my bathrobe. Samuel sleeps a lot, but that doesn't matter. I hold him in my arms most of the time, whether he's awake or asleep, because I'm so in love, I don't want to set him down. The depth of my feeling is inconceivable. I can barely fathom it. I never knew such love was possible. He's the most beautiful thing in the universe to me, and I can't stop staring at him…adoring him….

I carry him to the iPod dock in the living room and scroll through a few of my playlists. Samuel's eyes are open and he's watching me, but he's sleepy—I can tell, so I search for a calming ballad. I've been listening to a lot of classical music lately because that's what the experts recommend, but this afternoon I'm in the mood for something different.

Rod Stewart's album *If We Fall in Love Tonight* pops out at me, so I click on "For the First Time." I set the iPod in the dock and gently shift my newborn baby boy in my arms so that his cheek rests on my shoulder. When the music starts to play, I dance slowly around the living room, rocking him to and fro.

I feel such joy, I begin to wonder if I've died and gone to heaven.

How could this much happiness even be possible?

I never told Luke or Carter this, but there were times, in the weeks following the funeral, that I contemplated suicide. Part of the reason was because I didn't want to go on living without my sweet baby boy. I missed him terribly and my guilt was beyond excruciating. It was the worst kind of torture imaginable. I just wanted to end my suffering.

On another level, I wanted to be with Samuel again, wherever he was, even in death—but I'd heard that people who committed suicide went to hell, so I didn't want to risk ending up in the wrong place where I'd never see him again.

Did that mean I believed in heaven and hell? I still wasn't sure what I believed. All I know is that I didn't want to risk sending myself into a fiery pit of despair for the rest of eternity because I wasn't strong enough to stick it out, to keep on living until my time came.

I supposed that was still true today. As much as I wanted to be with Samuel, I'd never risk something like that. I'd simply have to be patient.

That didn't stop me from imagining what would happen if I got hit by a bus or went down in a plane crash. I sometimes fantasized about the beautiful white light that people describe, and seeing Samuel there, in the clouds, waiting to greet me. I dreamed about the joy I would feel when I held him in my arms again…

But would we even have arms in heaven?

~*~

My cell phone buzzed at work the following day, and I was surprised to see a text from Carter.

Hey. How are you?

I blinked a few times as I stared at his message. The last time we spoke, five months ago, we'd finalized our divorce, and since then, we'd had no contact with each other whatsoever, except through our lawyers.

I slowly typed a reply, feeling a need to be cautious: *Fine. How are you?*

I waited a few seconds, staring at the screen, wondering why he was getting in touch. Then my phone buzzed again. *I'm okay. Have you been watching the news?*

My belly did a little flip and my heart began to beat faster. I still wasn't sure why Carter was contacting me. Part of me feared he wanted to compare that situation to ours and rub my nose in it again, and I didn't want to engage him in that. I didn't want him to stir up my guilt. I could do that well enough on my own, thank you very much.

My response was brief: *Yes.*

I hit send and waited.

A co-worker came by my desk and asked for a specific report. I had to ignore my phone for a moment while I found it and handed it to her. When I picked up my phone, two more texts had come in.

Have you seen the stuff about the little girl who drowned?

Hello? Are you there?

I began to type a reply. *Sorry, I'm at work and someone needed something. But yes, I've been following it. I wish we knew more.*

Carter responded a second later: *It's kind of addictive. I can't stop thinking about it. I don't suppose you'd be willing to get together and talk? I promise I won't be a jerk.*

My eyebrows lifted at that, and I leaned back in my desk chair. Wow. Carter was admitting to being a jerk. I couldn't deny that I took some pleasure in reading those words.

But still, I needed to protect myself. I slowly typed a reply: *I don't know…*

Please? he asked. *You're the only person I can talk to about this.*

My hackles rose. *What about Melissa?*

This time I had to wait a little while before his response came in. I found myself tapping my foot anxiously on the floor.

Finally, my phone buzzed.

She doesn't really get it. She thinks it's a big hoax. Maybe it is, but I feel like I'm going crazy, wondering about it. Can we meet? Just for coffee or something?

I exhaled sharply. I certainly didn't feel that I owed Carter any sympathy if he was going through something—because he never offered any sympathy to me—but I couldn't ignore my burning desire for information. Maybe he knew something I didn't, or maybe he had a different perspective that would shed some light on what I was feeling.

But did I really want to talk to Carter about this? It was painful, revisiting old memories, and maybe he'd want specific details about the very moment of Samuel's passing.

At least with Luke, there was no blame about what happened. He always led me away from my guilt.

In the end, however, my curiosity won out. I needed to know what Carter thought about all this.

Eventually, I picked up my phone and responded. *Are you free after work?*

Seven

Emma

Carter and I arranged to grab coffees and meet on the bench across the street from the Empress Hotel. As I rounded the corner at the intersection, I saw him in the distance. He was already sitting there, reading on his phone. Eventually he looked up. When he spotted me walking toward him in the late-afternoon sunshine, he waited until I got closer—then he stood.

"Hi. It's good to see you."

"You, too." I spoke with a hint of reserve while I took in the fact that he'd grown a short beard. It was a bit of a surprise, because never, in all the years I'd known him, had he been anything but clean-shaven.

We regarded each other awkwardly for a few seconds, then he stepped forward and kissed me on the cheek, as if I were an old friend. I suppose that's what we could be to each other now—*friends*—if we managed to put our difficult past behind us and move on with other people. It was at least better than being hateful.

We sat down on the bench, facing the impressive front lawn and ivy-cloaked façade of the historic hotel. I pulled back the plastic lid on my coffee cup and took the first sip.

"How have you been?" Carter asked, squinting in the sunlight.

"Good," I replied. "You?"

He shrugged. "I've been okay."

We watched cars drive by on the street in front of us.

I looked up at the sky.

Carter gazed off in the other direction.

A couple of kids across the street horsed around, fighting over something in the backpack one of them was carrying.

"How are the wedding plans going?" Carter asked.

I made an effort to sound cheerful. "Pretty good. We're having it on New Year's Eve." I gave him a sidelong glance, and he chuckled.

"Whose idea was *that*? It couldn't have been yours."

I rolled my eyes a little, with chagrin. "It was Luke's. He's never been married before, so he wants to make a big deal out of it."

"No one will be able to get cabs, you know. Not after midnight."

I laughed. "I know. I did mention that. I'm hoping most of the guests will stay in the hotel."

Carter took another sip of his coffee. "Which hotel?"

I gestured toward the one across the street—the most famous and luxurious hotel in Victoria.

Carter whistled. "Seriously? You were able to book that for New Year's Eve? I can't even imagine what that must have cost. Unless they're putting you in the basement, or something." He sipped his coffee again.

"We'll be in the Ivy Ballroom," I told him.

He leaned back. "Wow. Ivy Ballroom. So...is my

invitation in the mail, or what?" He nudged me playfully, as if we'd leapfrogged back to the years before we lost Samuel, before we became so antagonistic with each other. For a moment, I was transported, but the feeling passed in an instant because we both knew we couldn't erase the last four years.

I wasn't quite sure what he was trying to do here.

I sipped my coffee and watched one of the yellow cabs at the taxi stand pull away from the curb.

"So," I said flatly. "You wanted to talk about the little girl in Nova Scotia."

He inhaled deeply. "Yes. It's been an interesting few days, watching the news."

He said no more than that, which frustrated me because, sometimes, getting Carter to talk about his feelings was like trying to get blood from a stone. Which was why I was so surprised he'd wanted to meet with me. But true to form, now that I was here, he expected me to pull it out of him.

"It's been interesting, for sure," I replied. "What do you think? Is she just trying to get attention? Making things up? Or do you think there is actually something to it?"

Carter faced me on the bench. "I can't deny, I want to believe her experience was real."

My heart turned over in my chest, like an old engine that hadn't worked in a while, finally sputtering to life. "Me, too," I said. "I want to believe it."

Carter stood up and walked to the concrete wall behind us to take in the view of the inner harbor and sailboats moored at the docks. I stood up as well and joined him there.

"But do we just want to believe it because we want to be

consoled?" he asked me. "That's what people are saying about this kind of thing, and it makes me feel like a fool for wanting to buy into it."

"Not everyone says that," I replied. "Plenty of people have an unshakable sense of faith and believe wholeheartedly that there's something more beyond this life. I just wish I were one of those people, that I had no doubt. It would make all of this so much easier."

A man puttered around on a sailboat that was docked below us. We watched him polish the seats with a blue-and-white cloth.

Carter turned toward me. "Listen, there's something I need to say to you."

"What is it?"

Carter sipped his coffee, then turned away from me. He crossed the sidewalk to throw the empty cup in a trash receptacle by the curb. Then he stood for a moment with his back to me, kicking the receptacle with the toe of his work boot. Finally, he returned.

"I had a dream about a month ago," he said. "Although…I'm not even sure it was a dream." He cleared his throat. "I was kind of freaked out."

"What was it about?"

He blew out a breath. "It's hard to talk about, Emma. I suppose it's part of the reason why I'm obsessed with that little girl's story."

I couldn't take the suspense. I took hold of Carter's arm. "What happened?"

He looked down at his boots and shook his head. "I dreamed about Sammy. Only it didn't feel like a dream. It felt real." He paused and turned toward the harbor again, resting his elbows on the concrete barrier. "I was asleep, and then I heard something—the creak of a door. I opened my eyes and sat up, and there he was in the doorway, wearing his blue pajamas. You know…the ones with Thomas the Tank Engine?"

I nodded.

"He was just staring at me," Carter continued, "and for a second I thought he'd had a bad dream and he wanted me to take him back to bed and tuck him in. Then I remembered that…he was gone. So it couldn't be happening."

Carter bowed his head and I could see that he was trying not to get choked up. I considered laying my hand on his back and rubbing gently, but resisted the urge.

"He just kept staring at me like he was really angry," Carter continued. "Then he walked away, back down the hall. I got out of bed to follow him, but of course he wasn't there. I kept telling myself it was a dream, but I'm sure I was awake."

"Wow."

"Have you ever had a dream like that?"

"I've had lots of dreams," I replied, "but I always knew I was dreaming. There was never any question about that." I inclined my head. "So, what are you saying? That you think he was really there? Like a ghost?"

Carter shook his head. "I know it sounds crazy. I probably need help."

"Don't we all." We stood in silence for a moment. Then I sat down on the bench again.

Carter followed. "I miss him," he said.

"Me, too."

I gazed up at the blue sky. A fluffy white cloud moved in front of the sun.

"But what does this have to do with the little girl on the east coast who went to heaven?" I asked. "*Allegedly* went to heaven."

"Well," Carter replied, "this is the crazy part. Ever since I heard about that, I've been doing research online, about the afterlife and near-death experiences."

"So have I," I confessed.

He nodded, as if he wasn't surprised to hear it. "I found this woman in Vancouver who's a psychic." Before I had a chance to say anything, he held up a hand to stop me. "Now, hear me out. She claims she can talk to people who have passed on."

I shook my head as if to clear it. "Wait a second. You're not actually thinking about going to see a psychic, are you? To try and talk to Sammy?"

He shrugged. "I don't know. Maybe. That dream really stayed with me. I felt like he wanted to tell me something. And if there is an afterlife, don't you want to know that he's okay? And that he's still…alive in some way?"

I stared at Carter in shock. "He's not alive. He's gone." A painful lump formed in my throat and I swallowed forcefully over it.

"Yes, I know that, but… You know what I'm saying, Emma. If he's present somehow. I want to know."

I sat back and stared across the street at the hotel. "I can't believe you're saying this. You were never one to believe in *woo-woo* stuff. I had to drag you to church most Sundays, and you made fun of anyone who believed in signs or fate."

He accepted that with a nod. "I know. You're right. But that dream… And listen…" He turned slightly on the bench to face me and hung his head low. "I realize it's kind of late for me to be saying this, but it's long overdue and it needs to be said." He wiped a finger under his nose. "I owe you an apology, Emma."

My stomach began to burn with unease. "For what?"

"For how I treated you. For the things I said to you." He faced the hotel and sat quietly for a moment while my heart pounded in my chest like a sledgehammer.

"When I look back on it," he continued, "I can't believe I was that messed up. I was so angry and...I was just wrecked. I just needed to blame someone."

My blood raced through my veins. I wanted to get up and run, but I wasn't sure why. "Please, Carter, you don't have to say this."

"Yes, I do. And you have to let me say it." He grabbed hold of my hand and squeezed it. "You didn't deserve all that. I was upset and the grief was too much, but at least I didn't have to deal with what *you* had to..."

I tried to pull my hand away. "Please stop..."

But he wouldn't let it go. "It must have been so much worse for you. I should have understood that. I shouldn't have been so selfish, because something like that could just as easily have happened to me. When I think of all the times I let him swing too high at the playground, or when I was busy in the front yard and took my eye off him for a few seconds. He could have run out in front of a car or something. I wasn't perfect. So, I was wrong to blame you like I did. I was an ass, Emma, and I'm so sorry."

My stomach was in knots because this was incredibly painful to talk about. I didn't want to think about what happened that day...how I left Sammy alone in the yard....how I panicked when I saw him in the pool.

Finally, I managed to pull my hand from Carter's grasp.

"Thank you. I appreciate that. But I don't want to talk about this with you. Not now. It's in the past and it's taken me a long time to get this far. I don't want to go back there."

I got up and started to walk away, but he followed. "Wait, Emma. Please, I'm sorry. I didn't mean to upset you."

"You didn't."

"Yes, I did. Obviously, I did, and I don't blame you for hating me."

I stopped in my tracks. "Hating *you*? Are you kidding me right now? You're the one who hated me all this time. It's why we're divorced—because you couldn't even look at me. You asked me to leave. You couldn't bear to live in the same house with me, and God knows I couldn't live there either." I held up both my hands in mock surrender. "Please, let's just leave things the way they are. You're in a good place. I'm in a good place. And I accept your apology. There. You're forgiven. Now I have to go."

I started walking again, hurrying down the street to my car. This time, I was relieved that Carter didn't follow.

I got into my car and sat there for a long moment gripping the wheel, staring in a daze through the windshield.

A short while later, I drove toward Luke's house in Oak Bay. I turned on the radio and fought to calm my nerves and settle my churning stomach. When I began to feel calmer, I thought back to what Carter had said about visiting a psychic in order to reach out to Sammy, wherever he might be.

Was that even possible? Or was it crazy? My conversation with Carter suddenly felt unfinished. I had a lot of questions.

Rather than go straight home to Luke, I decided to drive

around for a while, just to give myself a chance to ponder what Carter had said.

~⊘

"You're kind of late," Luke said when I walked in the door. He was wearing the chef's apron I'd given him for his birthday that said "Hot Stuff," and he was brandishing a barbeque spatula. He came to the door to meet me and gave me a kiss while the dogs circled around us with wagging tails.

"Sorry," I replied. "There was a problem with the computers today and we had to catch up on a few things."

I wish I could say I hadn't planned to lie to Luke about seeing Carter after work, but I did plan it. While I was driving to his place, I'd worked out a believable excuse, and I'm still not sure why I felt I couldn't tell Luke the truth. It's not as if I'd agreed to meet Carter because I missed him or wanted to reconcile. I simply didn't want to talk about what Carter had said to me. It was too painful to vocalize, and I'd become very good at avoiding painful things. I just wanted to enjoy dinner with my fiancé.

Later, when we sat down to eat on the patio, Luke mentioned one of the books I'd lent him. "So I finished *The Color of Heaven* today," he said as he served himself some salad.

"Yeah? What did you think?" I hadn't read that one yet. I was still working on the other one.

"Well, I don't want to give away any spoilers," he replied, "but I'm having trouble believing that it was real. I'm just not sure. What about the book you're reading? Do you believe it?"

"I don't know. The author certainly does. He makes a very good case, and he's a medical doctor, a man of science. It's hard to believe he would make all that stuff up and risk his reputation."

"Unless he knew he could make millions off the book. That's where it gets dicey. It's hard to figure out what people's motivations are."

I nodded in agreement, then couldn't resist asking Luke another question. "Here's a doozy for you. What about psychics? Do you think they can actually communicate with people in heaven, or help people talk to loved ones who have passed?"

He reached for the pepper mill and seasoned his steak. "*Hmm.* That is a doozy." I suspected he was stalling as he set the pepper mill back on the table and picked up his fork. "I'm not going to say I don't believe it, but I do have a problem with people charging money and trying to get rich off that kind of thing. I think it opens up opportunities for con artists who want to take advantage of vulnerable people who are grieving. And that steals credibility from the whole industry. Makes it all look fake."

"It's interesting that you call it an industry."

He inclined his head. "I guess that's just my perception."

"It's a reasonable one."

I decided to leave it at that and not mention what Carter had suggested about going to see that psychic in Vancouver. Especially because Luke didn't even know I'd met with him.

Later that evening, while I was in the kitchen puttering around and Luke was watching the news on television, I received another text from Carter. I picked up my phone and immediately went into the den to read it.

Hey. I'm sorry about today. I didn't mean to upset you.

I had to admit, I felt a bit foolish and embarrassed for running off the way I did, like a frightened bird.

I sat down in the leather reading chair by the window and thumbed a reply: *Thanks. But you'd think I'd have thicker skin by now. Believe it or not, I appreciated what you said.*

I started to type *It was a long time coming*, but I backed up and deleted that part, and just hit send.

His reply came a moment later. *We didn't really get to finish our conversation about the other stuff. I know this is going to sound crazy, but I'm seriously thinking about going to see that psychic in Vancouver. I don't suppose you'd be willing to come with me?*

I sat there, actually considering it, and typed uncertainly: *I'm not sure. When are you thinking of going?*

As soon as she can fit us in, he replied.

I felt heat and color rush to my cheeks as I thought about this. A psychic who spoke to the dead. Did I really want to invite that kind of thing into my life? I'd just spent the past four years fighting to overcome my grief and figure out how to live like a normal person again, to accept that my son was gone and never coming back, and that no amount of wishing was going to change that. Did it make sense that now I was going to try to communicate with him, from somewhere beyond the grave?

What exactly did I want to hear? That he didn't blame me for what happened? Would that make me feel better?

Yes, I suppose it would. But was I insane to get into this with my ex-husband, who was half the reason why I had such a difficult time overcoming my guilt and grief in the first place?

I slowly typed a reply. *I'm not sure it's a good idea.*

Why not? he quickly replied. *If it turns out to be a big scam, it'll be an interesting experience and we'll have a story to tell. At least we won't go through life wondering what if.*

Pulling my knees up under me, I glanced at the open doorway and listened to the sound of the television in the other room.

I couldn't imagine what Luke would think about this. He'd always been supportive of me in every way, and I doubted he would try and stop me if I really wanted to go, but would he think, deep down, that I was a nutcase?

Was I?

Maybe, because there was no way on earth I could let Carter go and see a psychic—and possibly talk to Samuel—without me. If that was going to happen, I wanted to be there.

I lifted my phone and responded: *If you're going to do it, I'll come. But I'm still not sure it's a good idea.*

I'm not sure either, he replied, *but I can't live with the curiosity. I need to know.*

I considered that for a moment, then I typed a response. *Me, too. Let's go ahead and try it. Let me know what she says.*

OK. I'll keep you posted.

I slipped my phone into my pocket and sat in the dim lamplight for a while, staring at the bookshelves and wondering if I should tell Luke about this. I certainly didn't want him to think I was keeping secrets from him so that I could sneak around with Carter, or that I wanted to rekindle my relationship with my ex. Nothing was further from the truth. There was too much ugly water under that bridge.

But I also didn't want Luke to think I was unhinged, trying to communicate with my son who had been dead for four years. Luke had always been very understanding about my grief, but I'm not sure he would agree that this was a good idea. I wasn't even sure it was myself. And I didn't want him to change his mind about marrying me.

In the end, I decided to sleep on it. Maybe Carter wouldn't be able to get an appointment. Maybe you had to book these things months or years in advance.

An hour later, while Luke was out walking the dogs before bed and I was in his bedroom changing into my pajamas, Carter texted me.

I just heard back from her. Are you free tomorrow night? Appointment at six. I can drive.

Eight

Emma

I was sitting up in bed, reading, when Luke returned from walking the dogs. They followed him upstairs and jumped onto the bed to sit with me while Luke brushed his teeth.

I patted each of them lovingly and scratched behind their ears. "Did you boys have a good walk?"

"It was a short one," Luke called out from the bathroom. "We met Mrs. Jenkins with her two dogs and chatted for a while."

A few minutes later, he slipped into bed beside me and Toby and Max jumped down to lie on their dog beds under the window.

"Are you going to read for a while?" Luke asked.

Of course, that wasn't the real question he was asking. He wanted to know if I was in the mood for romance. Usually I was, but with Carter's text sitting on the bedside table, I couldn't pretend not to be distracted.

"Actually, I need to talk to you about something."

"Sure."

He sat up the feather pillows and gave me his full

attention. I cleared my throat, nervously. "There's something I didn't tell you about why I was late today."

"Okay…" He regarded me uneasily.

"I don't know why I didn't tell you. I just didn't want to talk about it right then, I guess. But now I need to tell you what's happening."

"I'm listening."

I reached for his hand. "Carter texted me today while I was at work. He said he wanted to talk to me about what's going on with the girl who went to heaven. I guess it's been on his mind, too."

Luke's eyebrows lifted. "So, that's where you were after work? With Carter? There was no computer glitch?"

I sensed immediately that he was hurt, which was the last thing I wanted, and I felt terrible for not telling him the truth. "Yes. I'm sorry I couldn't tell you before. I should have."

"Why didn't you?"

Now I felt even worse. "I don't know… The whole thing was just horribly unpleasant. I haven't seen Carter since we signed the divorce papers, and it was just as awkward and uncomfortable as you could imagine. When I got home to you, I didn't want to think about it or talk about it. I wanted to forget it."

Luke seemed to relax slightly at that. He wove his fingers through mine. "What happened? Why did he want to see you?"

I dropped my gaze to our entwined hands. "He wanted to tell me about a dream he had about Sammy, which he wasn't even sure was a dream. He said he woke up one night to the sound of his bedroom door opening, and Sammy was standing there, staring at him. Carter was really freaked out by it, and all this stuff about that little girl going to heaven is making him think."

"Same as you," Luke replied, and I nodded.

"But that's not all," I added. "Carter also told me he'd been considering seeing a psychic about it, to find out if Sammy was trying to communicate with him about something."

Luke regarded me warily. "That's why you brought up psychics earlier."

"Yes. And then he texted me while you were out with the dogs to ask if I wanted to go with him to see a psychic in Vancouver. He made an appointment, and it's tomorrow night."

"*Jeez.*" Luke raked his fingers through his hair. "What did you say? You're not going to go with him, are you?"

I hesitated. "I don't know. I'm thinking about it."

His head drew back. "I'm trying to be understanding about this, Emma, but I don't like it."

"Why? Is it because I'm talking to Carter? Or do you think it's crazy to see a psychic?"

He let out a breath. "I don't know if it's crazy or not. But if you want to go and see someone like that, I'll go with you. You don't need to go with Carter."

"But..." I paused, and decided I had to speak my mind. "Carter was Sammy's father. It makes more sense for us to go together."

Luke frowned at me with disbelief. "But he treated you terribly. I don't want to see that happen to you again. I don't want you to feel demoralized and guilt-ridden. You don't deserve that, Emma. You've come so far. Just let him go on his own. If he had a bad dream about Sammy and wants help figuring it out, that's his issue, not yours. You don't owe him anything. He was a jerk to you."

I gazed down at my hands in my lap. "Actually, he apologized to me about...all of that."

Luke stared at me through a sudden ringing silence. "So...*what*? Now you're best friends?"

"No, of course not."

When I said nothing more, Luke tossed the covers aside and got out of bed.

"Where are you going?"

"Nowhere. Just downstairs. I need a glass of water."

He left the room and the dogs followed.

I sat there in the silence, wishing I'd handled this better. If he was angry with me, I couldn't blame him. I'd lied to him today about meeting with my ex-husband. It was a mistake to say I had to work late.

Sliding out of bed, I donned my robe and padded downstairs where I found Luke in the kitchen, filling a glass at the sink.

"I'm sorry," I said, standing behind him, hugging him, sliding my hands up his bare chest. "I should have told you where I was today. I just didn't want to talk about it because the whole thing was just...icky. I wanted to forget about it."

Luke turned around to face me. "How was it icky? You just said he apologized to you."

Sensing his displeasure, I lowered my hands to my side and stepped back. "He did, but it was too little, too late. I didn't want to stick around after that. If you had been there, you would have seen me walk away from him."

Luke stared at me for a long moment, then he stepped forward and gently pulled me into his arms. My body flooded with relief.

Neither of us spoke, and I hoped this meant he forgave me for not telling him the truth earlier.

When he drew back, he said, "I just don't want you to get hurt. And I don't want to lose what we have here, Emma. We're moving on together, and I'm happy about the future. I don't want him dragging you back there or...trying to steal you back."

I shook my head. "That's not something you have to worry about. He's not trying to get me back. First of all, he's with someone else now, and even if he wasn't, I'm engaged to you. He just..." I let out a breath, because I wasn't sure how to finish that sentence.

"He what?" Luke pressed.

It took me a moment to articulate my thoughts. "Maybe, because he's been blaming me all this time, he never got past the anger stage. Now he's actually grieving and he doesn't know how to handle it."

Luke took my face in his hand, stroked my cheek with the pad of his thumb. "I don't mean to sound cruel, but it's not your job to help Carter, because he certainly didn't help you."

I cupped his hand in mine and nodded. "I know that. But I'm not doing this for him. I'm doing it for me, because if Sammy is in heaven, I sure would love some proof of that. It would help me to know that he's okay and safe and happy. Maybe it would give me a sense of peace."

Luke pulled me into his arms again. "I want that for you, Emma. I really do, but I don't know if peace is ever possible when you've lost a child."

His words caused a swell of sadness in me because I knew he was right. I'd never stop missing my beautiful son. Not in this lifetime.

"Maybe not," I replied, "but I still need to do this. If I don't, I'll always wonder *what if.*"

Those were Carter's words, not mine, but they applied to me, too.

When Luke and I got back into bed, I told him when the appointment was. Thankfully, he accepted my decision to go, told me he loved me, and assured me that he trusted me.

I took the afternoon off from work, and Carter offered to pick me up at my apartment so that we could drive to Vancouver together. But I hadn't been living at my apartment for months. Luke urged me to have Carter pick me up in Oak Bay and admitted he wanted Carter to see with his own eyes that we were together. To know that Luke's home was my home now, and that this was where he could expect to find me from this day forward.

"He needs to know you're mine now," Luke said, holding me in his arms at the door while I waited for Carter to arrive.

When he finally pulled up, Luke walked me out and down the steps to the driveway.

Carter shut off his car and got out. With his typical manly swagger, he circled around the front, put his hands on his hips, and looked up at the house. "Wow. This is quite the place you've got here. I'm Carter."

He strode forward to shake Luke's hand and I realized I was holding my breath as I watched the exchange.

They shook hands. "I'm Luke. Nice to meet you."

They stepped apart, said nothing more, and it became instantly uncomfortable.

Carter turned to me. "We should probably get on the road."

"Yeah, for sure," I replied, trying to act casual as I opened the car door and climbed into the passenger seat.

Carter got in and started up the engine. "That wasn't awkward at all," he said, giving me a look as he turned the car around.

"At least you were civil," I replied, waving to Luke as we drove off.

"Me? I'm always civil."

"Sure you are," I replied, thinking of the many times he walked up to a guy in a bar who'd looked at me the wrong way and suggested the other guy leave before someone got hurt.

Yes, my ex-husband was territorial. But he'd lost that right the day he asked me to leave.

Carter and I chatted politely during the drive to the ferry. I asked about his landscaping business, and he updated me on his new equipment and other developments. He asked after my mom and my job. I asked about his parents and his sisters and Melissa. It was typical small talk.

After we boarded the ferry, which was a ninety-minute ride to the Tsawwassen Terminal on the mainland, we grabbed a bite to eat at the buffet. Mostly, we sat in silence, except for when we discussed a high school friend who had been injured in a cycling accident recently and was in rehab with a brain injury.

When we got back into the car for the final leg of the journey, Carter found a country music station on the radio, but switched to a rock station when they played one of our songs. We drove in silence after that, until I had to help Carter navigate to reach our destination.

~⊘

When we pulled up in front of the psychic's home and place of business, I had a bad feeling—but not because it was a sketchy neighborhood. In fact, it was quite the opposite. Neither of us could believe what we were looking at—a multimillion-dollar waterfront estate made of steel and glass, with ultra-modern sculptures in the yard, in one of the wealthiest neighborhoods in BC.

"It's not quite what I imagined," Carter said, peering at the upper stories with curved rooflines. "It looks like a space ship."

"Tell me about it. I was picturing a crappy little apartment somewhere downtown where we had to pass through a curtain of hanging beads. Wasn't that what the picture showed on the website? A psychic woman in a turban? Wasn't there a lava lamp vibe?"

Carter nodded. "Yeah. This is kind of disturbing."

I glanced up and down the street. "Are you sure we're in the right place?"

He checked his phone. "Yes. This is the address she gave me. Come on. Let's ring the doorbell."

I followed him along the flagstone walk to the front door, but there was a polished brass plaque that said:

WRONG DOOR

For Psychic Readings: Please Use Side Door

Below this, a long, boney finger pointed to the left, so we tramped down the flagstone steps, around the side of the house, down another flight of steps bordered by a tall cedar hedge, finally arriving at a basement entrance that looked like something out of a Walt Disney World theme park. The arched door was covered with a plastic substance that resembled tree bark. The trim was cloaked in ivy.

"It looks like a Hobbit house in Middle-earth," Carter whispered as he stepped forward to rap with the wrought iron door knocker. "It's not exactly consistent with the upstairs décor."

"Maybe this is a waste of time," I said, grabbing hold of his arm before he had a chance to knock.

He met my gaze squarely. "We came all this way. We might as well see it through."

Exhaling a deep breath, I lowered my hand to my side and waited uneasily for someone to answer.

The door creaked open and the woman from the website greeted us with a beaming smile. She looked to be about sixty and wore heavy eye makeup, gaudy dangling earrings, and a turquoise turban that clashed with her mauve kimono. "Welcome. You must be Carter and Emma. Please come in."

She led us to a waiting room decorated with every cliché in the book on psychics. On the walls were framed images of Tarot cards, crystal balls, and unknown galaxies with floating spirits. What surprised me most was how crowded the waiting room was.

We took a seat on a red velvet sofa, and the woman said, "I'll come and get you when Maria's ready for you."

"Oh," I said. "You're not Maria?"

She laughed. "Oh, good gracious, no. I'm Nell, her receptionist. Would you like a cup of coffee or herbal tea? We have cappuccino as well."

Carter cleared his throat. "None for me, thanks."

"Me neither."

Nell smiled. "Well, let me know if you change your mind. And FYI—she's running a little behind today. Just fifteen minutes or so. Please make yourselves comfortable. It shouldn't be too much longer."

Nell left the room.

I discreetly glanced around at the other clients waiting to see Maria. They were all women, sitting alone, except for one older couple in their seventies.

I leaned close to whisper in Carter's ear. "How much are you paying for this?"

He replied in a hushed voice. "Five hundred bucks. No refund policy."

My stomach did a somersault. "Seriously? Five hundred dollars for fifteen minutes?" I began to work through the math in my head. "If she works eight hours a day, like the rest of us, that's sixteen-thousand dollars each and every day."

Carter pulled out his cell phone and used his calculator. He whispered in my ear. "Assuming four weeks of vacation, that's close to four million a year."

I whistled. "No wonder she can afford to live in a space ship."

All this made me think of my conversation with Luke the night before, when he'd used the word *con artist*. I didn't want to assume that Maria was a scammer, but even if she was the real deal, how was it possible that she could talk to people in heaven every fifteen minutes, day after day, week after week? Did she have the hereafter on speed dial? And wouldn't she find it taxing on her brain?

Everything about this felt shady to me. But I had to hand it to her. No matter which way you sliced it, she was a shrewd business woman.

While Carter and I waited, I picked up a magazine from the coffee table. There were plenty of choices—decorating magazines, dog magazines, gossip tabloids. There was even a monster truck publication.

With every minute that passed while I flipped through *House and Home*, I grew less confident that this was a worthwhile use of our time and Carter's hard-earned cash. I promised myself that I would remain skeptical, but at the same time, I would try and keep an open mind, no matter what she said to us.

Nine

Emma

"Carter? Emma? Maria's ready for you now."

We rose from the sofa and followed Nell down a short hallway. She knocked on the door at the end, pushed it open, and gestured for us to pass through.

As I entered Maria's consultation area, I realized nothing was as I expected. I thought we'd pass through the curtain of beads into something resembling the inside of a genie's bottle, but this room was modern and massive with twenty-foot ceilings and an entire wall of windows that overlooked the water. The floors were shiny black marble and there were three sleek white leather sofas positioned in the shape of a U, facing a gigantic onyx fireplace. Beyond that, Maria's desk was made of glass.

She was seated in a white chair, typing something into her computer. There could be no denying that she was a breathtakingly beautiful woman. She had long, straight, honey colored hair and wore white slacks, a white blouse, white pumps, and an expensive looking Wedgewood-blue silk scarf.

She glanced up and smiled. Her eyes were a striking shade of light blue, and she had the irresistible charm of Jennifer Aniston as she spoke in a friendly tone. "Hi. Come on in. I'll just be one second."

Nell directed us to the leather sofas in front of the fireplace and offered us coffee again. "No thanks," Carter replied.

As soon as Nell was gone, he and I exchanged a look, communicating the same thing—that this was not what we'd expected.

Maria finished what she was doing and rose from her desk. "You must be Carter and Emma. It's a pleasure to meet you."

He and I stood up at the same time. Carter held out his hand to shake Maria's as she approached, but she drew back slightly, as if she were afraid of getting burned.

"If you don't mind," she said, "we'll need to hold off touching hands for a few minutes."

"I see," Carter replied. "My bad."

Maria sat down across from us. "No problem. Is this your first time seeing a psychic?"

"Is it that obvious?" Carter replied with a laugh as he sat down.

I wondered if he was as captivated by Maria as I was. I don't think I'd ever been in the presence of anyone so charismatic before.

"Not at all," she replied. "But you both look a little uneasy. Sometimes I wonder if I should have let Nell go wild with the décor in the waiting room. All that was her idea because she thought it would make clients feel more comfortable—that it would be more in line with their expectations and would look good on the website—but every time a new client walks in here from the waiting room, they do a double take." She glanced toward the door. "I'll probably redecorate out there soon, make it more consistent with the rest of the house."

Carter looked around at the modern furnishings. "This all looks great."

Maria laid her hands flat on her thighs. "Thank you. But enough chatter about interior design. Here's what's going to happen and it shouldn't take too long. We'll go sit over at that table in the corner and take hold of each other's hands. Don't worry, there's a bottle of hand sanitizer at the ready."

Carter laughed, and I knew he was charmed.

"Then," she continued, "I'll wait for a message from someone. And don't tell me who it is that you want to hear from. It's best if we figure it out together. But I need to warn you, there's no guarantee you'll hear from the person you want to talk to. They might simply not be available. Or they might not want to talk to you. And don't be offended if that happens. Sometimes they just want everyone to move on. I can't control that."

"Okay," Carter said, sounding hesitant and disappointed, which wasn't unreasonable, considering he was paying five hundred bucks for this. Obviously, Maria's no refund policy was set up for the days when spirits had better things to do.

"Great. Let's get to it, then." She stood up to lead us to a small round table in the corner of the room with three chairs surrounding it. She picked up the glass spray bottle that looked like a centerpiece from the Ming Dynasty, and squirted her hands, then she handed it to me. I used it and passed it to Carter.

When we were all germ-free, she spread her hands wide to take hold of ours and said, "Ready?"

I stared at her open palm for a few seconds and felt my heart begin to pound faster. "I'm not sure."

Carter frowned at me, probably because we were paying by the minute.

Maria sat back and folded her hands on her lap. "It's not a problem, Emma. Take your time. If you decide you don't want to do this, you can always wait outside."

Carter urged me with his eyes to be brave, so I took a breath, sat forward and held out my hand. "No, it's okay. I'm ready."

We all joined hands and Maria closed her eyes. I'm not sure what I was expecting—maybe for her body to jolt and shake, or for her eyes to roll back in her head. Or the lights would flicker. But it wasn't like that. She simply sat for a moment or two with her eyes closed, then nodded and spoke to us in a normal voice.

"You had a son who died a few years ago. He says hi, and he wants you to know he loves you both."

My heart exploded with a dizzying mix of panic and excitement—*Sammy! My boy*—but I immediately fought to remind myself that Maria wasn't telling us anything out of the ordinary. Maybe she'd looked us up on the Internet and already knew what we'd been through. The information was easily attainable. It was in all the local papers.

"He wants you to know he's fine and he's happy, and that heaven is wonderful, and you don't have to worry."

Was this really happening?

I was at war with myself. Part of me wanted to weep tears of joy upon hearing those words, but the other half was fighting to come up with reasons why I shouldn't believe in any of this. They were words Maria could say to every client who walked in the door. It didn't prove anything.

She continued to speak in a calm, natural voice. "He says he knows you don't believe what I'm saying—and he's talking to you, Emma—but that you need to believe it so that you can be happy again. He doesn't want you to be sad."

I felt my brow furrow with disbelief, but still, I tried to tell myself that Maria could probably sense my skepticism. I wasn't that difficult to read.

She was quiet for a moment, then inclined her head as if she were trying to hear someone whispering from a great distance away.

"Now he's talking to you, Carter. I'm sorry, he's speaking very quickly. This is difficult…" She continued to listen. "He's saying something about a…. A time out? He wants to give you a time out. He says you need to sit in the blue naughty chair."

My gaze shot to meet Carter's. His eyes were wide, his cheeks flushed with color.

Maria chuckled. "He says you're too big for the chair and you'd look silly, but that's okay. You need to sit and think about how mean you were to Mommy."

By now my stomach was doing flips and I was breathing very quickly. Carter and I stared at each other from across the table.

Maria continued. "He wants you both to be happy. Just be happy. He keeps saying that. He says life is beautiful. Be happy. Live a happy life. It's not your fault, Mommy. It was my mistake. I slipped. Daddy, you need to be happy. Have more babies."

Maria's eyebrows pulled together and she sat forward, straining to listen. "Oh... I think he wants to go now. That's all he wants to say. But he doesn't want you to come back here. He says he won't talk to you if you do. He says don't waste your money. He wants you to go and be happy and stop feeling so guilty. He says he'll see you again later." She cleared her throat. "He means in heaven."

Maria continued to listen, but then she opened her eyes and let go of our hands.

"That's it. He's gone. He was very sweet. Are you guys okay?"

We both regarded her with wide eyes.

"You look pale, Emma. Are you feeling faint? You could lie down on the sofa if you need to. Or would you like a glass of water?"

I shook my head. "No, I'm fine. That was unbelievable."

"It was, wasn't it," she said with a modest smile. "He was a very sweet boy. How old was he when you lost him? Seven? Eight?"

"He was four," Carter told her.

Her eyebrows lifted. "Really? He seemed older than that. Probably an old soul."

I buried my face in my hands and wept. "I can't believe he was actually here."

Maria rubbed my shoulder. "He was, but he made it clear that he doesn't want to come back again. He wants you both to get on with your lives and be happy."

While I fought to collect myself, Carter drew Maria's attention away, and I was grateful for the space, emotionally.

"Do you hear that same message a lot?" Carter asked. "From people in heaven? Or wherever they are?"

"All the time," Maria replied. "I don't like to consider my work predictable or tedious, but that's one thing that keeps repeating itself, day after day. *Don't worry. Be happy.*"

"There's a song about that," Carter replied.

"Yes." Maria stood up and I sensed she was eager to usher us out and invite the next client in. But I found it difficult to rise from my chair. I still hadn't recovered from what just happened. I was having trouble processing it.

"It was a pleasure to meet you both," Maria said. "I hope this was helpful."

It boggled my mind that she could have such a profound effect on our lives, but take it so lightly, and simply say "good-day" to us, and move on.

To Carter and me, it was a life-changing moment, a revelation of the highest order, and we would never be the same again. To her, this was just another fifteen minutes in her workday. She wasn't amazed by this.

Carter and I stood.

"Thank you," he said, holding out his hand to shake hers.

Maria smiled at him. "If you don't mind, I won't shake your hand. I'll just say it was a pleasure."

A few minutes later, we stood outside on the flagstone staircase between the house and the tall cedar hedge. All we could do was stare at each other with blank looks on our faces.

"Did that really just happen?" Carter asked.

"I don't know. I feel numb. It happened so fast."

We continued to stand there in a daze. Then we thrust ourselves into each other's arms and began to cry. We sobbed and wept uncontrollably, clinging to each other as if the world were about to end. I was afraid that if I let go of him, I'd dissolve into mist and sink into the ground.

Eventually we calmed ourselves and drew back, but continued to hold onto each other by the forearms.

"She mentioned the blue naughty chair," Carter said. "There's no way she could have known about that. It wasn't in the papers. And we never even had to use it, for pity's sake. It was just there in his room as a reminder to be a good boy, which he always was...." Carter's voice broke. He couldn't finish.

Holding hands, we started slowly up the steps. "Do you think it was real?" I asked. "Do you think Sammy actually spoke to us just now?"

"I don't know," Carter replied. "If it weren't for the comment about the naughty chair, I'd say no. But how could she know that?"

"Maybe she truly is psychic and can read people's minds, and she picked it up from you or me, but not from Sammy or from some other dimension. Were you thinking about it?"

"Not at all."

We reached the car, got in and buckled our seatbelts. Carter started the engine and pulled away from the curb.

"I'm still trying to be skeptical," I told him. "I can't quite believe it."

"Me neither. And as far as reading minds, I *was* thinking about how mean I was to you. She could have read that off me like I was shouting into a megaphone, because as soon as I thought Sammy might be in the room, I felt ashamed. I hated that he knew we were separated, or that we'd fought with each other. I guess, back when we were still married, I didn't think he was watching." Carter turned to me and touched my hand. "Honestly, Emma. I'm so sorry. I really am."

All I could do was nod my head and sit in silence, swallowing heavily over the painful jagged lump in my throat.

We didn't talk for a while, but we continued to hold hands. We drove all the way to the ferry terminal, waited in silence until it was time to drive on, then got out of the car and went up to the lounge area to sit in the comfortable chairs in front of the windows.

As the ferry pulled away from the terminal, the sun was setting and the sky was a spectacular panorama of pink and grey clouds with bright silver linings. The mix of color and light was mesmerizing—like a snapshot of heaven—and neither of us needed to say a word about it. We just looked at each other and understood that this sky embodied the true definition of the euphoria we both felt.

A short time later, Carter slouched low in his seat. "*Just be happy*. Maria said he was determined to be clear about that."

I inhaled deeply and looked up to watch the stars begin to come out.

Carter turned to me. "Are you happy, Emma? I mean…as happy as you can be, without Sammy?"

I focused on the brightest star I could see. "Yes. I'm happy. I'm in a good place. Are you?"

He paused. "I don't know. I want to be. For Sammy."

"And for yourself." I turned to him, but he continued to gaze out the window, not at me.

"I'll need to work on that," he replied.

We rode the rest of the way in silence, and didn't talk about certain other things Maria had said, pertaining to our futures. We chose to leave that alone.

CHAPTER

Ten

Bev

Halifax, Nova Scotia

It had been two full days, and the reporters were still outside my house.

Louise and I took cover indoors. I'd planned to keep her home from school anyway for a full week after the accident, and I'd asked for sick days at the hospital. Thankfully we had a private fully-fenced backyard with tall trees, so we were able to go outside with Leo and get some fresh air in a safe place with no cameras pointed at us.

One good thing came from our self-imposed lockdown: We had plenty of time to get creative with crayons. Over the course of two days, Louise drew dozens of pictures of her visit to heaven, and I tacked each one to the wall outside her bedroom.

To a stranger, they might have looked like any other drawings by a five-year old because they were images of colorful rainbows and yellow suns, trees and tall buildings—

just like what she'd described to me in the park. But to me, I saw something more.

Each time she finished a new picture, she handed the page to me and said, "This isn't as good as the real thing. I don't think I can draw it."

"Would it help if you had something better than crayons?" I asked, encouraging her to continue. "What about paint?"

"That would be good."

"Let's go to the art store tomorrow," I suggested.

In the meantime, she drew hearts everywhere to surround herself and her grandfather, who held her hand wherever they were—in the sky above the clouds or in an orchard with sunlight filtering through pink apple blossoms or rabbits in the tall grass. I could almost hear the sound of insects buzzing, grass swishing against my legs...

And she always drew a mustache on her grandfather.

By the end of the second day, the entire hallway was papered with Louise's colorful crayon illustrations, but now she was painting with oils on canvas—using an easel I'd purchased at the art store.

I spent a lot of time in the hallway, studying her creations, which she produced at an alarming rate. She drew birds and trees and meadows with colorful wildflowers and sparkling drops of dew. Oceans with turquoise water, dolphins and seagulls. Mountains with white, snow-capped peaks. Sunsets with spectacular clouds and silver linings.

On the third day, when I woke at six am to the sound of rain pelting against my window, I donned my bathrobe, went to the living room and peered through the slats in the blinds. To my relief, the street in front of my house was deserted. The reporters and news vans had departed.

Knowing my sister was an early riser on school days, I called her. She told me to turn on the television because it appeared we were no longer the top news story on every station. We'd been bumped aside by an earthquake in California the night before. I wasn't happy about the devastation, of course, but I was thankful to have our privacy back.

~*C*

As soon as I heard Louise stirring in her bedroom, I went to see if she might like to go shopping. A rainy day at the mall seemed like the perfect getaway after being holed up for two days. Maybe we'd even go to the indoor playground after lunch.

I knocked on her door, entered and found her sitting at her art table, drawing another picture, but this time with crayons. Moving closer, I knelt on my knees beside her. "Good morning. What are you drawing?"

She was so intent on the task of drawing clouds with rays shooting out from behind, that she ignored my question. Deciding to leave her alone until she finished, I kissed the top of her head and went to make us some eggs and toast.

When I served everything up, I called out to her. "Breakfast is ready! Do you want apple juice or orange juice?"

She didn't respond, so I called again. "Louise? Apple juice or orange juice?"

Leo lifted his chin off the floor and tilted his head at me. Then he rose to his feet and trotted to Louise's room.

I don't know why, but I panicked. For a blazing instant,

I feared my daughter had been sucked back to heaven in that vacuum cleaner she'd mentioned. I slammed the fridge door shut and ran to her room where I found her on her knees on the rug, smiling and rubbing Leo's belly.

Exhaling heavily, I laid both hands over my heart. "Louise. Why didn't you answer me?"

She looked up and smiled. "I don't know. I wasn't listening."

"You weren't!" I replied playfully because I didn't want her to know how irrational I'd been just now. I dropped to my knees to join her in the belly rub. We scratched Leo's underside together.

"Breakfast is on the table," I said.

"Okay." She rose to her feet and turned to her art table where her crayons were spread all over the picture she'd just finished. She slid it from underneath, and a bunch of crayons rolled off the table, onto the floor. I crawled on all fours to pick them up, and placed them back in the Tupperware box.

She handed me the picture. "Can we hang this one up, too?"

I took it from her, sat back on my heels, and stared at it.

It was different from the others. This time, there were four people, all holding hands. Louise was in the middle, my father with his gigantic mustache was on the left, and two others stood to her right. Above them, a cloud with a silver lining beamed rays across the sky.

"Who are these two?" I asked, pointing at them.

Louise stood before me at eye level, meeting my gaze directly. "Nanny and Papa."

I stared down at the picture. "But…"

But what? Did I mean to tell her that she didn't have

two other grandparents? All children in the world have four—two from the mother's side and two from the father's. That's how biology worked.

But Louise had never met her paternal grandparents. I didn't even know who they were or what their names were, whether they were dead or alive. That's how little I knew about her father, who had been a beautiful, reckless mistake I'd made one wild weekend five years earlier.

Although, I never considered it a mistake, because that's how Louise came into my life. Unexpected. Unplanned. If I hadn't gone out that night, drank too much wine and acted irresponsibly—which wasn't like me at all—I wouldn't be her mother today.

"What are their names?" I asked.

"Just Papa and Nanny." She spoke without the slightest hesitation.

"I've never met them before," I mentioned, trying to keep a cool head and not freak out. "What do they look like?"

She climbed onto the bed. "Papa is tall and skinny with white hair and glasses. He doesn't have a mustache. And Nanny has hair like yours, long and curly, but it's brown. She's not tall. She's very small." Louise giggled self-consciously. "That rhymes."

Louise rolled over on the bed and kicked her legs in the air.

"You're in a silly mood," I said good naturedly, reaching out to tickle her belly. "Is there anything else you want to tell me about Papa and Nanny?"

"Just that they're my daddy's mommy and daddy."

I felt the color drain from my cheeks as I stared at her. Only once had I mentioned her father to her, about a year ago when she asked if she had one. I told her yes, but that he lived very far away and we didn't know each other anymore. Thankfully, she had let the matter drop.

I'd never planned to keep the truth a secret from her, but I didn't see any point in bringing it up again or telling her anything about him because I'd decided long ago that I would raise her on my own. I didn't want any help from a man I barely knew—a man I'd only spent one night with. He'd been in town for a conference and was leaving the next day, and we never intended for anything to come of it. It was a one night stand, pure and simple.

He texted me a few times the following week, and we laughed about our crazy weekend. But that was it. Two months later I found out I was pregnant, but I had no desire to bring a stranger into my life. It felt dangerous and risky, because what if he was a psychopath? Or already in a relationship? He might have been married for all I knew. I just didn't want any drama, nor did I want to spend the next twenty years chasing down child support payments from someone I didn't even want in my life. So here we were.

"Do you want to ask me any questions about your daddy?" I asked Louise when she sat up on the edge of the bed. "I'll do my best to answer them if I can."

Her expression grew serious and she rose to her feet and wrapped her arms around my neck. "No, Mommy."

I held her close for a moment, rubbing her back. I couldn't resist asking. "Is there anything you want to tell me about your Papa and Nanny? What did they say to you?"

"Nothing."

"They must have said something."

She took a long time to answer. "Just that they loved me

and they wanted me to meet my daddy. That's why they sent me back here."

I held her away so I could look deeply into her eyes. "Why didn't you mention this before?"

"I did."

"No, honey. This is the first time."

She shrugged her shoulders and said, "I don't know. I forgot."

My belly began to roll with nervous knots, because obviously, she hadn't wanted to tell me about this.

"Do you want to meet your daddy?" I asked. "Is that why you drew that picture?" I'd always known this day would come, but I'd expected it to happen during her teen years. And who knew where we'd all be by then?

Louise shook her head. "No, I don't want to meet him."

I let out a breath and sat back on my heels again. "It would be okay if you did. I wouldn't mind."

"No, I don't want to."

"Why not?"

She shrugged a shoulder.

"Are you…shy?"

"I just don't want to."

I took a moment to let all this settle in and not say the wrong thing. She was only five, but this mattered. It wasn't something I wanted to mess up.

"He's not a bad person," I said. "I liked him when we knew each other. I just haven't seen him in a long time, and I don't know where he lives. He doesn't even know about you, sweetheart, but if he did, I'm sure he'd love you very much. Are you sure you don't want to meet him? I could find him if you want me to."

"I'm sure."

I nodded. "Okay."

I felt as if my whole world was spinning out of control, and all the decisions I'd made about raising Louise on my own were going to fly back in my face and knock me out.

"But you might change your mind someday," I continued, "when you're older, and if you do, we'll do whatever you want. I could contact him for you."

She nodded, but I sensed she was afraid of the idea. I realized that outside of her Uncle Scott across the street, she'd had no father figure in her life. I'd never dated anyone since she was born because I didn't want our home to become a revolving door of men coming in and out of our lives. All she had was me, Claire, and Scott—and my mom.

"How about some breakfast," I suggested, needing to change the subject so I could let this percolate. "And would you like to go to the mall today? We could have lunch there."

"Yes!" she cheered, and ran to the kitchen.

I took a moment to collect myself, and followed her out.

—❦

After Louise and I spent the morning at the mall and the afternoon at an indoor playground, she was exhausted. When we arrived home, I settled her in the living room to watch a movie, then I seized the opportunity to call Claire, because I needed to talk to someone about what happened that morning.

"You're kidding me," Claire said with surprise. "She drew a picture of her other grandparents? Have you ever mentioned them to her before?"

"Never. I couldn't even tell you if they're dead or alive, but I sure would love to know."

"Yes, because if they're both alive and well, then at least you'd know it wasn't true. I mean…the part about Louise going to heaven and meeting others who had passed on. As far as our father goes, she always knew he wasn't with us anymore. We've talked about him many times, so she could easily say she saw him in heaven and it would make sense. But her paternal grandparents…"

"I've never mentioned her father's family to her. I've rarely mentioned *him.*"

Claire considered all this. "What else did she say about it?"

"That these other grandparents wanted her to meet her father. That's why they sent her back. You can imagine how that hit me like a brick. I didn't know what to say."

"Oh, my gosh. Did she actually ask to meet him?"

"No, she said she *didn't* want to, which I was relieved to hear, even though I tried not to show it."

Claire was quiet for a moment. "But Bev… Was that coming from her, or you?"

I was taken aback. "What do you mean?"

"You know what I mean. You've always known how I felt about this whole situation. I thought it was a mistake from the beginning not to tell the guy that he was going to be a father."

My hackles rose. "And I explained to you why I didn't want to do that. I wanted to raise Louise on my own, and I didn't need help from a one-night stand I'd met in a bar. And believe me, I've tortured myself over that decision many times since she was born, and if I could do it again, maybe I'd do it differently. I'm not sure. But I can't change it now. It's water under the bridge. I just have to figure out how to move forward from here, with the way things are."

"But someday," she pressed, "Louise is going to want to meet her father. It's a certainty, Bev. And how would you feel if you were in his shoes? To find out that you had a kid and never knew it? Then suddenly out of the blue, a teenager or a grown woman shows up on your doorstep? That's not fair to him."

"I know that." I rested my forehead in my hand because this was a painful conversation. "But my decision was never about *him*. His feelings were not my top priority, because what mattered was what was best for me and Louise. I didn't want to risk bringing a total stranger into our lives. What if he was a terrible, abusive person? A drug addict, or a sleaze ball."

"But what if he wasn't?" Claire replied. "If you had such a fantastic time with him that weekend—and actually went to bed with him—you must have trusted him, at least a little."

I sat down and pinched the bridge of my nose. "Yes, I did. But some men are good at being charming."

Claire scoffed into the phone. "You know what I think?"

"No, but I'm sure you're going to tell me."

"Yes. I think you were just scared. Scared that he'd reject you, or that he wouldn't love you, or that he'd abandon you eventually."

"*Yes!*" I practically shouted into the phone. "That's exactly what I was scared of. And please don't start saying I have daddy issues because of what happened when we were kids. This isn't about that."

"Yes, it is, because you *do* have issues," she argued. "It's why you're still single, because you think any good man will be snatched away and your whole world will fall apart."

I tried to stop her. "Please, Claire…"

"It's true. Don't try to deny it. One day, you're running through the sprinkler and everything's wonderful, and the next minute, you're watching your father bleed to death in the ditch while your mother loses her mind."

Nausea pooled in my belly. "I didn't call you about this to be reminded of how miserable we were when Dad died. I just wanted to tell you about the picture Louise drew."

Claire didn't say anything for a long moment, but I could hear her breathing.

"I'm sorry," she finally said. "I didn't mean to be so hard on you."

"Well, you were. But forget it. I understand, and you're right. I do have issues. That's why I wanted to do my best to protect Louise. I never wanted to invite a stranger into our lives. I'm not a fan of unknowns."

"Life is full of unknowns," she replied. "You can't escape them, no matter how hard you try."

I stood up and went to the fridge to get some cranberry juice.

"So, what are you going to do?" Claire asked. "Will you just sweep this morning's drawing under the carpet? Or will you try to find out if the other grandparents are still alive? Or not."

I considered that for a moment. "I am curious."

Balancing the phone between my shoulder and ear, I poured the juice into a glass.

"Would it be hard to find them?" Claire asked. "Jeez.

You haven't even spoken about Louise's father in five years. Do you even remember his name?"

I shook my head at her and scoffed. "Of course I do. I remember everything about that night. He was a charming, handsome stock broker. His name was Luke. Luke Hawkins."

CHAPTER

Eleven

Luke

Oak Bay, British Columbia

They say time flies when you're having fun. When you're not, it can lodge itself into your psyche like a dark sludge.

When I finally heard a car door close out front, it was just past midnight. The dogs got up off their beds in the family room and barked as they trotted to the front door. I tried not to appear as eager as they were, but truthfully, I'd been watching the clock for hours, wishing Emma would just text me and let me know how things had gone with the psychic. But I hadn't heard a word from her.

I stepped into the foyer when she walked in.

"You're up," she said, appearing surprised to see me. "I thought you might have gone to bed." Closing the door behind her, she removed her coat and hung it up in the closet.

"How did it go?" I asked.

She kicked off her shoes and met my gaze. "It was unbelievable."

"In a good way?" I asked.

She nodded and without missing a beat, stepped into my arms.

I held her close, breathing in the scent of her hair. I buried my face in her neck. "I missed you."

"I missed you, too, but I'm really tired. Can we go upstairs? I'll tell you about it in bed."

"Sure. I'll just let the dogs out one more time. I'll see you up there."

I watched her go upstairs.

A short while later, I walked into the bedroom to find her under the covers, lying on her side with her eyes closed. At first I thought she was already asleep, but she slowly sat up and watched me get ready for bed.

"I don't even know how to describe it," she said, as I brushed my teeth. "When I tell you, it's going to sound crazy. I'm afraid you'll think I'm nuts for buying into it."

"It sounds like you think she was the real deal," I replied as I dropped my toothbrush back into the cup and wiped my mouth on a hand towel.

"Yes, even though the rational part of my brain keeps trying to convince me to be skeptical, I can't ignore what my gut is telling me."

I grew more curious by the second and slid into bed beside her. "What happened?"

She took a deep breath and sat up straighter against the pillows. "Well, her name was Maria, and she's a very shrewd business woman—incredibly successful and rich—which made me suspicious when we first got there. All I could think about was what you said about con artists and it being an 'industry.' Anyway, there was a crowd of people in the waiting room, so she was shuffling clients in and out every fifteen minutes, which seemed completely impossible to me—to imagine that she could have any sort of meaningful encounter with any of us. It felt like a money grab, because we were all paying five hundred bucks each."

"Five hundred dollars?" I replied, dumbfounded.

"Yes. But Carter paid for it because it was his idea. So, when we finally got in to see her, she was direct and to the point, and the three of us sat down together at a table, and we all joined hands—"

"Kind of like a séance?"

She paused. "Well…yes, except that we were in a brightly lit space with giant windows and a beautiful view, so there wasn't anything creepy about it. It wasn't like a haunted house or anything. Not like what you'd imagine." Emma reached for my hand and held it. "So, then she just started telling us that our son was there too, and that he wanted us to know he was fine, and that he wanted us to be happy. That was the main message."

"She could say that to everyone," I mentioned. "For that matter, you or I could start a psychic reading business and say that to everyone. All we'd need is a website and some smart marketing materials."

Emma held up a hand to stop me. "I know that, but then she said something that blew my mind. She said Sammy wanted to put Carter in the blue naughty chair because of how mean he was to me." Emma regarded me expectantly. When I said nothing at first, she sat forward to explain further, and her tone grew increasingly passionate.

"The blue naughty chair was something we introduced when Sammy was two—for time outs—but we never even used it because he was such a good kid. There was no way Maria could have known about that."

I stared at Emma for a moment because I wasn't sure how to respond. It did sound remarkable, but maybe Maria had an assistant who was very good at research. I was still skeptical.

"Wow," I managed to say. "So, that's what made you believe in it?"

"Yes. And I know you can't possibly understand this, Luke, because you weren't there—and I can tell by the way you're looking at me that you think it's a bunch of malarkey—but I felt Sammy in the room with us. Everything else Maria said seemed to come directly from him. Things he wanted Carter and me to hear. Things she could never know."

I wanted genuinely to understand and believe her, but I was having a hard time with this. I'd never been much of a church goer, and though I tried to be open minded, the idea of heaven had always seemed like wishful thinking to me. Even the books she had shared hadn't convinced me completely. "Like what?"

"Like…" Emma slowly slid her hand from my grasp. "Sammy wanted Carter and I to forgive each other." She held me in her intense gaze for a few seconds, as if she were testing me—waiting to see how I would take that. Then she looked down.

"Should I be worried?" I asked.

"Of course not," she replied, shaking her head. "I love you and this is where I want to be. With *you*. But it was an incredible experience today. I'm still not over it, and I'm not sure I ever will be. I don't think I can ever look at life the same way again."

Her eyes lifted and they were wet with tears.

All I could do was slide closer and wrap my arms around her. "I don't want to lose you."

"I don't want to lose you either, and you won't, I promise. But I'm glad I went there today and I'm sorry I couldn't bring you with me, but it was something I had to do with Carter."

The mention of her ex-husband's name caused a pang of unease in me, but I pushed it away. "So...*did* you?" I asked.

"Did I what?"

I sat back and looked her in the eye. "Forgive each other."

Emma watched me for a long moment, then she nodded. "Yes."

She offered nothing else, but I wanted more. I wanted to know every last word they had spoken to each other during the trip there and back. Did they cling to each other? Did she cry on his shoulder and tell him she was sorry for leaving him? Did he ask her to come back to him?

Another part of me didn't want to know what was said. I wasn't sure I could take it.

"I'm so tired," she said apologetically, making it clear she wanted to end the conversation at that. "Can we go to sleep?"

"Sure." I rolled away from her and switched off the lamp.

She snuggled close and laid her head on my shoulder, draped her leg across my thighs. I fell asleep praying that she had gotten the closure she needed today, and that everything would be okay for us from now on.

A few weeks later, the lease finally ended on Emma's apartment in Victoria. I'd been asking her to move in with me, officially, for months, but she hadn't wanted to take the plunge. She hadn't changed her address at the post office, and though she stayed at my place most nights, many of her personal belongings were still at her apartment. But now it was time at last for us to take things to the next level, and I was glad.

When the movers delivered everything, we asked them to put the furniture into my garage until we figured out what to do with it. Emma thought she might like to give the sofa and chair to her cousin Lori who planned to renovate her basement over the winter.

All the boxes containing smaller items were brought into the house, and we spent all day Saturday going through everything while it poured rain outside.

"How much of this do you want to keep?" I asked as I opened a box full of kitchen utensils and plastic bowls.

Emma came to inspect what was inside. She withdrew a wooden spoon. "I don't know. You have a fully equipped kitchen. Maybe we should just give it all to charity."

"Or we could hang onto it and store it for our kids," I replied, "for when they move into their first crappy apartment twenty years from now."

She gave me a funny look. "You certainly like to plan ahead."

"Go figure. I wasn't even a boy scout." I kissed her on the cheek.

Using the utility knife, she sliced through the packing tape on another box and found a casserole dish inside. She wanted to keep that one in particular, but everything else was a duplicate of what I already owned and we decided to part with it.

That night, when everything was unpacked and put

away—or boxed up for the Salvation Army—we sat down on the sofa to watch television.

"I'm glad you're here, finally," I said, reaching out to her.

"Me, too." She snuggled close and rested her cheek on my shoulder.

Breathing in the fresh scent of her shampoo, I said, "I want you to feel like this is your home, too, Emma, and if you want to change anything or redecorate, we can do that."

She looked up at me and smiled. "I love it here. I wouldn't want to change a thing. Except maybe the paint color in the bedroom, along with the drapes. It's kind of manly."

I chuckled at that. "Whatever you pick out will be fine with me."

Over the coming weeks, we settled into a comfortable routine together and focused on our wedding plans and honeymoon.

We didn't talk about what happened with the psychic. I certainly never brought it up, and neither did she. It wasn't that Emma didn't want to share it with me, or that she felt I didn't believe in it—although I wasn't entirely convinced it was real. I think she just wanted to move on and let go of the past. It was what I wanted too, because I was ready to build a future with her. I couldn't wait to be her husband.

"I have to fly to Toronto on Wednesday to meet with some clients," I told Emma when she came home from work one evening and found me in the kitchen making spaghetti.

"How long will you be gone?" She stood behind me at the counter and wrapped her arms around my waist.

"Just a couple of nights. I'll fly back Friday." I turned around to give her a passionate welcome-home kiss. "You could always come with me. We could see a stage play or go to a comedy club."

She considered that and let out a sigh of defeat. "I'd love to but it's crazy at work this week. Maybe next time, if I had a bit more notice."

"Sure."

"When will you go next?"

"Probably in December."

"Cool." She kissed me again, then went upstairs to change out of her work clothes.

A few minutes later, when the pasta was ready and she hadn't returned, I went upstairs to check on her. I didn't find her in our bedroom or in the shower, so I made my way down the hall, peering into each guest room. I finally found her in the smallest room at the end, sitting in the rocking chair, staring at the wall.

She jumped when I entered. "You scared me. I didn't hear you come up."

"Sorry about that." I slowly walked to the window and looked out. "You know, I always thought this room had the best view because it's on the corner of the house, and the sun sets right over there." I pointed at the horizon.

She continued to sit quietly, rocking back and forth in the chair.

"That rocker belonged to my grandmother," I told her as I faced her and leaned on the window sill. "Apparently, she used to rock my father to sleep in it when he was a baby."

Emma squeezed the armrests in her hands. "I didn't know that."

"When my parents died, I took everything that had sentimental value. A lot of the stuff in this house came from them."

Emma tipped her head back and regarded me sleepily. "You must miss them. I can't imagine how difficult it must have been to have lost both of them at the same time. And you were so young."

"I was nineteen," I replied, "and yes, it was rough. It didn't help that I was an only child. Suddenly, I didn't have an immediate family. I had some uncles and aunts, but it was mostly friends who got me through the worst of it. And their parents. There was always a sympathetic mother who wanted to invite me for Thanksgiving dinner or Christmas."

Emma inclined her head at me. "Why didn't you ever get married, Luke? I'm still astonished that you were single when I met you. Because you're an amazing catch."

I turned to glance over my shoulder, out the window. "It's not that I didn't *want* to get married. I was in a serious relationship for most of my twenties and I honestly thought she was the one, but then…" I faced Emma and gestured with a hand. "Well, you know what happened there. She cheated on me with some older guy, and I was gun shy after that. I had a hard time trusting women. And once you hit thirty, it gets harder to meet people that you really click with. So I just tried to focus on my work. Then you came along. And there was something so—I don't know—*vulnerable* about you. When you told me about what happened to Sammy, I understood that kind of grief and I just wanted to make you happy again. I wanted us to make each *other* happy."

Appearing serene, Emma continued to rock in the chair.

I turned and looked out the window again. "You know, this room would make a great nursery someday."

She slowly stopped rocking and stroked the armrests with her open palms. "You already have the chair for it."

"*We* already have the chair." I watched her carefully. "Have you given any thought to when you might like to start trying? To have a baby, I mean?"

I would have been raring to go that very night if she was keen because I wanted children more than anything. I wanted to be a dad. But I knew it was a sensitive subject for her. I would have to ease her down that path gently and gradually.

Emma's eyes traveled up the walls and fixed on the ceiling. "I don't know. It's a big step. Let's just get married first. Then we'll see." She stood up and smoothed out her skirt. "I'm hungry. Can we eat now?"

"Sure." I couldn't deny that I felt disappointed as I followed her down the stairs. I didn't like the sound of those words: *we'll see*.

When I returned home from Toronto on Friday night, the house smelled like an Italian restaurant. I'd already texted Emma when I landed and she told me she was cooking something special, but she hadn't mentioned what it was.

"Welcome home." Wearing a flowery sundress and high-heeled strappy sandals, she greeted me at the door, wrapped her arms around my neck and kissed me hard. The feel of her soft curves made me extremely grateful to be home.

"I got you something." I reached into my pocket for the small gift-wrapped box from Birks.

She gave me a flirty look. "*Ooh.* What is it?"

"Open it and find out."

She took my hand and led me to the kitchen where I noticed a bottle of my favorite California cabernet, open and breathing on the counter. Next to that was a loaf of cheesy garlic bread on a pan, ready to be slid into the oven.

Emma untied the gold ribbon, peeled away the paper and raised an eyebrow at me. "This is unexpected fun."

"It certainly is," I replied, admiring her full lips and long eyelashes.

She opened the box and found a pair of diamond earrings—one full carat each—that matched her princess-cut engagement ring. She laid her hand over her heart and gasped. "Oh, my goodness. Luke."

"Do you like them?"

"Are you kidding me? Of course I like them. I *love* them." She removed the silver hoops she was wearing and moved to the mirror in the hall to put them on. "Look how they sparkle. I can hardly speak right now." Turning to face me, she hugged me. "I'm so glad you're home."

"Me, too." I kissed her neck and held her close.

That night, we enjoyed a candlelit dinner at home. Then we took the dogs for a walk in the moonlight before falling into bed, entwined in each other's arms.

⟶❧

I woke alone in bed the next morning. Checking the clock

to see how late I'd slept, I discovered it was only 8:15. The sun was shining so I decided to go for a run before breakfast.

Downstairs, I found a note from Emma on the kitchen table.

Good morning. I was up early and didn't want to wake you. I went to the gym for a yoga class but I'll be home by nine. I'll bring croissants!

That sounded good. I put on my sneakers and took off out the front door.

An hour later, I returned and passed Emma's car in the driveway and hoped she hadn't been kidding about the croissants. I paced around outside for a few minutes to catch my breath and wipe the sweat from my face with the bottom of my T-shirt. Then I climbed the steps and went inside.

The dogs must have been out on the back patio because they didn't bark or arrive at the door to greet me. I was about to call out to Emma when I overheard her in the den, talking on the phone with the door closed.

She spoke in hushed, intimate tones. Something in me tightened with apprehension. I couldn't keep from leaning closer to listen.

"I know," she softly said, "but I guess I never really imagined this day would come." She paused. "I know, you're right, but it's hard." There was another long pause. "I don't know what to say. Yes, of course I want to be involved. No, please don't do that." There was a long, drawn-out silence. "I haven't talked to him about it. No, not at all." She started to cry. "I'm so sorry, I can't have this conversation right now. Please don't do anything yet. Yes, I know. We need to do it together. Okay, I'll talk to you soon."

She ended the call.

I quickly tiptoed to the kitchen to get a glass of water, because I didn't want her to catch me eavesdropping. Glancing around, I didn't see any croissants.

At last, the door to the den opened and she emerged with puffy, bloodshot eyes and a balled-up tissue in her hand. She stopped abruptly when she spotted me standing at the kitchen sink.

"Hi," I said, facing her squarely.

"Hi. I didn't hear you come in."

I gestured toward the den. "The door was closed." We said nothing for a few seconds, and it was painfully awkward. "Is everything okay?"

She wiped her nose with the tissue and moved past me to switch on the coffeemaker. "Not really."

When she didn't elaborate, I squeezed her shoulder. "Why? What's going on?"

She moved to the fridge to get the coffee cream. "Carter wants to sell the house."

A tense silence ensued. I stood there, measuring her for a few seconds.

"I thought that was what you wanted. It was all laid out in the divorce settlement—that you would sell the house within a year and split the proceeds fifty-fifty."

"Yes, that's right," she replied, moving about the kitchen without ever meeting my gaze. "I just didn't expect to feel this way. I can't stop thinking about the little playhouse in the backyard and how we had such big plans for it when Sammy got older."

I wanted to say: "But Sammy's gone now and he's never coming back," but I bit back those harsh words because I couldn't be that insensitive with her. It wouldn't help things, and she might never forgive me for such a comment.

At the same time, my frustration was on the rise. I'd been waiting a long time for her to truly move on, to focus on our wedding, and to dream about playhouses for *our* children in the future. It was what she said she wanted when we first met—a new beginning—and she had taken great strides forward every day.

Until she saw that psychic. With Carter. Things had been different since then. I felt like I couldn't really reach Emma.

She stood at the coffee maker, waiting for her cup to fill. I told myself this was just a speed bump, and once the house was sold, her life with Carter would be a thing of the past.

Moving closer, I laid my hand on her back and spoke gently. "I understand. It's not easy, but I think it's the right thing. You just have to get through this, and then I promise, when we have a child of our own, I'll build you the best playhouse this town has ever seen. And a monster swing set in the backyard. All the neighbors will be jealous."

The corner of her mouth curled up in a small smile, and she turned around and stepped into my arms. Our bodies melted into each other's.

"I don't know what I would do without you," she said in a shaky voice. "And I'm amazed that you can put up with me. I'm such a wet rag sometimes."

"You're not," I replied. "You loved your son more than anything in the world and that's why I fell in love with you in the first place. It's why I want to have children with you."

She stepped back and wiped at her eyes. "The next few days are going to be rough. I'll apologize to you in advance, because you might not see me much."

My stomach dropped. "Why not?"

"Because I told Carter I want to be there when he cleans out the attic and the basement and Sammy's old room. His room is still… It's the way it was when…"

Still the way it was?

I moved away from her and leaned back against the center island. I tried not to frown. Maybe I didn't understand how these things worked because I'd never lost a child—I'd never even been a parent—but I figured they would have taken care of that by now. It had been four years, for pity's sake. How could they just forget about it?

I supposed that was the point. They hadn't been able to forget about it or confront it. They were still hanging on, and that's why she'd been crying in the den.

Emma poured cream into her coffee cup and took a sip. "I'm going to spend Saturday over there, and maybe Sunday. It depends how long it takes."

I cleared my throat. "Would you like me to go with you and help? I'd be happy to."

Her gaze turned cool, almost horror-struck. "No. But thank you for offering, Luke. It's something I need to do on my own."

Like going to see the psychic with Carter.

I tapped my finger a few times on the counter top. "Will Carter be there?"

"Of course he will," she firmly replied. "We need to decide what to do with everything. So, I don't think you should be there. It would just be awkward, and it's going to be hard enough as it is."

I felt my blood pressure rising, but I didn't want to be that guy who was jealous of his fiancée's ex-husband. I trusted Emma. Truly, I did, and I knew she loved me. I just wished she'd lean on me more and let me be a part of these things that were difficult.

Although sometimes it felt as if she had purposely drawn a bold line in the ground to divide her life into two halves: the time before we met, and the time after. She didn't want me to cross that line. I had to stay put, right here on this side, while she crossed back to the other side alone.

It wasn't easy, but I knew I had to let her go and face this last thing without me.

"Okay," I finally said, working hard to trust her and convince myself that this was the final hurdle, and once we were over this, everything would be different. This was a positive thing. It would bring us one step closer to the new beginning she had been searching for.

I just needed to be patient. I needed to trust her.

Twelve

Emma

Victoria, British Columbia

When Carter opened the door to Sammy's bedroom, it was like stepping back in time. The small bed was neatly made up with the familiar blue-and-white striped comforter we'd bought for him after we moved him out of his crib. His LEGO blocks were stored in the large plastic container under the window, and the red beanbag chair looked as if he'd flopped onto it only yesterday.

Standing in the doorway, I closed my eyes and breathed in the scent of the room, allowing myself to take it all in while working hard to keep a stiff upper lip, because we had to get through this and I didn't want to fall apart in the first five minutes.

"It's so clean," I said to Carter as he moved to stand beside me. "I wasn't expecting that."

"My mom comes in here to dust sometimes. She never says a word about it. She just does it."

I turned to look at him. "Have you always been keeping the door closed?"

That's how it was when I lived here. Neither of us could bear to look inside.

Carter slid his hands into his jean pockets. "Pretty much. But ever since you and I went to see Maria, I've been leaving it open. I come in here and look around and just think about things. That's why I thought it was time, Emma. I knew that Sammy wouldn't want us to keep dwelling on the past. I think that's what the dream was about. He was trying to lead me back in here."

"He wants us to be happy," I replied, realizing I was speaking about our son in the present tense, which would have seemed bizarre to anyone except Carter. "To know that he's in a good place."

Carter understood and nodded his head with a smile.

I found myself smiling, too.

~*~

Five hours later, the bed was dismantled, the mattress was leaning against the wall, and everything was boxed up and labeled for delivery to a local charity.

Carter and I had each taken a few sentimental items to hold onto. I chose some of Sammy's clothes: the Peter Pan sleeper he wore home from the hospital as a newborn, his white leather baby shoes and his winter hat with the bunny ears. I also kept all his artwork which I planned to paste into a scrapbook, as well as a few LEGO blocks. Carter let me have Pooky, the soft blue teddy bear that Sammy couldn't sleep without. That was the most treasured item.

Carter had taken Sammy's dinosaur collection which

they'd worked on together, a few of the crayon drawings, and the *Thomas the Tank Engine* pajamas.

When the work was done, we stood up and looked around at all the boxes. "I can't believe we finally did this," I said.

Carter laid his hand on the back of my neck and squeezed, then he regarded me with pride. "I'm sure he's happy about this."

Before I knew what I was doing, I turned to Carter, wrapped my arms around his neck and wept. Hot, salty tears streamed down my cheeks and simply wouldn't stop.

"Baby," Carter whispered affectionately, stroking my hair just like he used to, which seemed like another lifetime. In other ways, it felt like yesterday. "Don't cry. It's all good now. Everything's going to be fine."

I wanted to stop crying, but I needed to let it out. All of it. Every last tear. I told myself that once I was finished, that would be that. There would be no more tears, no more looking back with overpowering sorrow. Instead, I would look to the future and remember Sammy with joy.

Carter held me and I was grateful for the strength of his arms and the compassion in his voice. It was what I had needed from him so desperately when we lost Sammy—and something I never received.

Eventually, I drew back and wiped the tears from my cheeks. "I'm so sorry," I said, laughing in embarrassment.

"Don't be sorry," he replied. "It was a big day. Gargantuan." With the pad of his thumb, he wiped a tear from my cheek. "I think we need to go to the kitchen and get something to drink."

Carter took my hand and led me out of the room. He didn't ask what I wanted. He simply went to the fridge, withdrew a bottle of Pinot Grigio, and poured us each a glass.

He raised his for a toast. "To Sammy. And to us."

We clinked, and I took a sip. "I'm sure he's looking down on this with a smile."

"I'll bet he is."

We made light conversation for a little while. Maybe it was the wine, but I felt relaxed and rejuvenated. Then Carter pulled out his phone. "I meant to ask if you'd seen this." He typed a few words, then began to scroll through a website.

"What is it?"

"This." He handed me his phone and showed me a picture of an attractive blond woman with her daughter. They were smiling into the camera and posing in a playground.

I read the title of the article:

GIRL WHO WENT TO HEAVEN IS JUST LIKE YOU AND ME

My eyes lifted. "This is her?"

"Yes, I thought you'd like to see what she looks like. It says her mother is still trying to protect their privacy, and this info came from an anonymous source who claims to know them personally. I suspect the source was paid big bucks for the picture."

I read through the article, which described the little girl as happy and healthy and suffering no long-term ill health effects from the ordeal.

I zoomed in on the photo to get a closer look at their smiling faces. "They seem happy. The mom's pretty."

Carter stood for a moment, watching me intently. I handed his phone back to him. Then he turned and gestured for me to follow him onto the back deck.

The last time I was in this house, we had just signed the divorce papers and I couldn't even look out the window at the backyard. Today, I found myself wanting to see it, one last time.

We stood outside together in the soft September breeze, side by side, sipping our wine. I looked at the spot on the grass where the blue paddling pool had been. I stared at it for a long time.

Then I shaded my eyes and squinted through the late afternoon haze, to try and see the playhouse, but it was too far back in the woods and the foliage was more overgrown than ever. I couldn't see it.

"What are you going to do after you sell this place?" I asked Carter, lowering my hand to my side and taking another sip of wine. "Will you move in with Melissa?"

He scoffed. "God no. I thought you knew about that. I figured Lori would have told you by now. Melissa and I aren't seeing each other anymore."

My eyebrows lifted. "I'm sorry to hear that. When—?"

"The week after we got home from our trip to see the psychic. She kept insinuating that you and I must have slept together, but I kept telling her we didn't, but she just couldn't believe me. That wasn't the worst of it. She never really understood the situation with Sammy. She was always pushing me to get over it, hounding me to clean out his room, but it was none of her business. Nobody can push you to be ready. You're ready when you're ready. What's more, she wanted us to do all that together, but that just wasn't going to happen."

"Luke wanted to come today as well. I had to tell him no."

"How did he take it?"

I shrugged a shoulder. "He's always very understanding, so he pretended to be okay with it, but I think it bothered him. I also think he's been biding his time, waiting for this to be over, so that he and I can move on."

Carter sipped his wine and regarded me directly. "It'll never be over, you know. You're always going to love Sammy. You'll never stop thinking about him. He'll always be your firstborn son."

I nodded in resignation. "I know. But at least if I can think about him without wanting to drown myself, that's something."

"It is." Carter clinked his glass against mine again.

"So, when are you going to call the real estate agent?"

"I'll wait until Monday," he replied. "Then I'll have to start looking for a new place to live, I guess."

"You going to be okay?"

"Of course," he said. "It's time for me to go. Lately, it just hurts to keep living here with all my regrets."

His eyes held a whole universe of melancholy and I felt it, too—a great and terrible sadness. This was followed by a wave of discomfort, because I wanted overwhelmingly to step into his arms again and apologize for everything. To somehow find a way back to what we once were to each other.

We were supposed to love each other forever. I'd always believed we would, that we were inseparable. Soul mates from the first moment our eyes met. How did this happen?

Standing there with him now felt like I was experiencing another death. Somehow, I had to find a way to say good-bye to him and to all of this—to bury our history deep in the ground. I reminded myself that it was impossible to go back. We weren't the same people we once were, and I was engaged to Luke now. I loved Luke. I truly did. He had been the one to pull me out of the abyss.

Carter and I stood for a moment, staring out over the yard while my heart beat thunderously in my chest. Before I did something unthinkable—like reach out to touch Carter—I finished my wine and said, "How about we take a walk to the playhouse? I'd like to see it one last time before someone else takes possession."

Carter nodded. He took hold of my hand and led me down the deck stairs. As we walked across the yard to the gate, my heart seized up with sadness, because I knew this was truly the end.

It would be our final good-bye.

CHAPTER

Thirteen

Luke

Oak Bay, British Columbia

After Emma spent the day with Carter, packing up the tangible remnants of their marriage to prepare their house for sale, she returned home exhausted—both physically and emotionally. She didn't want to talk about her day, except to say that it was both grueling and therapeutic. She didn't mention Carter at all. When I asked how things had gone with him, she shrugged a shoulder and said, "It was fine. I'm just glad it's over."

She showed me a box that contained a few of Sammy's belongings she had held onto as keepsakes. I suggested she find a better box for the items—something nicer than cardboard. An antique chest perhaps? I proposed that we go shopping together the next day. When she said yes, I was relieved to be allowed into that part of her life.

Three days later, Emma was late coming home from work. When she didn't call, I began to worry and sent her a quick text.

I'm about to fire up the barbeque. Are you on your way?

I set my phone on the kitchen counter and tried not to fixate on it while I waited for a response. When it buzzed a moment later, I was in the other room and returned to pick it up.

Sorry, I should have called. I'm working late. I'll be home around seven.

I hated myself for it, but I couldn't forget the day she'd said something similar when she was secretly going to meet Carter. She'd confessed the truth later, but that didn't erase the fact that she'd lied about it initially.

I raked my fingers through my hair, reminding myself that just because a girlfriend had cheated on me in the past, it didn't mean all women were untrustworthy or destined to be unfaithful.

I texted her back: *OK. See you soon.*

When she arrived home, everything seemed normal. She kissed me on the cheek before hurrying upstairs to change out of her work clothes. We enjoyed a nice dinner together with wine, and I chastised myself for not trusting her. I told myself these were my issues, not hers, and I couldn't let them get the better of me.

The following Saturday, I came home from a morning run and couldn't find Emma or the dogs anywhere in the house. Dripping with sweat, I went outside to the back patio and spotted her down on the rocks, pacing back and forth, talking on her phone. The dogs were sitting at the edge of the lawn, looking out over the water.

I called out to her, but she couldn't hear me above the sound of the waves on the rocks. I went back inside for a glass of water and returned to the patio. She was still talking. She didn't look back at the house.

Later, when she finally came inside, I asked if she wanted to go out for brunch. She said yes and we went to one of our favorite greasy diners in Oak Bay.

The waitress arrived with glasses of water and took our orders. Then Emma sat back and stared out the front windows at the cars passing by.

She seemed distracted. Subdued.

"Is everything okay?" I asked. "You've been quiet."

She immediately perked up. "Oh, I'm sorry. I don't mean to be. Everything's fine. It was just a long week at work."

I sipped my coffee. "You were on the phone for a while. Who were you talking to?"

God, I hated how I sounded—like a jealous, possessive boyfriend, trying not to sound jealous and possessive.

Emma rolled her eyes and shook her head. "That was my cousin Lori. She's dating some guy who doesn't call her often enough, in her mind. I had to talk her off the ledge."

"Ah."

Emma launched into a detailed explanation of where Lori had met the guy, and why Emma thought he was all wrong for her. It was good to see her speaking animatedly, sitting forward, gesturing with her hands.

Again, I chastised myself for being so paranoid. I needed to get a grip. Everything was fine.

~C

A week later, everything wasn't fine.

I had traveled to Vancouver for a meeting with some clients visiting from Toronto and was supposed to take the evening ferry home, but the meeting ended early and I managed to get on the late afternoon boat. I wanted to arrive home before Emma did, and surprise her with her favorite sushi and a bouquet of flowers.

When I pulled into the driveway, a strange car was parked out front. I recognized it immediately. It was Carter's.

My gut twisted into a tight, coiled knot but I fought not to assume the worst. Maybe they'd had an offer on the house and he was just dropping off papers for her to sign.

I parked my car and checked my phone to see if she'd texted me to let me know, but there were no messages from her.

Swallowing over my apprehension, I gathered the flowers and sushi up off the seat, got out of the car and shut the door quietly with my elbow, which was another show of mistrust, because if there was something going on, I wanted to surprise them and catch them in the act. That would be best. It wouldn't leave me with any doubts or unanswered questions.

I ascended the stairs slowly and slipped my key into the front lock, but the dogs started barking, so I knew my game was up.

Pushing into the foyer and setting my briefcase on the

floor, the sushi and flowers on the hall table, I greeted Toby and Max, while waiting for Emma to come and greet me as well.

When she didn't appear, I moved silently toward the kitchen. I glanced up the stairs, while my anger and suspicion escalated with every passing second.

Where was she? Were they up there, in our bed? Or was I being paranoid and irrational? That was still a very real possibility.

I reached the back windows, looked out, and saw her at last. She was running up the lawn from the rocky waterfront. Carter was behind her, also running. They must have heard the dogs barking. Was Carter chasing her?

I opened the sliding glass doors and stepped onto the patio. Emma ran up the flagstone steps from the lawn below. She was out of breath when she reached the top. She halted with her hand on the railing. Our eyes locked and held.

"You're home early," she said. The panic in her eyes was sharp and distinct. She was terrified of what I must be thinking.

I half expected her to say "This isn't what it looks like," but she didn't say a word. She simply stood there, breathing hard, staring at me with wide eyes.

"What's going on?" I asked, trying to sound casual, but letting her know I was suspicious.

Carter reached the top of the stairs. "Hey, Luke," he said, as if we were friends.

By this time, I didn't know what to think. Carter seemed at ease. Maybe it wasn't what I thought. Maybe they actually were just signing papers for the sale of the house, which would be a good thing—one step closer to complete closure.

"Hey," I replied.

But then Carter glared at me with challenge, and my back went up.

Emma strode toward me. Her cheeks were flushed. She was still breathing quickly. "I'm sorry, Luke. I should have told you he was coming over."

I couldn't speak, but my fists were clenching.

As Carter moved past her, he touched the small of her back, held his hand there for a moment. The gesture was intimate, right in front of my face, and it sent a ripple of anger down my spine.

"I should go." He shouldered his way past me toward the sliding glass doors.

I wanted to follow and grab him by the shirt, shove him backwards into the wall of the house and tell him to get off my property, but I resisted the urge and faced my fiancée.

"What's happening here, Emma?"

Her eyebrows pulled together with shame and remorse. It was obvious she was fighting not to cry. "I'm so sorry. I don't know what to say. I feel terrible."

My gut churned. "Why? Are you still in love with him?"

Her lips parted, but she couldn't seem to find the right words to answer my question.

"Are you?" I shouted, taking a step forward because I needed to know the truth. I couldn't go on like this.

"I don't know," she shakily replied. "Maybe."

Pressing the heels of my hands to my forehead, I turned away and strode to the glass railing. I gripped it tightly and bent forward with my eyes shut, clenching my teeth together, willing this not to be happening.

I'd honestly thought this was the real thing—that Emma was the one I'd been waiting for, and that it would all work out. I thought we'd have a family together. I had wanted it so badly. I was ready.

But that couldn't happen because she still had feelings for her ex-husband, and I felt like I was reliving a nightmare. At least this time, I hadn't found them in bed together.

Emma moved to stand beside me. "I do love you, Luke. You have no idea how much this is killing me."

I shot her a cold look. "It's killing you? That's hard to believe when you're the one at the helm, steering the ship."

Emma laid her hand between my shoulder blades. I wanted to brush it away, but I forced myself to remain calm. Maybe we just needed to work through this.

Another part of me said *no*. There was no coming back from this. She still loved Carter. This was the end of us.

"If you love him, you should go and be with him," I said harshly. "There's no point dragging this out."

She stepped back. "I never wanted to hurt you. You've meant everything to me, Luke. I really can't bear this."

"Sure you can," I said callously. "Besides, it doesn't matter." I moved away from the railing and faced her. "You want what you want, Emma, and it appears that it's Carter, not me. I get it. I was just some sort of bridge for you. A way to get over what went wrong between you and him."

"No, please don't think that—"

I held up a hand. "Just tell me, when did you realize it? When did you know that you wanted to go back to him?"

She shook her head, as if she wasn't sure.

"Was it when you went for the psychic reading?"

She shook her head again. "I don't know."

"Yes, you do. Tell me."

She wet her lips. "That was the start of it, I guess. And when he apologized. When we cleaned out Sammy's room, everything felt different. All the bad stuff just disappeared. I remembered the way we used to be, before all the pain."

"And the past was more important to you than what we have now?" I asked.

Hesitantly, she nodded. "There's just so much history between Carter and me."

I faced her squarely. "It can't just be that. You always said you wanted to move forward. You wanted a new beginning. Don't tell me you want to go backwards, that you're loyal to promises you made years ago. If you do want to be with him, don't sugarcoat it. If there's no hope for us, I need to know. Tell me that you love him. That you're always going to love him. You're going to have to hit me over the head with a sledgehammer, Emma, or I'll just keep fighting for you. I'll keep waiting and hoping."

Her eyes filled with tears. "Please, don't make me do this."

"Why not?" I spread my hands wide. "Is it too painful for you? Because if it is, I don't care. Just give it to me straight. Be honest with me, because the worst thing you could do is lie to me."

She bent forward and started weeping, but I made no effort to comfort her. Not this time. Any sympathy I might have felt had been trampled. My heart was flattened.

She struggled to pull herself together. Then she met my gaze and spoke in a quavering voice.

"I did love you. You were so good to me and you helped me move on. But I can't explain it. Carter is part of my identity. I think our souls are meshed. He knows me better than anyone and we've been to hell and back—maybe not together. We had to do that separately. But he and I suffered the same."

I turned away from her and began to pace around the patio, because this was torture. Maybe I shouldn't have pushed her to be straight with me.

"I admit, he and I were cruel to each other," she continued, "because we were both suffering and angry. And you've been nothing but kind. You're the kindest, most amazing man I've ever known, but the fact is..." She paused. "You don't cherish Sammy's memory like Carter does. That's what he and I share. And I want to have another child, but part of me can't imagine having a baby with anyone but Carter—because he's my soul mate. He understands. We're in the same place. And if we have a child, it would be Sammy's brother or sister. Something in me wants that. I'm so sorry Luke." She paused, then delivered the final blow. "Last week, after we packed up Sammy's room, we went to the playhouse together and that's when we both knew we couldn't say good-bye. We couldn't sell the house. So...we're not going to."

I turned to her. "So, it's just going to be a shrine to the child you lost?"

"No, it won't be like that. And you don't understand. But we're not going to try to bury the memories either, because we know Sammy's still with us."

Well, there it was. I couldn't compete with a ghost. And maybe I was better off this way. Maybe I was meant to be alone. Maybe a family—a child of my own—wasn't in the cards for me. Maybe I needed to get that through my thick skull once and for all.

If this was what Emma wanted and needed—to be with Carter—I wasn't going to stand in her way.

I took a few minutes to collect myself, then I faced her and spoke more calmly. "I appreciate the honesty. That's all

I wanted. And if this is the way it is, and you're sure—*if you're absolutely sure*—then I want you to be happy."

She broke down again, strode forward and hugged me while she cried. I clung to her—not to comfort her, but because I was heartbroken and needed to hold on. I didn't want to let her go, though I knew I had to.

When she stepped out of my arms, it felt as if my heart had been ripped out of my chest. Yesterday, I thought she would be my wife. I even thought we might have a child of our own a year from now—that I would be a father at last. But none of that was going to happen. She would leave me now, and I would be alone again.

CHAPTER

Fourteen

Luke

Emma had said she'd return the next day to collect her things. I had asked what time she planned to arrive because I wanted to make arrangements to be elsewhere. We had settled on a time after supper, then she said good-bye to the dogs and walked out the door.

That night, after our breakup, I couldn't sit home alone. I called my friend Wayne, a high school buddy who lived in Victoria, told him what happened and asked if he wanted to go out for dinner and drinks. *Lots* of drinks. He had a wife and two kids at home, and it was a weeknight, but he told me he'd meet me in an hour. I called my neighbor to let the dogs out before bed, just in case I didn't make it home.

I wasn't normally the type to pour my heart out in public places, but Wayne and I spent the entire evening at a very expensive restaurant talking about Emma and my previous cheating girlfriend, Gwyneth. We rehashed how that relationship had crashed and burned, and discussed why I didn't see the signs with Emma. How could I not have recognized that she wasn't as committed as I thought? Why hadn't I been more cautious and guarded at first? I'd jumped in with both feet after the first date, which wasn't like me at all. Not after what happened before.

"Look at it as a positive thing," Wayne replied. "You're finally over what Gwyneth did to you, and I think you've been ready for a long time to have a family. You've been wanting it but you just haven't met the right girl. As it turned out, Emma wasn't her, but at least you tried." He pointed a finger at me. "What I don't want to see is you throwing in the towel. If you were a bridge for Emma, then let her be a bridge for you. Don't just give up. Get back on your feet and try again." He picked up his wine and took a sip. "Because I'm telling you, man. Being a dad is great. I can't imagine my life without Jenny and the kids. She's the best thing that ever happened to me."

After dinner—followed by far too many cocktails at a trendy martini bar—Wayne let me sleep on the sofa in his basement, but at six in the morning, I woke hungover with a raging headache and thought about Toby and Max. Rather than stick around for breakfast with Wayne and his family, I left a note thanking him for the use of his sofa, and said I'd call him later. I got into my car and returned to Oak Bay.

The dogs were at the front door when I walked in. They greeted me with wagging tails and wet tongues. I immediately let them out through the back door to the patio and they ran down to the lawn below.

While they took care of business, I made a cup of coffee.

A moment later, I stood at the patio railing, watching sea-kayakers paddle by along the rocky coastline. It was a beautiful September morning with a light mist over the water. Dew on the grass glistened in the early sunlight. There was something almost magical about the day and I tried to appreciate it, even though my insides felt like cold stone.

When I finished my coffee, I whistled to call the dogs in, poured kibble into their bowls, and cooked an omelet for myself. I sat down to eat at the breakfast bar, but the house was depressingly quiet, so I got up and turned on CBC radio to listen to *The Current* while I ate.

After breakfast, my hangover got the best of me. I collapsed on the sofa and slept for two hours. When I woke, I dragged myself to the kitchen and guzzled a large glass of water, then I thought about going for a swim in the pool because it was a warm day. I got into my trunks, but when I padded across the pool deck and looked down at my reflection in the water, I decided instead to relax on one of the lounge chairs under the canopy, where I could lie back and read the newspaper. The dogs lay in the shade under one of the patio tables.

I don't know how much time passed while I lay there. I might have fallen asleep again. I wasn't sure.

When I opened my eyes, it was mid-afternoon. Emma told me she planned to hire professional movers to collect the furniture in my garage, which would happen later in the week, but that night, she'd be cleaning out drawers, picking up her toothbrush. Stuff like that.

I didn't want to be in the house when she arrived, so I had to make other plans, but I had no idea what to do with myself. I didn't want to call Wayne again because I doubted Jenny would appreciate me dragging him out two nights in a row. Maybe I'd take in a movie. I'd think of something.

The sky turned dark and the temperature cooled, so I rose from the lounge chair, whistled for the dogs, and went back inside.

The house was silent and dismal. Or maybe it was just my mood. In an effort to liven up the place, I found a major-league baseball game on TV. The white noise of the cheering crowd and the sound of the commentator was a welcome distraction, but then I turned and saw Emma's sneakers beside the sofa. The sight of them was like a knife in my gut.

If she were here right now, we'd probably be cooking something in the kitchen or talking about our honeymoon. Making plans. Maybe we'd get the bikes out and go for a ride, or we'd take the dogs to the park. Maybe pick up some groceries on the way home.

The next thing I knew, I was wandering around my house, taking an inventory of the things she would collect—things that wouldn't be here when I returned. I found her trench coat in the front closet and a bunch of her shoes and boots. In the den, the book she was currently reading lay on the table next to the brown leather chair. I picked it up and opened it to the bookmarked page. She was about halfway through. I read a couple of paragraphs, then set it down again.

When I went upstairs to our bedroom, it hit me that it was no longer *our* bedroom and I had to learn to stop saying "us" and "we" all the time.

I stopped short in the doorway.

Because I hadn't come home the night before, the bed was still made. Emma's silky blue nightgown was draped across the footboard and her laptop was on her pillow. She must have forgotten about it when she left in such a hurry, but there it was.

I walked toward it and opened it. The screen lit up and I couldn't resist. I clicked on her email program.

I don't know what I was searching for—love letters perhaps? Secret messages to Carter where they discussed and plotted how they could be together again, and how she would break the news to me?

There were no such emails. If there were, she had permanently deleted them.

Feeling like a pathetic voyeur for scrolling through her inbox, I shut down the email program and shook my head at myself. *Don't do this to yourself, man. Move on.*

But when I opened my eyes, a website page was staring back at me. Or more particularly, it was a woman whose face was startlingly familiar. She was posing and smiling outdoors with a little girl who appeared to be her daughter.

The recognition was immediate and caused a rush of exhilaration in my veins.

Bev Hutchinson.

Halifax.

That conference a few years back…

Why was this picture on Emma's laptop? Is this why she wanted to go back to Carter? Because she'd been looking into my past, had discovered this brief fling I'd had, and decided I was a player when it came to one-night stands? Was that it?

I scrolled up to the headline and discovered this was a recent article on a major news site. There was a photo of the ship that had gone down in Nova Scotia. I read the headline:

GIRL WHO WENT TO HEAVEN IS JUST LIKE YOU AND ME

My mind shifted into overdrive. I started reading the article and quickly realized that the little girl Emma had been obsessing about was Bev's daughter. What were the odds?

The article described how Bev had performed CPR to bring her daughter back from the dead. This made me recall my conversations with Bev about her work. She loved being a nurse.

She'd had a daughter? She must have gotten married…

I read through the whole article. It commended her as a single mother.

I scrolled back up to the image and zoomed in on it.

Two beautiful smiling faces. A sweet little girl. Five years old. I was mesmerized.

Then my mind began to scramble through the math. When was the conference?

Almost six years ago.

Was it possible that…?

No, it couldn't be.

I stared at the image again—those two beautiful faces. The little girl who had drowned and allegedly gone to heaven. I couldn't take my eyes off her, nor could I leave it at this. I needed to know more.

CHAPTER

Fifteen

Bev

Halifax, Nova Scotia

I 'll never forget where I was when the text came in. It was eleven o'clock at night and I had just finished an evening shift at the hospital. Still in my scrubs, I pulled my purse out of my locker and checked my phone, but the battery was dead so I shoved it into my back pocket and figured I'd charge it in the car.

I wasted no time getting there and plugged it in right away, just in case Claire had called. Whenever I worked a night shift, Louise slept over at my sister's place, but this afternoon, Louise had been complaining of a stuffy nose, so I wanted to make sure she was okay.

I turned the key in the ignition and sat in the dark, waiting for my phone to charge. At last the screen lit up. A moment later, a few texts came in. I tapped on Claire's message right away: *Louise is feeling better. She went to bed no problem. Get a good night's sleep and if she's okay in the morning, I'll take them both to school.*

I quickly thumbed a reply: *Thanks for letting me know. I just got off work and I'm heading home. Call me if she wakes up and needs me through the night. I can come and get her, no prob.*

I hit SEND, then scrolled through the other messages. There was something from one of my colleagues who wanted to trade a night shift with me next week, and another from my mom, inviting us for dinner on Sunday. I responded and accepted her invitation.

Then I tapped on a text from an unknown number and was surprised to see a very long message.

Hi Bev. Hoping you remember me. It's Luke Hawkins. We met in Halifax five years ago when I was in town for a conference.

My stomach went *whoosh* and my heart started to pound. It was partly excitement because I hadn't heard from Luke since we were together, and I'd never forgotten the chemistry we shared. But the initial thrill turned instantly to panic, because I'd been living in fear of this day since before Louise was born—when I'd made the decision not to tell Luke that I was pregnant.

I'd always planned to tell him eventually, but I wanted the time to be right. When Louise was a baby, I was too preoccupied and exhausted all the time. I was so in love with her, I wanted her all to myself. Later, I imagined it would be best to wait until she was old enough to understand.

But we weren't there yet. She was only five.

I continued to read Luke's text.

I just tried calling you but there was no answer, so a text will have to do. It's been a while so I hope this is still the correct number. I saw a news article about you tonight. What a shocker. I had no idea you were involved in the accident where that ship went down. The story of you and your daughter was all over the news here in BC when it happened, but I didn't know it was you. I'm glad you're okay. It must have been a terrible ordeal, especially with what happened to your daughter. It's a good thing you have medical training.

The text ended there, but there was another that came after it, which appeared to be a continuation of the first. He said: *Can we chat on the phone? I'd really like to talk to you. You can call me anytime at this number. I'll try again tomorrow if I don't hear from you.*

That was the end, and by now my heart was racing so fast, I felt nauseous.

Did he know? Maybe he didn't. Maybe he just wanted to reconnect and catch up.

Oh, God. What was I supposed to do? I didn't want to call him at that moment. I needed time to think it through.

I texted Claire. *Are you still up?*

She replied right away. *Yes. Watching tv.*

You're not going to believe what just happened, I replied. *Is Scott there with the girls? Can you come over? I need some advice.*

Yes, he's here. I'll meet you at your place in five minutes.

I texted her back and said *OK*, then I backed out of my parking spot and headed home.

"My God," Claire said after she finished reading Luke's messages. "Do you think he knows?"

"I don't know. You can't tell, based on what he says in the texts." I sat down at the kitchen table. "I'm not sure what to do."

Claire set my phone down in front of me and went to fill a glass of water at the sink. "I hate to say I told you so, but I always knew this was going to come back and bite you in the ass one day."

My gaze lifted. "That's not helpful. And believe me, I knew it would too, and if I had a dime for every time I wished I'd just come clean in the first place, I'd be a rich woman today." I buried my forehead in a hand. "Oh, God. I should have told him. What was I thinking? Why was I so afraid?"

"We both know the answer to that," she said as she sipped her water.

I waved a hand through the air. "Okay, okay. Let's not rehash it. Let's just try to figure out how I should handle the situation *now*."

"There's nothing to figure out. If you're going to talk to him, you have to tell him. If I were in your shoes, I'd call a lawyer first thing in the morning."

I exhaled heavily. "This is exactly what I wanted to avoid in the first place. I don't want to go through a custody battle, and I certainly don't want Louise to have to deal with that. It doesn't help that she said she didn't want to meet him."

My cell phone rang on the table in front of me, and I jumped. I picked it up and darted a glance at Claire. "It's him."

"Him, who? Luke?" Her mouth fell open and she set her water glass on the counter.

It rang a second time. "I have to answer it. Stay here. I'm going in the other room."

I hurried to my bedroom where I closed the door behind me, then I swiped the screen. "Hello?"

There was a brief pause on the other end. "Hi, is this Bev?"

My heart raced like wildfire, and I couldn't deny that the quiet, smoky sound of his voice caused a commotion in me. It was familiar and surprisingly intimate.

"Yes, this is Bev. Is this Luke?"

"Yeah," he replied. He took his time before he added, "It's been awhile. How are you?"

"I'm good. How are you?" I spoke too quickly and my cheeks flushed with heat.

"I'm all right," he said. "I'm glad you answered. I wasn't sure if this was the right number…if it still worked. God, I hope I didn't wake you. It's late there, isn't it? I didn't think."

"No, it's fine," I replied. "I was at work tonight and I just got home a little while ago. What time is it where you are? And where are you exactly? You mentioned BC in your text."

"That's right," he replied. "I live out here now. It's eight-thirty."

All the way on the other side of the country. I fought to breathe in a slow and steady pace. "You were in Toronto before, weren't you? What made you decide to move out west?"

This was painful small talk, but it was necessary. I had to be polite and keep it together. Just make casual conversation.

"I guess I got tired of the noise and the constant smell of exhaust in the city. And this is where I grew up."

"That's right. I remember you told me that."

I was tempted to add: *I remember everything.* But I swallowed the words.

"Are you still working as a stockbroker?" I asked.

"I'm retired from that. Now I just do a bit of financial consulting here and there. I still travel back and forth to Toronto a fair bit."

I managed a small laugh. "You seem too young to be retired from anything."

"Maybe," he conceded. "But I like being my own boss. Better hours."

Suddenly, I didn't have a clue what to say next. I was completely thrown by the fact that we were talking on the phone after all this time, as if we were casual acquaintances who hadn't made a baby together.

But this was Louise's father. She had his DNA.

If I were open and honest right now, I would thank him, a hundred times over.

I bowed my head in shame. How was I going to explain this? If only I could turn back time.

"You're probably wondering why I'm calling," he said.

I took a deep breath and resigned myself to whatever was about to occur. "Yes, I am…"

He hesitated. "Well, this is probably going to sound crazy, and I apologize in advance if it does, but I saw a picture of you on a news website a few hours ago, and you were with your daughter in a playground."

My stomach tightened into knots. "Really? I've been trying to keep a low profile, especially where Louise is concerned. There were a lot of paparazzi around after the accident, but I didn't want all that publicity."

He was quiet. "Bev, I don't know how to ask this, so I'm just going to come right out and say it. Your daughter… When we were together…" He cleared his throat. "Is she mine?"

I squeezed my eyes shut and lay back on the bed. Swallowing heavily, I tried to come up with a straightforward response, but none of this was straightforward. It was complicated and agonizing. "Luke…" I whispered. "Yes. I'm sorry. I should have told you. I wanted to, many times, but I didn't know how to. I was scared."

He said nothing and my heart pummeled my ribcage. The room was practically spinning.

"Are you still there?" I asked, sitting up again.

"Yes, I'm here. I'm just in shock." There was another long pause. "What were you scared of?"

I ran my fingers through my hair, pushing it straight back off my face. "I don't know. Everything, I guess. I didn't know you very well."

This was excruciating. I was still terrified about what could come of this.

"I wish you had told me," he said. "I really can't believe it."

Rising to my feet, I paced around the room. "I know…it must be a shock to you. I'm sorry."

Heaven help me—I couldn't stop apologizing.

"Does she know about me?" he asked.

"Sort of. She knows she has a father, but I told her that you live very far away and that we don't really know each other very well."

"That's kind of a weird explanation," he replied. "We spent the night together, Bev. But you don't think you know me?"

My stomach muscles clenched tight. "She's only five. I can't explain those kinds of adult things to her now."

He was quiet for a few seconds. "I suppose not."

I paced around the room, and when he didn't completely freak out at me, I began to wonder what I'd been afraid of all these years. Maybe everything was going to be all right after all.

"Are you still there?" I asked again, because he hadn't spoken in the past fifteen seconds.

"Yes. I'm here."

"I'm a bit surprised," I said, feeling my heartbeat begin to slow to a more normal rate. "I've been dreading this conversation since I found out I was pregnant. I didn't know what to expect. I thought you'd be more angry than this. Or upset."

He scoffed bitterly. "You can't see me right now, Bev. Believe me, I'm upset."

Oh God.

"It's been quite a week," he continued. "And this conversation is the icing on top of a really *bad* cake."

My insides began to burn. "I see." I wasn't sure if I was incensed or relieved. It was a bizarre combination of both, I suppose. "Listen…you don't have to worry about a thing. I don't expect anything from you, and this doesn't have to affect you at all. I won't even tell Louise who you are if you don't want me to. I can't guarantee she won't want to track you down later in life, but for now, I'm happy to keep things just as they are. I'm okay raising her on my own. In fact, I prefer it that way. So, we can just hang up the phone right now and pretend this never happened."

He was silent. When he finally spoke, his voice was raspy and brimming with bitterness. "God, you *really* don't know me."

"What? I'm sorry, I—"

"I think we should end this conversation now, Bev. But this isn't over. I promise you'll be hearing from my lawyer."

The line went dead. "Wait! No!"

I tried to press the call button to get him back, but he was gone. My entire body erupted in a firestorm of dread and fear. I ran out of the room.

I found Claire sitting on my sofa in the living room,

watching the news. "He was mad," I told her. "He said I was going to hear from his lawyer."

Her eyebrows pulled together in a frown and she sat forward. "Oh no. We need to call Scott right away. He'll be able to find you a lawyer too. We need to get you the very best in the city."

I held up my hands. "Wait, wait. I don't want it to come to that. Luke had every right to be angry. I'm the one who screwed up. I shouldn't have kept this secret from him. I need to call him back."

"No! Don't do that!" Claire leaped off the sofa and snatched the phone from my hands. "You need to call a lawyer, first thing in the morning. Let them handle this."

I stared at her with wide eyes while my blood coursed hotly through my veins. "This is exactly what I was afraid of. It's why I didn't tell him in the first place. I never wanted to get into a custody battle. I'm sure I just need to talk to him, work this out." I grabbed the phone from my sister and headed for my bedroom.

"But that's what lawyers are for!" She followed me down the hall, which was still papered with Louise's crayon drawings of heaven.

I hurried into my room. "I need to call him back. I have to try."

She shook her head at me, but I shut the door in her face and locked it.

"Please, Bev!" She knocked hard. "Just calm down and take a breath. Think this through."

With trembling fingers, I found Luke's number and pressed the call button. It rang once, twice, three times...

"Please answer." I paced anxiously around my room.

At last, a click sounded in my ear. "Hello." His voice was stern and unfriendly.

"Hi, Luke, it's Bev again. Please don't hang up. Let's just talk for a second."

"I don't think that's a good idea."

"Yes, it is. Please. I'm so sorry. Before…when you said this was the icing on top of a bad cake, I thought you meant you were annoyed by this and you didn't want the responsibility or something. But if I misunderstood and that's not the case, let's talk about it, because I don't want this to get ugly, and I'm sure you don't either. We don't need to be enemies."

He didn't say a word. Not a single word. With every passing second, my heart beat faster and I grew more desperate.

"I admit…this is my fault. I'm the one who messed up. I should have told you a long time ago."

I was rambling now and breathing heavily. If I had a lawyer present, he'd probably slap his hand over my mouth to shut me up.

"I don't even know what you want," I continued, "but let's try to figure this out. We can figure it out together."

There was nothing but silence on the other end. I was in such a state of panic, I feared I might vomit.

"I don't know," he finally said. "My gut's telling me to call a lawyer. And I'm going to want a paternity test."

I sat down on the edge of the bed and tried to speak in a calm voice. "I don't blame you. You have every right to be angry and I get that, but believe me, she's yours. I was wrong not to tell you, and I've been struggling with that decision since Louise was born, but like I said, I was afraid. I didn't know what you'd do if I told you."

"What did you think I'd do?"

"I don't know. Call a lawyer? Demand custody?"

"Would that have been so wrong?" he asked.

I exhaled heavily. "No, of course not. It's your right, legally. But I was selfish and I wanted to avoid conflict, and I wanted her all to myself. I didn't want to have to answer to anyone when it came to raising her—especially a man I barely knew. Mostly, I just wanted Louise to be happy and safe."

"Is she?" he asked. "Happy?"

I tried to slow my breathing. "Yes, very. We have a good life. She's an amazing little girl."

I sat on the bed, tapping my foot on the floor.

"You could have asked for child support, you know," he said. "I would have paid it."

I flopped onto my back and covered my eyes with my hand. "I'm sure you would have, but I was okay financially. I have a good job and a good support system."

"What kind of support system?"

I felt like I was on trial. I needed to plead my case, convince him not to go to war with us. "My sister and her husband live across the street and they have a daughter, too. The girls are about the same age, so they're very close. My sister helps me out a lot with child care. So does my mom."

"What about…?" He paused. "Is there someone who fills the father shoes for Louise?"

The question caught me off guard. "What do you mean? Am I seeing someone? No. There's no one. It's just me. There's never been anyone. But my brother-in-law is a father figure, I suppose. Her Uncle Scott. Across the street."

Luke said nothing.

Sitting up, I spoke in a softer, warmer voice. "Luke. If

you want to come out here and meet her, why don't you fly in for a visit. You could book a room at a hotel and stay for a few days or a week, or as long as you want. It's up to you. I'd explain the situation to her—that you're her father—and we could spend some time together. We could keep it casual and fun, because I'll be honest—the last thing I want is for the family courts to force Louise to get on a plane and fly across the country to meet a total stranger. Let's do this right. I don't want her to think of you as the enemy, and I promise you—that's what you'll be to her if you take me to court and we get into a battle over this."

"That sounds like a threat."

"Not at all. It's just a fact. And it would break my heart to put her through that. I'm sure that's not what you want. It's not what I want either."

I sat up and saw the shadow of Claire's feet under the door and realized she'd been listening to my conversation this entire time.

"We'd still need to bring lawyers into this," Luke said. "Because I have rights."

"I know you do," I replied. "And I won't fight you on that—not if we can work this out in a way we're all comfortable with. I'm willing to be reasonable if you are."

"I'm always reasonable," he replied.

I let out a breath of relief. "That's good to hear."

"But don't get too comfortable. That doesn't mean I trust you. You kept my daughter from me for five years. I'm pissed off and I'm still getting a lawyer."

I felt my shoulders slump. "Fine. If that's what you want to do. But if you want to be a part of Louise's life, she's going to need to trust you, and take my word for it, you're going to need my help with that. So…just work with me, okay? Her happiness and wellbeing is my top priority, and I hope it will be yours too. That's why I want you to meet her in a casual situation—because if this turns into a power struggle between you and me, she'll sense it and she'll take my side. And that's not a threat. It's just the way it will be. But like I said, I'm reasonable, Luke, but we *both* need to be if this is going to work."

He paused. "Okay. That sounds fair. I'll go online tonight and check on some flights. I'd like to come right away. Tomorrow, if possible."

Tomorrow? My stomach turned over with apprehension because I was still terrified that in the end, this man would try to take Louise away from me. At the very least, even if things went well, he would encroach upon our relationship and I would have to share her with him. Nothing would ever be the same.

But I had no choice. Luke was Louise's father and he had rights. And unless he turned out to be a psycho maniac, it would be a losing battle to try and fight him. Besides, it was only a matter of time before Louise would want to know him, so I wanted to lay the groundwork to make sure it would be a pleasant experience for her. More than anything, I wanted it to be a positive thing. Lawyers and courtrooms would get in the way of that.

"Let me know what time you'll be arriving," I said to Luke, "and where you'll be staying. We'll figure out the next step from there."

We hung up, and I opened my bedroom door to find Claire staring at me.

"You heard that?"

She nodded.

"He's coming tomorrow," I said, "and I'm scared out of my wits."

She pulled me into her arms for a hug.

I decided to bring Louise home for breakfast before school, rather than let Claire drive her, because I needed time to explain what was about to occur—that her father would arrive on an airplane that afternoon, and she would meet him for the first time. Recalling our previous conversation about Luke—when she'd informed me that she didn't want to meet him at all—I was uneasy about delivering the news.

"How are your pancakes?" I asked, sitting across from her at the kitchen table.

"Yummy. I like the chocolate chips. We don't usually have chocolate for breakfast."

I smiled at her. "Well. Today's a special day."

She reached for the maple syrup and tipped the bottle over her plate. I sat back with my coffee and let her pour as much as she wanted. "Do you want to know why it's a special day?"

She swirled her pancake through the syrup and nodded.

"Because we're going to have a visitor. It's someone who really wants to meet you. He's flying here on an airplane, from very far away."

She didn't look up. She was too focused on her sopping pancakes. "Who is it?"

While I didn't want to make a big deal out of it and give her reason to feel anxious at school, I didn't want to make light of it either. That would be a pretense. It was a difficult balancing act.

"It's your father," I explained in a calm, matter-of-fact voice. "He'll be arriving this afternoon, and I'll go and meet him. Uncle Scott will pick you up after school. Then I'll bring your daddy here and we'll have supper together."

"All of us?" she asked. "Auntie Claire and Uncle Scott, too?"

I cleared my throat. "No, just the three of us. You, me, and Luke. That's your daddy's name."

"Okay," she replied, calmly, as if I'd just told her it was time to go and brush her teeth.

She picked up her knife and cut her pancake while I sat there trying to comprehend what she might be thinking. Could it really be this easy? Was she truly okay with this? Or was she nervous and trying to hide her ambivalence from me?

You're over-analyzing it, Bev. Just let her be and try to relax. Don't make too much of it.

"Do you have any questions you'd like to ask me? About meeting your dad?"

Louise inclined her head as she mulled it over. "What does he look like?"

I set my coffee cup down. "That's a good question. I'll do my best to answer it, but it's been a long time since I've seen him, so he might have changed. But the last time I saw him, he had dark hair and friendly brown eyes. His eyes sparkled when he smiled, and that's something I liked about him. He made me laugh."

"Did he tell jokes?"

"Sort of," I replied. "He said some funny things. He was a nice person and a lot of fun."

"How come you didn't marry him?" she asked. "Aren't most mommies and daddies married?"

"Yes," I carefully replied. "That's usually the way it happens. But not all families are the same. We're different because your daddy lives very far away."

It was a simplistic explanation, but it would have to do for now.

Louise said OK again and finished her breakfast with no further questions.

"If you're done," I said, "why don't you go brush your teeth and put on your shoes. We don't want to be late for school."

She slid off her chair and ran to the bathroom, while I sat for a moment, finishing my coffee and wondering how this day would play out.

Luke

It was disorienting, getting on a plane at midnight and flying across the country to meet a daughter I hadn't known I had. Shortly after takeoff, when we were above the clouds and surrounded by darkness, I started to wonder if there had been some mistake and it wasn't true—that I wasn't a father and I'd jumped the gun when I booked this flight. Maybe I should have taken steps to verify the facts first.

Then I thought about it *not* being true. Heaven help me, if it wasn't, I'd be devastated. I couldn't even begin to comprehend how let down I would be, which surprised me, because I knew almost nothing about this little girl, and I'd only seen one picture of her, which I'd found on the Internet.

On the flipside, I was furious with her mother and not the least bit enthusiastic about seeing her again. Not after the secret she'd kept from me. I would have preferred to deal with her through lawyers, but I couldn't argue with her rationale on the phone—that I needed her on my side in order to earn Louise's trust and affection.

The more I thought about that, the more infuriated I became. First off, I couldn't accept the fact that a woman I'd slept with—a woman I'd genuinely cared for, despite the brevity of our relationship—had willfully shut me out of her life and prevented me from knowing my own daughter. As a result, I'd missed the first five years of Louise's life. I would never get those years back.

How do you recover from something like that? How do you walk into your daughter's life for the first time and make her love you? Was that even possible?

~C

I woke to a blinding orange sunrise in the window of the aircraft. I squinted and lowered the blind, then glanced up groggily at the flight attendant, who offered me a breakfast tray.

An hour later, we touched down in Toronto for a sixty-minute layover. Then I boarded another plane for the second leg of my journey—a two-hour flight to Halifax. It was 12:30 p.m. local time when I finally arrived.

As soon we landed, I powered up my phone and sent a text to Bev to let her know I'd made it and that I'd take a cab to my hotel. We arranged to meet in the lobby at 3:00 p.m., which would give me time to drive there, check in, grab a quick shower, and prepare myself to play nice.

Bev

Nervous butterflies fluttered in my belly as I made my way up the stairs at the main entrance to the Lord Nelson Hotel. I had no idea what to expect when I saw Luke. When we spoke on the phone, he'd made it clear that he was angry, so I worried that this could escalate into a heated argument. I hoped that wouldn't be the case, but I was prepared for anything.

A doorman in uniform greeted me at the entrance. I smiled in return and walked into the historic lobby, where I paused on the marble floor and glanced around at some guests who were gathered at the registration desk. It had been five years since I'd seen Luke. I hoped I would recognize him.

When I didn't spot him right away, I turned to my left and crossed toward The Arms Restaurant—an upscale English-style pub—climbed the steps and peered inside. There were only a few patrons at tables, so I turned around and wandered across the lobby to the other side. Peering into the elegant Georgian Lounge, I found it empty, so I turned around again.

Then I saw him, emerging from the elevators. He stopped in his tracks when our eyes met.

He hadn't changed a bit. He was still as handsome as I remembered, and my whole body began to hum. There was just something about this man that knocked me off my feet. That's why I'd behaved so recklessly five years ago— spending the night with someone I'd only just met. It wasn't something I ever thought I would do. I'd always been very straight-laced, except for that one night.

I reminded myself that I was no longer the woman I had been back then. I was a mother now—the farthest thing from reckless—and I had to handle this situation with tremendous care.

Slowly, I walked toward him. We met in the center of the lobby, under an enormous crystal chandelier.

"Hi," Luke said, his gaze roaming over me from head to foot. "You look the same."

"So do you," I replied.

We stared at each other for a few seconds and it was painfully awkward.

"So," he said, "we have a lot to talk about. Where do you want to do this?" He glanced around the lobby and gestured toward the restaurant. "Do you want to get a drink or—?"

"No. Why don't we go across the street to the Public Gardens? It's a beautiful day." Not only that, but I needed to stay on my toes. A drink would not help.

I led the way and he followed me out the main doors.

We descended the steps, walked toward the busy intersection and made small talk along the way.

"How was your flight?" I asked.

"Long. I'm going to be jet-lagged."

"And it's a four-hour time difference. That makes it rough."

There was a lot of traffic and pedestrians gathered on the corner as we waited in silence for the light to change. When we finally crossed the street and arrived at the giant wrought-iron Victorian gates, Luke looked up and said, "This is incredible. You'd think Saint Peter would be here to usher us through."

I laughed. "You're right. This is a little slice of heaven. It's my favorite place in the city. I bring Louise here all the time to see the ducks."

As soon as the words crossed my lips, I worried that I should be more guarded about what I shared and how I shared it, because maybe the mere mention of Louise's name might remind Luke of what he had missed—because of the choices I had made.

We strolled along the gravel path and stepped onto the upper bridge with elaborate balusters and concrete urns full of pink flowers on the four corner pedestals. Without saying a word, we stopped on the arched deck to look over the rail, into the fish pond below. Everything was lush and green. The vibrant-colored rhododendrons were awesome and striking. The whole world seemed vivid all around us.

"So, where do we start?" Luke asked.

"I don't know," I replied. "What would you like to know? Ask me anything and I'll tell you."

He faced me and inhaled deeply. "All right then. What's she like?"

I gazed into his pained eyes and felt a fresh wave of guilt. I couldn't imagine what it must be like to be in his shoes, knowing nothing about his own daughter. He must hate me.

"Well…" I said, "you've seen that picture of her online, but I can show you some more if you like. I have my phone in my purse."

I made a move to reach for it, but he put his hand on my arm and stopped me. "First, tell me in words. What's her personality like? What should I expect when I meet her? How should I act with her?"

The question was like a knife in my chest because he seemed genuinely nervous about meeting Louise for the first time and making a good first impression. I wanted more than anything to help him, to try to make amends.

"Well. She's very mature for her age," I told him. "You'll be surprised. She was never the type to throw temper tantrums during the so-called terrible twos. She's thoughtful. Calm. Artistic. She loves to draw pictures and she can read well beyond her grade level. I mean…she's not into Dostoyevsky yet, but we've been reading picture books every night since she was a baby, so she gets it."

Luke was listening intently with a slight frown.

"She likes to watch movies," I continued.

"What's her favorite?" he asked.

I had to think about that for a moment. "That's a tough question. I'd say the top five are *Frozen, Cinderella, Beauty and the Beast*, and get this…she loves the original *Oliver Twist* from the 1960's. And, of course, *The Sound of Music*, although the Nazi stuff is over her head."

"She likes musicals," Luke said.

I turned to him. "Yes, that's right. Those are all musicals. I never thought of it that way."

We started walking again and strolled toward the Victorian bandstand in the center of the Gardens.

"I'd like to bring her a present," Luke said. "I didn't

want to get her anything at the airport because I didn't know what she might like, and it's all touristy stuff anyway. Is there anywhere around here I could find something?"

"Absolutely. We can walk down Spring Garden Road and there are all sorts of shops, and a great children's bookstore. I can help you with that."

"Thanks. I honestly have no idea what a five-year-old girl would be into these days."

So far, this was going far better than I'd expected. Luke wasn't combative, nor was he reminding me of the fact that he'd wanted to take me to court the night before. I prayed it would continue this way—that he wouldn't suddenly turn into a monster who wanted to screw me over.

We continued walking along the grand path toward Griffin's Pond.

"Is that the *Titanic*?" Luke asked, stopping short.

I chuckled. "Yes, it's a model. The actual *Titanic* sank off the coast of Newfoundland so there are a lot of artifacts in the city. There's a graveyard where some passengers are buried. And the Maritime Museum of the Atlantic has a display on the waterfront if you're interested. That's something we could do with Louise. Or wait, maybe not after what we just went through. I'll think of something else for us to do together."

"That would be great," he replied. "Whatever you think she'd enjoy. I just want this to be…" He looked up at the sky, but didn't finish.

"What?"

"I don't know," he said. "Easy. I don't want her to be afraid of me."

"She won't be. And I don't want that either."

We continued along the tree-lined path, past weeping

willows, slowly making our way toward the Boer War Memorial Fountain.

"Since we're talking about feeling comfortable," I cautiously mentioned, "there's something I should probably prepare you for, because it might come up when you meet her. It's kind of...way out there. I don't want it to catch you off guard."

Hands in pockets, he slid me a glance. "Should I be nervous?"

I let out a heavy sigh. "I don't know. I'm nervous about everything right now, Luke. This is all..." I shook my head. "There's so much to say and I don't know where to begin. I feel like you must hate me."

"No." He spoke matter-of-factly, which didn't make me feel any less uncomfortable.

"Then you're a better man than I would be in your position," I replied. "If you really want to know, I've been going crazy trying to figure out what to say to you today, and how to say it. So, I'm just going to spit it out. I know there's no possible way for me to make up for what I did, but I want you to know that—"

He shook his head, cutting me off. "Please, Bev. You don't have to say anything. There's nothing to say, really. We can't change it."

"But that sounds so hopeless," I replied.

He shrugged a shoulder.

I stopped on the path. "I hope that in time that you might be able to forgive me."

He gazed off in the other direction, toward the iron fence along the perimeter of the park. "I don't know. We'll see. Let's just get through this day."

A lump formed in my throat—not because he wasn't

willing to forgive me yet, but because he seemed almost broken. Was this all my doing? Had I robbed him of his belief in people? If so, how would I ever fix that?

We reached the fountain and found a bench to sit on.

"Is that what you wanted to tell me?" Luke asked. "You said you wanted to prepare me for something—something that might catch me off guard."

I shook my head as if to clear it. "I'm sorry, I got sidetracked. But this is important, and I'm not sure how to tell you, or how to ask…"

I dug deep for the courage to explain. "Obviously, you must have read about what happened to Louise when the *Dalila* went down. If you saw the news and that picture of us, you must know what all the hoopla was about."

"I think so. Everyone was saying that Louise went to heaven while you were performing CPR on her. Is that true?"

I looked down at my feet. "It's hard to answer that question definitively, because I still don't know. You'd think I would because I'm her mom, but it's just so hard to believe. But what I'm about to tell you—and ask you— might help shed some light and answer that question, once and for all."

He turned toward me and rested an arm along the back of the bench. "I'm listening."

"Okay. After Louise told me about what happened to her, I encouraged her to draw pictures to help me see what it was like up there—in heaven—and to help her remember, because she was afraid she might forget as time went by." I looked down at my hands in my lap. "She drew dozens of pictures of rainbows and trees. Blue skies, blue water, clouds with silver linings, but she also drew pictures of people she says she met up there. One was my father, who died when I was a child."

Luke listened raptly. "I remember you mentioned that."

"Yes. She never met my dad in real life, of course, but after she woke up in the rescue helicopter, she told me what he was like and it was very accurate, but still... She'd seen pictures of him and she knew about him, so I can't be certain that she wasn't describing what she'd heard from stories we might have told her."

Luke studied me with a slight frown, waiting for me to continue.

"After that, she drew another picture of her *other* grandparents." I turned to look at Luke. "Maybe you know where I'm going with this, but I had no idea if she was drawing your parents or just a fantasy of two extra grandparents, like other kids have. She said she saw them in heaven and that they were her father's parents, which was odd because I rarely ever spoke of you. She called them Papa and Nanny. She said her 'Papa' was tall with white hair and glasses, no mustache, and that her 'Nanny' was a small woman." I studied Luke's expression. "So, I guess the question is—are your parents still alive? And if so, is that what they look like?"

His mouth fell open and his face paled. "My parents are dead. They died in a car accident when I was nineteen."

My heart began to pound. "I'm so sorry. Why didn't you tell me that when we were together? I thought we shared everything that night."

He shook his head. "I don't know. You told me about losing your father. I didn't want to bring it up. I don't talk about it much."

I stared down at my lap and labored to process this. "It's awful that you lost them. Both of them at the same time. I'm so sorry."

"It was a long time ago, but thank you."

The lump returned to my throat and I took a moment to gather my composure and remember what started this discussion.

"What did they look like?" I asked. "Was your father tall?"

Luke nodded. "Yes. And my mom was extremely petite. The top of her head barely reached his elbow."

I couldn't even blink. My heart was racing like a runaway train. This felt like proof of the heaven Louise had described, but still, I couldn't fully believe it.

Why not?

I covered my eyes with my hand. "I don't know what to say right now. I'm a bit flabbergasted."

"Me, too."

We sat in silence, staring at our feet. A flock of pigeons came by, pecking at the ground around us.

"So…you never told Louise *anything* about my parents?" Luke asked.

"How could I? I didn't know a thing. I never mentioned them at all. That's why I was so shocked when she drew that picture."

"Can I see it?" he asked.

"Of course. I have all her pictures tacked to the wall outside her bedroom. It's quite something to look at them all at once—it's an incredible body of work for a five-year-old. They're very beautiful. So colorful."

A crowd of teenagers walked by, laughing about something.

"This is a lot to take in," Luke said, after they passed. "What a week it's been."

I thought back to our conversation the night before, when I'd made a few erroneous assumptions about how he felt.

"You mentioned that on the phone—that this was the icing on a bad cake. Is there something else that happened to you Luke? On top of this?"

He gazed off in the other direction again, and I was forced to look at the back of his head.

"Yes," he answered curtly. "But it's not something I want to talk about." His tone was firm.

"I'm sorry, I didn't mean to pry."

"Don't worry about it." He stood up and checked his watch. "I don't know what time the shops close around here. Maybe we should get going."

I stood up as well. "Sure. Why don't we go to the bookstore first? We can find something for Louise there. Then, if you're ready, we'll take my car and go pick her up at my sister's."

I watched him start off ahead of me and realized he was not the same man I'd met five years ago. That man had been charming, flirtatious, good-humored and open. We'd spent the entire night laughing. That's what I remembered most about him—his smiling eyes.

The Luke before me now seemed to live inside a dark thundercloud. Obviously, he was angry with me for what I'd done, and he was tired from his flight. And he was definitely shaken by what I'd told him about the picture Louise had drawn.

But I was curious about what, exactly, he didn't want to discuss just now.

He stopped on the path and turned. "Are you coming?"

"Yes." I hurried to catch up.

~⊘

It was almost five when we pulled into my driveway. "This is it," I said to Luke as I shut off the engine. "This is where we live."

Gift bag in hand, he stepped out of my car and gazed up at the front of the house. "It's nice."

"We like it. It has a wonderful fenced-in backyard with big trees. I'll show you that later—and the picture of course—but let's get Louise first. Are you ready?"

He nodded and we started off across the street. We climbed Claire's steps and rang the doorbell.

It was Scott who answered. "Hey Bev, come on in. You must be Luke."

While they shook hands, I tried to play it cool. "This is my brother-in-law, Scott."

"Nice to meet you," Luke said, glancing past him at the vaulted white ceiling and the massive stone fireplace in the living room. "This is a great spot you have here."

"Thanks. It's a quiet street. Great for the girls."

Just then, Claire emerged from the basement. "You're here at last. The girls are just finishing a movie. You must be Luke." She strode forward to shake his hand. "I'm Claire, Bev's sister. It's nice to meet you."

"Likewise," Luke replied.

Claire glanced down at the gift bag.

"That's for Louise," I explained. "We just went to Woozles."

"Oh, you picked a great store," Claire said to Luke. "We

go there all the time on Saturday afternoons." She paused. "Would you like to come in for a bit?"

She gestured to invite us into the kitchen, but I shook my head at her. "Um... Actually, we should probably get going. I have supper in the slow cooker and poor Leo hasn't been out since noon."

Luke turned to me. "Is Leo your dog?"

"Yes. I didn't mention that, did I? I hope you're not allergic or anything."

"No, I love dogs. I have two of my own."

"Really? What kind?" I asked.

"One's a black lab and the other's a curious mix—maybe part German Shepherd, part Lab? We're not sure. They were rescue dogs."

"Ah. That's nice."

The conversation stopped dead and I felt suddenly self-conscious because Scott and Claire were standing there, watching us. I turned to my sister who seemed to read my feelings.

"Why don't I bring Louise over to your place in about ten minutes?" Claire suggested. "As soon as the movie's over. That way you can let Leo outside and get settled."

"That's a great idea," I replied, gratefully.

This whole situation was more than a little awkward and I wished I'd planned it better. At least Claire had the sense not to bring Louise upstairs right away. It might have been even more awkward for father and daughter to meet for the first time in my sister's entry hall.

We thanked Claire and Scott, and walked out. A moment later, Luke and I stood on my front step while I rifled through my purse for my keys.

"I'd like to see the picture Louise drew when we get inside," Luke said.

"Yes, I'll show it to you right away."

When I finally opened the door, Leo was in his usual spot on the welcome mat, eager to greet us.

"Hey there." I dropped to one knee and scratched behind his ears.

Leo sniffed Luke excitedly, and Luke got down on a knee as well.

"He likes you," I said.

"I like him, too. Hey there, big guy. Aren't you gorgeous."

Leo rolled over onto his back and Luke laughed softly and rubbed his belly. I realized it was the first time I'd heard Luke laugh since we'd greeted each other in the hotel lobby over an hour ago.

I rose to my feet. "He needs to go out. Don't worry about your shoes. Leave them on. We'll take him out the back door. Then I'll show you the picture."

Luke followed me through the front hall to the kitchen, where he set the gift bag on the table. "It smells good in here."

"Barbequed chicken thighs—slow cooker style. I don't know what I'd do without my slow cooker."

We walked out the back door to the deck. Leo ran down the steps and charged around the yard in circles.

"Look how excited he is," I said with a smile, moving to the deck rail. "He loves company."

Luke joined me and took in the play structure and sandbox in the far corner of the yard, and the wooden bench and birdbath in the opposite corner. The marigolds and hydrangeas were still in bloom along the fence, and the leaves on the ancient oak trees whispered in the breeze overhead.

"You were right," Luke said. "This is a great yard. It's very private."

"We love it."

"How long have you lived here?" he asked.

"Since I found out I was pregnant with Louise. It's a long story, but Claire was separating from her first husband at the time, so she was alone and needed moral support, and I was pregnant and needed my big sister. Then she married Scott across the street and moved in with him, so she rented this place to me for a while until I offered to buy it. She gave me a good price. I owe her, big time."

"It's nice that you have each other."

While Leo performed his business in the bushes, I turned to Luke. "You don't have any brothers or sisters, do you? I seem to recall you telling me that you were an only child."

"I am."

"It must have been difficult after you lost your parents. Did you have any other family?"

"I had some uncles and aunts," he explained, "but I was nineteen so I was ready to be on my own anyway. I didn't need a guardian. I was in college. It was my friends who became my family."

"Where are they now?" I asked. "Do you still keep in touch?"

"Yes. I have one good high school friend in Victoria, and the others are all in Toronto. That's where I went to university."

Leo finished and came bounding up the deck stairs. "Good boy," I said, patting him on the head. Then I turned to Luke. "Let's go see the picture."

We walked inside to the hall outside Louise's bedroom, which was papered from floor-to-ceiling with depictions of heaven—as seen through Louise's eyes. I switched on the hall light and Luke stood there, astonished.

He inhaled deeply and whistled. "This is unreal."

"It is, isn't it? Every day, when she produced more and more of them, my mind was blown. They're all so vivid and gorgeous. Of course, I'm her mother, so I'm biased, but I really think there's something special here. I don't even know the right words to describe them."

He moved along the wall, taking his time, studying each one. Then he turned to me. "Do you think this is what it's really like?"

I shrugged. "I don't know. Is heaven even real to begin with? Or is this something from her imagination?"

"Either way, she's a gifted artist."

He gazed over all the pictures and I knew exactly what he was searching for. "Which one is it?"

"This one." I turned to the opposite wall, reached up, pulled the tack out, and handed the page to him.

He stared at it for a moment. Then he shook his head with disbelief.

"This looks exactly like them." He pointed. "That's my mom's curly brown hair. She was short and tiny and my father was tall and lanky. They were quite a pair. He wore glasses, just like these. He was a college professor. He taught chemistry. My mom was a mom. She stopped working when I was born. She had the most beautiful eyes."

I stood in silence, watching him and wishing I knew the right thing to say, but this was an experience unlike any other.

After a moment, Luke tacked the picture back on the

wall. "What else did she say about them? Besides what they looked like?"

I spoke in a steady, lower-pitched voice. "Louise said they told her that they loved her, but that she needed to come back to this world because they wanted her to meet her father. She said that's why she was sent back here."

He bowed his head and closed his eyes for a moment. "This is insane. I'm having a hard time believing it."

"Me, too."

Luke's shoulders rose and fell as he inhaled. Then he lifted his head and his eyes blazed at me. "Bev. Would you have *ever* told me about Louise if I hadn't seen the picture online and called and asked you, point blank, if she was my daughter?"

My lips fell open and I felt a thickness in my throat. I pressed my hands against my cheeks. "Yes. I would have, eventually. I've felt guilty about it for a long time now, more and more with each passing day, especially since Louise drew that picture. I've been struggling with how to handle it, but I've been caught up just trying to protect her from all the publicity. It was so much all at once. I had to tread lightly. Slowly."

He frowned. "So, you would have told me, *eventually*? When? When she was in high school? Or when she was old enough to seek me out on her own? When I'd missed out on her whole life?"

My knees went weak and I began to tremble. "I don't know. I'm sorry. I'd already dug such a deep hole for myself. I didn't know how to get out of it."

"How to get out of it? You just pick up the damn phone and call me. Or you send a text. I can't believe I was the one who had to call *you*. What if I'd never seen that picture?"

We heard the front door open.

"Hello!"

It was Claire. I recognized the sound of Louise dropping her backpack on the floor and kicking off her shoes.

The gravity of this moment was considerable. I didn't want Louise to sense the tension, and I couldn't imagine what Luke must be feeling outside of his anger toward me.

"She's expecting to meet you," I whispered to him. "She's been excited all day. Please, let's put this aside for now."

I gestured for him to follow me to the entrance hall, where I greeted Louise. "Hey cutie! How was your day?"

"Great!" she replied. "We just watched *Frozen*."

"Again?" I folded my arms and gave her a playful look. "Aren't you getting tired of that movie by now?"

"No!" She giggled, then peered past me toward Luke, who stood in the archway, leaning a shoulder against the jamb, his hands in the pockets of his jeans. He pulled one hand out and waved at her with a friendly, eager smile. Despite our argument just now, my heart melted.

"Louise, this is Luke," I said. "Why don't you go and say hello."

With a confidence beyond her years, Louise strode forward.

Luke bent at the waist and held out his hand. "Hi Louise. It's very nice to meet you."

They shook, then she returned to me and wrapped her arms around my waist.

"Are you hungry for barbequed chicken?" I asked while I rubbed her back.

"Yes."

"It's her favorite," I said to Luke. "That and French fries, right?"

"I *love* french fries," she announced. "With *lots* of ketchup."

"I love French fries, too," he told her. "Do you like them when they're crinkly cut? Or straight cut?"

"I like them crinkly," she replied, seeming amused by the question.

"Cool. I like 'em that way, too."

Louise giggled and hid her face in my belly. I turned to Claire. "Thank you for bringing her over."

"No problem. Have a nice supper. Call me later. I'll come over if you need me." She turned to leave. "Bye, Luke. It was nice to meet you."

"You, too," he replied with a nod.

As soon as she was out the door, he gave me a look. "What did she mean—she'll come over if you need her?"

I fumbled to explain in front of Louise. "Oh. She knows I have to drive you back to the hotel. She said she'd come over and babysit if Louise is asleep by then. Which you will be, right?" I said to her. "If it's past your bedtime? You'll be off to dreamland?"

She grinned up at me. "Maybe."

I wiggled her nose. "Why don't you go wash your hands? Then you can help me set the table."

"Okay."

While she ran to the bathroom, I moved toward Luke and slid by him in the narrow archway. "You can help, too, if you like."

"Sure." He followed me into the kitchen.

I quickly busied myself. "When Louise comes back, maybe you could set the table together." Feeling anxious and uncomfortable, I laid my hand over the cupboard doors next to the fridge. "Plates and glasses are here, cutlery's over there, and Louise can show you where the napkins are. Otherwise, I have everything taken care of. I just need to cook the fries. I apologize. It's not exactly a gourmet meal."

"It's fine," he replied. "I wasn't lying when I said I love french fries."

I was overcome with relief that he seemed willing to move past our disagreement just now and keep things light, for Louise's sake. "Maybe you can give her your gift after we eat?"

"Yeah." He seemed in a bit of a daze, watching me. "She has my mother's eyes."

My heart skipped a beat. "Really?"

I wondered if he'd still want that paternity test.

Louise entered the kitchen and approached me. "Mommy, can I show Daddy my room?"

I blinked a few times—mostly because she'd used the word "Daddy" as if she'd been using it all her life.

"Of course." I met Luke's gaze. "Would you like to see Louise's room?"

"I sure would," he replied with enthusiasm. "Lead the way, sport."

Watching them go off, I had to force myself to stay put and focus on dinner when I would have preferred to follow them and be a fly on the wall. But I knew I had to give them space and time to get acquainted. Without me hovering and worrying.

I moved the gift bag to the top of the fridge, then I emptied a bag of frozen fries onto the cookie sheet and slid it into the oven. I set the timer for twelve minutes, then set a carton of orange juice and the Brita water pitcher on the table. My stomach was churning with anxiety the entire time as I wondered what they were talking about. What was Luke saying to her? How would any man begin to talk to a five-year-old daughter he'd just met for the first time?

Leo sat by the oven, watching me intently. He tilted his head this way and that.

"Yes," I whispered. "I'm freaking out."

Five minutes later, Luke and Louise returned to the kitchen.

"I showed him my dollhouse," Louise informed me. "And my teddy bears."

"You did!" I said excitedly.

"It's quite a collection," Luke replied. "A lot of names to remember. Are you going to quiz me later?"

She laughed, and an awkward silence ensued.

"Why don't you and your daddy set the table?" I suggested, unnerved by the fact that I had just referred to Luke as her "daddy." But Louise had set the tone earlier. I didn't want to disrespect that.

"Okay."

It was interesting to watch them interact. Luke was good with Louise—*really* good. This made me wonder what was wrong with me. Why had I chosen to keep this secret from him? How could I have justified it for so long? And why hadn't I even *tried* to see what might come of it? What was I so afraid of? Whatever it was, it couldn't have been worse than this.

After dinner, we put away the dishes, then moved into the living room to open the gift Luke had brought for Louise.

She stood at the coffee table and pulled the sparkly ribbon loose, drew out the pink tissue paper and uncovered a large picture book about fairies. With wide eyes, she raised it up and admired the exquisite cover art, then reached into the gift bag and pulled out a Tinkerbell doll. With a gasp of delight, she began to dance around while she hugged the book and doll to her chest. "I love fairies!"

Luke watched her with a smile and I knew he was completely enchanted, just as he had been during dinner when Louise told stories about school and all the fun things she liked to do.

I realized there was no one else in the world, besides me, who had ever looked at my daughter that way. My mother was a close second, but this was different.

"I'm glad," he replied. "I wasn't sure what you'd like, but your mom helped me out."

I turned to Louise. "What do you say?"

"Thank you!" She set the book on the coffee table and dashed forward to hug Luke. His cheeks flushed with color and he shut his eyes as he held her tight. He looked as if he might weep.

I felt such guilt and empathy for him in that moment— for all that he had missed out on, which was all my fault. Again, I berated myself for the choices I had made and I feared whatever repercussions were heading my way. I deserved them.

When Louise drew back, she picked up the book and climbed onto Luke's lap. "Can we read it now?"

"Sure." As he opened it to page one, his eyes lifted and met mine. He regarded me briefly, but with a clear look of scorn.

My stomach lurched with dread and I started to worry

that his civility through most of the day had been a pretense—that in truth, he was harboring a bitterness far worse than I imagined, and that he might not be amicable when it came to making a decision about the custody of our daughter.

I wanted to do the right thing and make amends in some way, but what if he was just here to gather ammunition to use against me so he could play hardball? Claire had warned me about that. She'd tried to convince me to call a lawyer rather than communicate with Luke directly, but I still hadn't picked up the phone to call one.

My nerves continued to whir as I watched Luke flip through the pages of the book I'd helped him pick out. Terror began to bubble up within me. What if he tried to take her away just for revenge? Would he do that?

My hands trembled, so I stood and went to the kitchen to get a glass of water. I needed to take a breath and calm myself.

My beloved retriever found me at the kitchen counter, staring off into space. He wagged his tail and turned around in a circle.

"Do you need to go outside again?"

He trotted to the back door. I opened it for him and he hurried out to the yard. I waited until he returned before I joined Luke and Louise in the living room again, where they were still seated in the chair by the fireplace, utterly absorbed in the book.

If I wasn't petrified that he might want to steal my daughter away forever, it might have been a picture-perfect moment.

"It's getting late," I found myself saying in a cool, inhospitable voice.

They both looked up at the same time, and the similarity in their eyes nearly knocked me over. I had to fight to appear casual.

"And it's time for you to get ready for bed, young lady," I added, as cheerfully as possible. "Why don't you brush your teeth and get into your pajamas. Then you can come and say goodnight to Luke."

He regarded me with a frown. Only then did I realize I hadn't used the word "Daddy" this time.

It wasn't a strategic move. I wasn't nearly that crafty. It just came out that way.

Louise slid off Luke's lap and said mournfully, "Okay, but can Daddy read to me tonight?"

Jealousy washed over me. Reading to Louise at bedtime had always been my thing. I was hurt, rattled and afraid.

Still, I couldn't say no. That would be petty and far too revealing. "Of course," I replied. "As long as you're quick to get into your jammies. No dawdling."

"I'll be fast as lightning!" She bolted from the room.

I stood for a moment, watching her disappear down the hall. Then I met Luke's gaze.

"Did I do something wrong?" he asked.

"Not at all." But there was no fooling him. A blind man could have seen right through my response.

I moved to sit down on the chair opposite him. "Listen. I'm sorry. This was tense tonight. I just don't want Louise to get hurt."

"Why would she get hurt?"

Speaking in a quiet voice to make sure she heard nothing from down the hall, I said, "I don't know. This is complicated. Before today, it was just her and me. We were two peas in a pod. Now, you're here and it's obvious you're angry with me, and I don't know what your intentions are. And I'm worried she's going to feel torn between the two of us. I can see it now—you and me, fighting over her." I paused. "I don't want to add stress to her life. I just want what's best for her. I want her to be happy."

"And you think I don't want that?"

"I don't know." I inclined my head at him. "I saw the way you looked at me a little while ago. You're pissed."

He lounged back in the chair, regarding me in silence while my heart nearly pounded out of my chest.

"I didn't realize I was that transparent."

I spoke frankly. "Well, you are. And I'm trying to be sympathetic here, because the fact is…you were wronged. I don't deny it. I feel terrible about that. You have to believe me. I do. And I wish I could turn back time. If I could, I would handle this differently. But here we are, with no time machine. Louise is my daughter and it's been just the two of us since the day she was born. I *want* to invite you into our lives. Truly, I do, because it's the right thing to do and I believe Louise wants to know you better, but I can't let you wreck what we have. Please, don't try to do that."

His eyebrows pulled together with a frown. He sat forward, elbows on knees. "That's not my goal."

Louise entered the room just then and I jumped.

"I'm ready," she said. "You can come and read to me now. Mommy, you come too."

My head drew back in surprise. "You want both of us?"

"Yes." She turned and waved for us to follow. "Come on."

Luke and I exchanged a look. Then we both got up from our chairs.

~*e*

We sat on Louise's bed, one of us on either side of her, and read two chapters of the fairy book before she began to drift off. Then I closed the book, switched off the light and we both kissed her goodnight.

After we left her room, I quietly shut the door behind us.

"Listen," Luke said as we reached the kitchen and sat down at the table. "I'm not here to destroy you or take Louise away from you. I just want to be a part of her life, and I don't know how that's going to work. We live on opposite sides of the country and I won't lie. I don't like you very much, Bev, and it wasn't easy to be polite today. Your only saving grace is that you're Louise's mother and obviously, you've done a good job raising her so far. I'm grateful for that, but this was weird tonight. I mean…it was good in a lot of ways. Louise is incredible and I loved meeting her, but it's obvious that she wants us to be her mom and dad. In the conventional sense. And that's going to be a problem."

I felt sick to my stomach. "Yes. So how do we handle it?"

He shut his eyes and pinched the bridge of his nose. "I don't know. I need to talk to a lawyer. And you should, too."

My pulse accelerated. "Wait. Can't we try to figure this out without lawyers?"

"I don't know how that would be possible." He waved a hand through the air. "Like I said, I live in BC. You live here. You want what you want and I want what I want, and we're not exactly on good terms. So, I don't think we can work this out between us. We're going to need a mediator. Someone objective."

I buried my face in my hands. "This is exactly what I was always afraid of. It's why I never told you about her." I took a moment to slow my breathing and think this through. Then I looked up. "Do we really have to decide this right now? Can't we just take the week to see how we feel at the end? To see how Louise feels? Then maybe we'll both have a better idea how to proceed."

We sat in silence. He tapped a finger on the table.

"I don't know," he said uncertainly.

"You're here in town anyway. You've come such a long way. Don't you want to spend more time with Louise?"

"Of course I do." He surprised me by standing up. "I should go."

"No, wait. Please..."

"Don't worry. I'm not going to drag you to court tomorrow. I'll stick around for a bit and we'll see. Okay?"

I let out a tightly held breath. "Okay." I stood up as well. "Let me give Claire a call and I can drive you back to your hotel."

"No, don't bother. I'll take a cab. That'll be easiest."

"Are you sure? Claire won't mind."

"Honestly." He pulled out his cell phone. "Do you know a number?"

I recited the one I knew by heart and Luke called them. Then I walked him to the door.

"Thanks for having me," he said, which surprised me. "And thank you for showing me that picture. Louise is amazing."

"Thank you. I appreciate you saying that."

We stood in the entry hall, waiting for the taxi while Leo watched through the screen door.

Luke turned to me. "So, can I see Louise tomorrow?"

I drew back slightly. "Yes, but I can't just hand her over to you. What kind of mother would I be?"

"I get that," he replied. "But what are you doing? I could just meet up with you somewhere."

I considered that for a moment. "It's Saturday. She has a swimming lesson at eleven, then we usually go for lunch at the Farmer's Market and then, if the weather's nice, we go to the playground or take Leo for a walk at Point Pleasant Park."

He said nothing, but it was obvious he was waiting for me to invite him.

"I could text you in the morning," I suggested, "and we could pick you up on the way to swim class, if you want to come and watch. She might like that because she's been nervous about getting in the water since the accident. You'd be a good distraction."

"That would be great." The cab arrived and Luke pushed the door open and walked out. "Thanks. I'll talk to you tomorrow."

As I watched him get into the cab and drive off, I marveled at the fact that he had thanked me again. It was not something I felt I deserved.

Luke

When I arrived back at the hotel, I rode the elevator up to my room, turned on the television and found a game to watch. I'd brought my laptop with me and had some consulting work to do, but I wasn't in the right headspace. As I lay on the king-sized bed watching the game, all I could think about was Louise and Bev and their cozy little house and shady backyard, and their dog Leo, and Bev's sister Claire and her husband Scott across the street. It was a pleasant environment and they all seemed happy.

In my mind, I replayed different moments from the day and thought about things Bev had said to me when we discussed the situation.

No question about it, I was still angry with her, but I had to concede that she was exceptionally levelheaded and I respected that. It was something we'd promised each other on the phone initially—that we would be reasonable. All things considered, we *had* been. I didn't get the sense that Bev was playing games with me or trying to manipulate me in any way. Nor was she emotional or hysterical—thank

God for that. She was self-possessed and forthcoming about her fears and regrets. We may have argued, but at least we never got into a screaming match. No one stormed out or slammed any doors.

That didn't make up for what she had done, of course, and I was determined not to feel sympathy for her. If she had regrets, so be it. She deserved to break out in a sweat for what she did to me.

At the same time, I wasn't going to be a jerk about it and seek some form of revenge. No good could come of that. To be honest, I preferred not to hold a grudge against her forever. That would drive me insane. I'd rather just accept things the way they were and try to make the best of a bad situation.

Although it wasn't all bad. There was a bright spot in all of this because I had a daughter—and today I got to meet her and read her a bedtime story.

She couldn't have been more perfect and amazing. Every minute with Louise was pure bliss, and I couldn't wait to see her again.

In the end, as much as I wanted to play nice with Bev, I had to protect my rights. Over the next hour, I sat at the desk in my hotel room, researching some top family lawyers.

Bev

As soon as Luke drove off in the cab, I called Scott and asked him about finding a good lawyer. He told me to put it in his hands because he knew people in the right places, and he offered to help me out financially if I needed it. I thanked him and went to bed.

The following morning, the sun shone brightly. There wasn't a single cloud in the sky. Luke was waiting for us on the hotel steps when Louise and I arrived to pick him up before her swimming lesson.

"Good morning," he said, climbing into the passenger seat, shutting the door, and turning around to smile at Louise while he buckled his seatbelt. "Did you dream of fairies last night? I did. Or maybe it wasn't a dream. Maybe they were actually in my room."

"What were they doing?" Louise asked.

"Cleaning up," he replied, without missing a beat.

Louise giggled. "I don't think so. Fairies live in the woods. Not hotels. And they don't clean."

"Everybody has to clean."

"Not fairies! They have magic pixie dust!"

"Are you sure?"

"Yes!" She laughed. "I'm sure!"

Luke and I exchanged a look of amusement, and I hoped this would set the tone for the rest of the day.

Flicking my blinker, I turned onto the street. "How are you doing this morning? Jet lagged?"

"Oh yeah." He looked out the windows as we moved along South Park Street. "It's 6:00 a.m. to me, so I might need a coffee later."

"I'm a hospital shift worker. I can definitely fix you up."

As we drove toward the pool, I pointed out a few of the downtown landmarks like Citadel Hill, the Garrison Grounds, and the Town Clock. It was a quick drive, only about five minutes, and when we parked in the lot, Luke helped Louise out of her booster seat. She jumped down to the pavement and walked between us, holding our hands, swinging from them, as we made our way to the door.

Luke and I exchanged another glance because this felt like a staged "mommy and daddy moment." He raised an eyebrow at me, and I found myself struggling not to notice how handsome he was—why did he have to be *exactly* my type?—because this was complicated enough as it was.

Once we were inside, I directed him to the stairs to the viewing area while I took Louise into the girls' locker room to get changed. A short while later, I found him seated midway down the length of the bleachers.

"It's Olympic size," he said, sounding impressed. "I didn't know where to sit."

"This is perfect." I took a seat beside him and set my purse on the bench. I glanced to my right and waved at the group of mothers I usually sat with on Saturday mornings.

They all waved back while observing and ogling the drop-dead gorgeous man I'd brought with me today. Luke didn't seem to notice.

"Her class is right down there." I pointed when the instructor led five girls between the ages of four and six to the far corner.

"It's a small class," he said.

"Yes. She's a great teacher, too, very kind and patient, which has been a godsend. Louise always loved to swim but she's had some fears lately, since the accident. I've had to encourage her to get back on the horse, so to speak, and she's been a real trooper. Very brave."

We watched her smiling and laughing with one of the other little girls.

"I used to call her my water baby," I said, "but she doesn't like that anymore."

"Too grown up for that?" he asked with a grin and a sparkle in his eye that reminded me of our night together, years ago, when we had hit it off spectacularly from the very first moment. It was nice to know the Luke I remembered still existed somewhere behind that dark cloud.

The girls jumped into the shallow end of the pool, and we both turned our attention that way.

"Look at her go," Luke said. "She knows what she's doing. She's a fantastic swimmer for her age. She doesn't seem nervous at all."

He rested his elbows on his knees, and I watched him watch her. He was completely focused and captivated, which I found incredibly attractive—because what could be more wonderful than someone thinking the world of your child?

"I have a pool in my backyard," he told me. "Louise

would love it. You guys should come out and visit sometime. Have you ever been to Victoria?"

Surprised by the suggestion, I cleared my throat. "Um, no. I've never been west of Toronto."

"Really? You'd like it. It's similar to Halifax because it's a port city. Lots of yacht clubs and a touristy waterfront. Louise would enjoy seeing the seals."

"That sounds really nice."

I was pleased he wanted us to visit, but at the same time, I was afraid to commit to something like that, or to even imagine that we could work this out with such ease. I didn't want to get my hopes up.

A few minutes later, he glanced at me briefly. "So, tell me some stuff about Louise. What have I missed? You must have some stories."

The question was like a knife in my heart because I couldn't begin to fathom how I'd feel if I had missed out on Louise's life up to this point. I didn't want to rub salt in that wound.

"I wouldn't know where to start," I replied.

"How about the day she was born? Was your sister with you?"

I picked up my purse and held it on my lap. "Yes, she was, and it was an easy labor, as far as labors go. Louise came out quickly and she was healthy in every way."

"What was she like as a baby?"

I thought back to those early days and how I was so utterly, madly in love with her. The love had knocked me over like a hurricane the first second I held her in my arms. I cried like a baby and sobbed all over her. I never knew such love could exist in the world, and that love had only grown deeper with time.

But I couldn't say any of that to Luke. I couldn't tell him about all the profound joys and miracles he had missed out on because I had not allowed him to be a part of our lives. For one thing, that would be cruel. For another, it might make him feel more bitter toward me, but for Louise's sake, I wanted him to focus on the joys of today, and what still lay ahead.

So, I endeavored to stick to the facts. "She was a great baby. I breast fed, but only for the first six months because I had to go back to work. Between Claire, Scott and my mom, childcare was taken care of, so I never had to put her in day care. Claire and I were each other's free childcare providers, so Louise and Serena have been raised more like sisters than cousins."

She looked up at us just then and waved. We waved back and laughed. Then I told Luke about our camping trips with Claire and Scott and Serena the past two summers. By that time, swim class was over and I hurried down to meet Louise in the locker room.

The Farmer's Market was a short, ten-minute drive away, and as usual for a Saturday, it was crowded. Louise held Luke's hand the entire time as we made our way through the crush, past the vendors' booths, then stopped to listen to a young cellist playing for coins.

I bought Luke a coffee, then we ordered lunch at an organic eatery where we all had eggs and toast with tomatoes and avocadoes. Luke bought an interesting wood carving from a local artisan, and I bought some fudge and a jar of maple butter.

Later, when we left the market, Louise asked if we could go to the playground.

"Sure, but let's swing by the house first and pick up Leo," I replied as I buckled her into her seat.

"Can we get ice cream too?" she asked.

I laughed and messed her hair. "Maybe afterwards."

Moving around to the driver's side, I got in and turned to Luke. "How's the jet lag? If this is too much for you... Maybe you'd like to go back to your hotel for a bit."

"Are you trying to get rid of me?"

"No. I just don't want to assume that you want to hang out with us all day."

"Yes, he does!" Louise shouted from the back seat. "Right Daddy?"

He turned in his seat and smiled at her. "Yes, you're right. I absolutely *do* want to hang out with you today. Playground, here we come."

She threw her hands over her head. "Yay!"

Leo was thrilled to leap into the cargo area of my SUV, knowing we must be going somewhere fun.

When we arrived at the playground, Louise asked Luke to push her on the swings, so I took Leo for a short walk around the park. Then we stopped at a bench and sat down. I watched Luke go with Louise to the play structure, where she found one of her friends from ballet class.

Eventually, Luke joined me on the bench while the girls lay on their bellies on the grass, searching for four-leaf clovers.

"This is a great spot," he said. "You must come here a lot."

"Yes, even in the winter, we're here with our snowsuits and hats and mittens. There's a large skating oval on the Commons. We go there a lot, too."

He leaned back and rested his arm along the back of the bench. I leaned back, too, and was intensely aware of his hand near the nape of my neck. I felt his thumb move through my hair and a sudden flash memory of our night together came hurtling back at me. There was a tingling in all my nerve endings.

Oh, who was I trying to fool? I was still wildly attracted to this man, and no amount of sensible, rational thinking was going to smother the electricity I felt whenever he was near. He was handsome. There was no arguing that point, but it was much more than that. I'd met plenty of handsome men in my life, but none had sparked an excitement in me like this one did.

I couldn't explain it. There was just something about him. And he was the father of my child and Louise wanted him in her life. I couldn't blame her. Based on our first twenty-four-hours together, he was an absolute dream father, and he would probably be a dream husband, too.

I shut my eyes and shook my head at myself. *Why didn't I contact him five years ago? Where would we be right now if I had? What would our lives look like?*

His phone rang just then, and he reached into his pocket. It wasn't my intention to spy, but he was sitting beside me and I couldn't help but glance at the screen.

The call was coming from a British Columbia area code. It was a woman named Emma. There was a picture of her. She was, of course, beautiful.

Luke frowned at the screen while it flashed and

vibrated, as if he weren't sure he wanted to answer it. Then he turned to me. "I should take this."

He swiped the screen, stood up and walked a few paces away.

I tried not to stare. I pretended I wasn't listening and kept my eyes fixed on Louise, even though I was straining to hear his conversation.

"Hey. How are you?"

His voice took on an intimate tone that was clearly not platonic, and though I had no right, I felt a spark of jealousy. I didn't know who this woman was, but obviously, she meant something to him.

Discreetly, I glanced in his direction. His head was bowed low. He looked down at his feet as he paced around and rubbed the back of his neck. I wished I could hear what he was saying, but he was too far away.

Eventually he ended the call and stood on the grass for a few minutes, watching Louise and the other kids and parents in the park. He checked his phone again, then slipped it in his pocket and returned to the bench. He sat down, heavily.

"Is everything okay?" I asked, carefully.

He squinted into the sunlight and bent forward to rest his elbows on his knees. "Life sucks sometimes."

By now, my curiosity was getting the better of me. I was desperate to know more about the woman named Emma.

"It certainly does." I gave him a moment, then I said, "Do you want to talk about it?"

He let out a heavy sigh and sat back. "It's a woman I was seeing."

"*Was* seeing?"

"Yes. But it's over now. Which wasn't my choice."

I found myself gazing off in the other direction, fighting to hide my jealousy which I had no right to feel, because I'd made my bed. I was the one who had chosen not to be with him.

"Do you mind if I ask what happened?" I watched a few teenagers gather on the grass to throw a frisbee around.

"She dumped me for her ex-husband."

I shot him a look. "She was married?"

"Divorced," he replied. "And she and I were engaged. We were supposed to get married on New Year's Eve. We had the church booked and everything."

My head drew back in surprise. "I'm sorry to hear that. Wait a second... Is that what you were talking about when you said it was a bad week? This just happened?"

He nodded.

"Oh, God."

We sat in silence, watching the teenagers with the frisbee. Leo perked up, no doubt wanting to dash off and catch it in the air. I gave him a pat on the head and made sure I had a good grip on his leash.

"I thought it was totally over between them," Luke added. "When I met her, they were barely speaking, and the way she described it, they hated each other. But I guess somehow they decided to work it out."

"But they decided this while she was engaged to you?"

"Yes, and that's what stings the most, because I had no idea what was going on. Or maybe I did. I had suspicions, but I kept telling myself I was paranoid."

A squirrel scurried down a tree and scampered across the grass in front of us. Leo made a move to run, but I held onto him.

"How long were you with her?" I asked.

"Not that long. Only about a year, but I honestly thought it was the real thing. What a schmuck, right?"

"No, Luke…"

"Anyway, I'm having a hard time with this." He was quiet for a moment. "When she called just now, I thought maybe…"

"You thought she might have changed her mind?"

He nodded.

I waited a few seconds before I asked the question. "Did she?"

"No. She just wanted to let me know when the movers were coming to get her stuff out of my garage."

I paused. "I'm sorry about that."

But was I? Really?

He shrugged a shoulder. "That's life, I guess. You never know when you're going to get kicked in the face."

A little boy filled his shoe with pea gravel and poured it down the slide. His mother scolded him and led him away.

"If she *had* changed her mind," I said, turning to Luke, "would you have taken her back?"

He squinted through the afternoon sunlight. "I don't know. Maybe."

I tried to imagine how that would change the dynamic here. If Luke wasn't a single man, living alone, the courts might view this situation in a different light. They might see a more stable, complete family for Louise to be a part of, especially if Luke and Emma had children. How would I feel about that?

Louise stood up just then, waved good-bye to her friend and ran to us. She rested her small hands on my knees. "Can we get ice cream now?"

I pushed a lock of her hair behind her ear. "That's a great idea. Then let's go home and sit around. Maybe turn on TV and watch a movie?"

"Can we watch *Frozen*?"

"You just watched that yesterday."

"I know, but I like it."

I chuckled and touched my forehead to hers. "No kidding. Let's get going."

Luke stood up and held out his hand to Louise. She took hold and walked beside him to the car while I followed from a short distance, just wanting to watch them.

After we ate our ice cream cones and got back in the car, I started the engine and asked Luke if he wanted me to drop him off at his hotel, or if he'd prefer to come to our place for dinner.

"I don't want to impose," he replied.

"You won't be. I wouldn't invite you if I didn't want you there. But I understand if you just want to be alone."

He stared out the passenger side window for a moment, then met my gaze. "No, I'd love to come for supper. Thank you for asking."

"It won't be fancy." I gave him a sidelong glance, hoping to lighten the mood a bit. "I'm just going to take something out of the freezer. I think I have some steaks in there."

"I saw a barbeque on your back deck, didn't I?"

"Yes."

"Well, then." He grinned at me, which caused a rush of

heat in my blood. "I suppose it's my duty to inform you—I make a perfect steak every time."

I chuckled. "Then you are totally hired."

~⊘

It was past four by the time we arrived home. Louise went straight to the television and turned on *Frozen*, then she collapsed onto the living room sofa with Leo.

"Would you like a glass of wine?" I asked Luke as I rifled through the vegetable drawers in the refrigerator to see what I had.

"I'd love one."

I moved to the cupboard for a bottle of cabernet, popped the cork and poured two glasses. I held mine up for a toast. "To life not sucking so much in the future."

He held his glass up as well. "I'll drink to that."

We took the first sip.

"This isn't bad." He checked out the label on the bottle.

"Are you a wine connoisseur?"

"No, I just like what I like."

"Me, too."

We chatted about wine for a few minutes while we decompressed from the day. Then I apologized in advance for the french fries two nights in a row, and he laughed as he went to fire up the barbeque. I set to work chopping vegetables for a salad. All the while, music from *Frozen* reached us from the living room.

While we waited for the steaks to cook, Luke asked me about my work as a nurse and I talked about it for a while. After the wine kicked in, he started me down the path of sharing some of our ordeal on the *Dalila*. I described it all—

from the moment we boarded the ship until Louise was examined by the doctor in the ER, and him wanting to send her to a psychiatrist.

"I'm glad you headed that off at the pass," Luke said, pouring himself a second glass of wine and topping mine up as well.

"Me, too. I'd never want her to think she's different in any way, even though she is."

"She definitely is. She's extraordinary. Gifted artist, smart, and don't get me started on her swimming capabilities."

I laughed and we clinked glasses. "No bias there."

When the steaks and fries were cooked, we called Louise to the kitchen and ate supper together, chatting about silly things while Louise snuck morsels of meat off her plate and dropped them to the floor for Leo to gobble up. Luke and I pretended to turn a blind eye.

"Can I go finish my movie now?" Louise asked after she ate everything on her plate.

I said yes, but asked her to put her plate and cutlery in the dishwasher first. She took care of that, then off she went.

Luke and I remained at the table. He talked about his consulting business and his frequent trips to Toronto. We also conversed about all sorts of random things. Maybe it was the wine, but I shared an embarrassing story about Leo in the park, when he squatted and pooped on the grass in front of an outdoor theatrical performance that summer, and the audience had applauded.

Before I realized it, the sun had set and we were sitting in the dark. I heard music from the end credits on *Frozen*, so I got up to check on Louise. Luke followed me into the living room, and there we found her, asleep on the sofa with her arm around Leo, who was also sleeping.

"What do you do in a situation like this?" Luke whispered in my ear.

I leaned close to him and spoke softly. "I carry her off to bed and let her sleep in her clothes, without brushing her teeth."

I felt his breath, hot in my ear, as he chuckled. "I'm all over that. Do you want me to carry her?"

"That would be great, if you don't mind."

He moved forward and bent to scoop her gently into his arms. The sight of them together sent my heart into a frenzy. I never imagined I could feel such delight, watching a man cradle my daughter in his arms.

But this wasn't just any man. This was her father, and I felt his love for her in the depths of my soul. It matched *my* love for her in perfect synchronicity. It was intense. Beautiful. Impossible to describe in words. And he'd only just met her.

I followed quietly as he carried her down the hall, through our small gallery of heavenly depictions. Maybe this was heaven on earth, I thought to myself as I followed them, because seeing Louise loved so much by her father made me feel like I was floating on a cloud.

He set her down on the bed, placed her teddy bear in her arms, pulled a blanket up to cover her, and kissed the top of her head. She rolled over and remained asleep, and we both backed out of the room.

I quietly closed the door and we returned to the living room without speaking a word.

The house was dark so I turned on a lamp and pressed my knuckles to the bridge of my nose. "I'm sorry. I don't

think I can drive you back to your hotel. I've had too much
wine."

"It's all right," he replied. "I can take a cab again." He
checked his watch. "It's 8:00 here, but only 4:00 my time."

"Well, gosh. Don't go yet."

He laughed softly at me. "Did you just say 'gosh'?"

I was definitely tipsy. "I think it's a Nova Scotia thing.
Everybody I know says it."

He laughed again. "Really? Are you sure about that?"

"Probably not."

He nodded his head, knowingly.

"Come on out to the kitchen," I said. "I have trail mix
and I can make us some coffee."

"Coffee might keep me awake," he said. "What else
have you got?"

"I have tequila, but that might be a bad idea. How about
a beer?"

"Perfect."

I turned to face him. "Do you want to get a couple of
bottles from the basement? At the bottom of the stairs,
there's a little white fridge from my college dorm days."

"I have something like that in my basement, too," he said.

I showed him where to go, and a moment later, we were
seated at the kitchen table under the glare of the hanging
light, with a bowl of nuts and raisins between us, and two
bottles of beer.

The clock ticked loudly in the living room and Leo
stretched out on the floor at my feet.

Luke took a swig of beer. "You know, I always had fond
memories of you. For months after that night we met, I
wanted to call you, Bev, but you were on the other side of
the country, and you didn't call or text me, so I just left it.

Then, after a while, I started to romanticize that night. You were this perfect woman I'd probably never see again, and I think that's what I was looking for when I met Emma— another version of you." He looked at me with an unnerving intensity. "But now it feels like someone pulled back the curtain and you've turned out to be *not* what I thought you were. Neither was Emma, for that matter."

I set down my beer. "Please don't say that. I understand that all women must seem like the devil to you right now, but I'm not a bad person. If I was, I wouldn't feel so guilty over what I did to you."

He leaned forward. "Then why did you do it, Bev? Why didn't you call me?"

My heart raced. "I don't know. I think, maybe, I was afraid of wanting you in my life. Afraid of needing you. I didn't want to be dependent on anyone—and I don't mean financially. I didn't want to depend on you for love or support, or for my happiness."

"Why not? Did you think I wasn't dependable? That we couldn't be happy together? Because it was a pretty great night."

"Yes, and I *do* think we could have been happy. I think that *now*, but I was scared back then. I was young. Getting pregnant when I was single and on my own… I somehow got it into my head that I had to stand on my own two feet, because I'd learned at an early age that the rug can get pulled out from under you just like *that*." I snapped my fingers. "And your whole world can fall to pieces. And maybe part of me was afraid that if I asked you to be with me, you might say no."

"I wouldn't have. I would have come here and given it a shot, at least."

I let out a sigh of defeat. "I didn't know that. I thought

maybe that night we spent together was all just a fantasy. Maybe in real life, we'd have nothing in common."

"Like we have nothing in common *now*?" he asked, sarcastically.

I looked away and shook my head. "I romanticized you, too, Luke. I thought about that night, and I started to believe you were too good to be true—that it was all just a dream. Then I didn't want to be disappointed or let down if I contacted you and you were with another woman, or if you weren't interested in anything permanent. It was a one night stand, remember? I didn't want my heart to get broken. I couldn't let myself pine away for some guy I met in a bar. I needed to be a rock—for Louise."

He bowed his head. "I wasn't just some guy you met in a bar. It was more than that. At least it was for me, and it wasn't a dream. It was real, but you didn't tell me I was a father. Now, that changes everything—the way I look back at that night. The way I think about you."

My stomach tied up in knots, and I wanted to cry.

Rising from my chair, I moved to the counter and stood with my back to him for a moment. I wanted nothing more than to make this right, but it seemed impossible.

Turning around, I spoke frankly. "Here it is in a nutshell. I made a mistake, Luke. I was young and stupid and I should have told you, and now that I'm a mother, I don't think I'll ever forgive myself for what I took from you. But I didn't have that wisdom back then. I didn't know it would be like this. And now I'm kicking myself for wrecking what we could have been. I wish I could go back—that God would give me a do-over and I could contact you as soon as I found out I was pregnant. If I could, we might be together right now. We might be a family."

He stared at me, frowning. "There are no do-overs, Bev. And I don't know what to do with this information. One minute I'm laughing with you. The next minute, I'm remembering what you did and I resent you for it. And then Emma calls me and..."

He reached into his pocket for his phone.

"What are you doing?"

"I'm going to call a cab. I think I should leave."

My stomach dropped. "Why? You don't have to go."

He looked up at me, darkly. "Just give me some space, okay? I can't just forgive you. It's not that easy." He shook his head. "And it's been one of those days."

Because Emma called.

I held up my hands in mock surrender and backed up a few steps. "Okay."

He called the cab, and stood. "Will you tell Louise I said goodnight? And she can text or call me tomorrow if she wants to. Will you let her do that?"

"Of course. I'll let her use my phone."

He turned and made his way to the front door to wait for the cab. I followed and stood beside him.

"Luke, please, no matter what happens, I'm glad you found us. I'm glad that you called me, and I want you to know that I won't get in the way of you being a father to Louise. Whatever it takes, we'll work it out because I know she wants you in her life. I want to make sure that happens."

The cab pulled up and Luke looked down at me in the dim light from the streetlamps outside.

"Thank you."

I shook my head at him and almost laughed. "No. I'm the one who should be thanking *you*. Thank you for giving me Louise."

To my surprise, he pulled me into his arms and hugged me. My heart raced as I clung to his broad shoulders, breathed in the familiar, intoxicating scent of his body. I didn't want to let go, but he pulled away all too quickly and walked out the door.

I stood in a daze, breathing hard, watching him get into the cab and drive off. Then I shut the door and returned to the kitchen, knowing this wasn't over. I would try again tomorrow. If he was still angry with me, I would try again the next day, and the day after that.

And I would not fight him where Louise was concerned. He was her father and in my heart I knew he was a good man. I wanted him to be a part of her life. I owed him that, and I owed it to Louise as well.

No matter what it took, I would do my best to make amends.

Twenty

Bev

I had to work a night shift the following evening. Normally, Louise would sleep at Claire's house, but with Luke in town, I wanted to try something different. I called him at his hotel and asked if he wanted to stay with Louise at our place overnight. I suggested he could sleep in the guest room.

I was thrilled when he said yes, so I invited him for supper, too.

He arrived with an *I Spy* book for Louise which got the evening off to a fantastic start. While they immersed themselves in rhyming riddles and a hunt for hidden objects in the pictures, I put the final touches on our spaghetti dinner—without a single french fry in sight.

While sitting with Louise at the table, Luke and I refrained from discussing any of our personal issues. We behaved as if everything was hunky-dory, and it was a relief to simply enjoy the meal and talk about mundane things.

"If you have any problems," I said as I gathered up my purse in the entry hall, "Claire's phone number is on the fridge and she's home tonight, so don't hesitate to call her if you need to."

"Don't worry," Luke replied as he stood in the archway with Louise. "We won't get into any trouble. We're just going to play with some matches later. And maybe we'll run around with the scissors before bed."

Louise laughed herself silly.

I strode toward her and wiggled her nose. "It sounds like I'm going to have to put *you* in charge. You keep an eye on him, all right?"

"I will," she replied with a gigantic grin.

I slid my purse strap over my shoulder and headed for the door. "Don't forget to let Leo out before bed."

"I got it covered," Luke replied.

"Great. I'll see you in the morning. I'll be back at seven, in time to take Louise to school."

Luke waved good-bye to me at the door, and I forced myself to get in the car, go to work, and not worry.

During my shift, whenever there was an opportunity, I checked my phone to make sure Luke hadn't texted to tell me something awful had happened. Somehow, I managed to resist the urge to call and ask how they were getting along. I wanted to trust him, and I also wanted him to enjoy some quality father-daughter time with Louise.

When my shift ended the next morning, I couldn't get out of the hospital fast enough. Still wearing my scrubs, I drove home and hurried up the steps.

As soon as I opened the door, I smelled pancakes. Leo greeted me with a wagging tail and I patted him on the head, then dropped my purse onto the hall table. "Good morning," I said.

I entered the kitchen where Louise and Luke were just sitting down to breakfast.

"How was work?" Luke asked.

"It was great."

"Are you hungry?" He gestured with his chin toward the stove. "I made enough to feed an army."

I glanced at the top-heavy pile of pancakes on a serving platter, and noticed a bowl of fresh strawberries and sliced ham on the table as well. "I'm starved."

"Have a seat, then." He filled a plate and set it in front of me.

"How was your night?" I asked Louise expectantly as I popped a strawberry into my mouth.

"Fun," she replied. "We took Leo out in the backyard and threw a frisbee for him. He jumped in the air and caught it in his mouth a whole bunch of times."

"Do we even own a frisbee?"

"I brought one with me last night," Luke mentioned. "So now you own one."

My eyebrows lifted. "Cool. What else did you do?"

Louise swallowed another bite of her pancake. "We played with my teddy bears, and then I painted another picture of Papa and Nanny."

Feeling suddenly breathless, I met Luke's gaze. "Really?"

He nodded and there was a look of total serenity on his face.

"Then I got in my jammies," Louise continued, "and I

brushed my teeth, and we read the fairy book. Then I went to sleep."

"That does sound like a fun night." I picked up the maple syrup and doused my pancakes. "Could I see the picture you painted? Is it in the hall?"

"No, I gave it to Daddy. I told him he could keep it."

I touched my daughter's hand. "That was very nice of you, Louise."

"I'll show it to you after breakfast," Luke offered. "What time do we need to leave for school?"

"Oh, I can take her," I replied, because I was used to doing everything myself.

He gave me a look. "Why don't we both take her?"

My heart felt suddenly light and full of hope as I swirled a bite-sized piece of pancake through the syrup. "Okay."

As soon as we cleared the table and Louise went off to brush her teeth, I spoke quietly to Luke. "Could I see the picture now?"

He reached on top of the fridge, pulled it down and showed it to me.

I observed a tall man and a small woman holding Louise's hands as they ran across a colorful meadow full of wildflowers. There were butterflies and dragonflies flitting about, shafts of golden sunlight shooting out from behind white clouds in a lavender sky. I could almost hear the swish of grasses blowing in the wind, and my heart swelled with elation. Tears filled my eyes. My voice shook as I spoke. "I get choked up every time she paints a new one."

"The same thing happened to me last night," he said. He pointed at the hearts in the meadow, hidden in the wildflowers, which I hadn't noticed at first glance. "She says she draws hearts because she doesn't know how else to paint the love in a way that we'd be able to see it."

I shook my head in amazement as I scrutinized it further and found more hearts within the paint strokes of the sky, and in the woman's hair. I was overcome as I handed the canvas back to Luke. "And these look like your parents?"

"Yes, it's them. She talked about them, too, and the way she described them and what it was like there…" He bowed his head and took a moment to collect himself before he continued. "I believe her, Bev. I believe she was with them. And I believe she came back because of you. And for me, too."

A warmth radiated through my body and I felt weak in the knees. I had to sit down at the table where I began to laugh and cry at the same time. "Do you really, truly believe it?"

He nodded. "Yes, I do. Don't you?"

Tears streamed down my face and I found myself nodding. "Yes, I think I do now."

He squeezed my shoulder, and urged me to get up and go to the hall to look at more of her paintings. "Do you see the hearts?" he asked.

I stared at the pictures. The early ones were drawn with crayons and paper, but the newer ones were on canvas, painted with oils.

Like the hidden treasures in the *I Spy* book, her works contained hearts in everything—in the hull of a boat, in a cloud, a flower, a door, a babbling brook, the wings of a bird. The hearts were all different colors, shapes and sizes.

"This is incredible," I said. "How did she do this?"

"I don't know. She's an artist. Did she have this gift before?"

"Not like this. I mean, she always liked to draw pictures, but these are…"

"Inspired," he finished for me.

"Yes." Eyes wide and glowing, I continued to stare. "It's all so beautiful. They move me to tears."

Louise came out of the bathroom just then and placed her small hand inside Luke's larger one. "Will you pick me up after school, too?" she asked him.

His eyes met mine. "I don't know. You'll have to ask your mom."

A flutter of joy rose up within me. "Are you available to pick her up?"

He looked back down at Louise. "I'm always available for anything where this little one's concerned."

"Then yes," I said to her as a lump formed in my throat and happy tears filled my eyes again. "He'll come with me to pick you up today. But if we're going to pick you up, we need to get you to school in the first place and not be late. So, go and get your backpack and put on your shoes."

Louise hurried off to get ready, and together, the three of us got into my car and headed off.

~ C

After we dropped Louise at school, I explained to Luke that I needed to go home and sleep for the day. "But thank you so much for staying with her last night. She really loved it."

"I loved it, too."

I turned left at an intersection and we ended up behind a city bus.

"There's something else I should tell you," Luke said while we paused in the morning traffic.

"What is it?"

He turned to me. "That woman I was seeing—Emma—she's the reason I found you."

"I don't understand."

He inhaled deeply and began to explain. "The reason I found that picture of you online was because Emma had become obsessed with what happened to Louise and the possibility that she went to heaven. The picture was on Emma's laptop and I stumbled across it after she left me. She was following your story because she had a son who died."

My heart sank. "I'm so sorry."

He nodded. "She had a four-year-old boy named Sammy who drowned in a backyard swimming pool, and when she heard about Louise drowning and being brought back to life, it made her think of her own son, and that's why she and her ex-husband started seeing each other again."

"I see."

"But there's more to it than that," Luke continued. "They went to a psychic who told them that Sammy was still with them, in a sense, on the other side of this life. The psychic claimed she talked to him, and that he wanted his mom and dad to forgive each other. When Emma told me about it, I tried to be supportive, but I didn't really believe in it, so I think maybe that played a part in what made her pull away from me. We weren't really on the same page. But now I'm changing my mind about it, because of what Louise has told me, and the pictures she's been painting."

"She's turned you into a believer?" I asked.

"I guess so. And she's also made me understand the connection that Emma had with her son, and with her husband, because of how they both couldn't let go. I didn't really get that before. Now I do. I understand the profoundness of parental love."

I wasn't sure what to say in response. All I could do was reach for Luke's hand and squeeze it.

A moment later, he said, "We should talk about where we go from here, because I can't go home at the end of the week without some kind of plan. I want to be a part of Louise's life."

"I want that, too," I assured him as I braced myself for whatever he was about to say next. Maybe I would need that lawyer Scott had recommended, sooner rather than later.

Luke tapped his thumb on his knee. "I spent some time online last night, searching for condos."

I shot him a look. "Condos for sale in Halifax?"

"Yes. They're shockingly affordable compared to BC."

"That's for sure," I replied. "There's a huge difference in the housing market. So..." I regarded him curiously. "What are you thinking?"

"That maybe I could buy a condo here and visit often. I could get something with two bedrooms, and when I'm here, maybe Louise might want to stay with me?"

I chewed on my lower lip, almost afraid to hope that this could work out. "Did you talk to her about it last night?"

"No, I wanted to talk to you first. See what you thought."

"I think it's a great idea," I told him. "How often would you come?"

"I don't know about that yet. It's a long flight to get

here. It's not something I could do every weekend, but I work in Toronto a lot, which is more than halfway here, so I could combine business travel with visits here."

The bus in front of us pulled over to pick up some passengers, and we were forced to wait behind it.

"What about Louise going to visit you in Victoria?" I asked. "Is that something you would want?"

We'd definitely need lawyers for that...

Luke considered it briefly. "I'd love to have her, but from what I've seen over the past few days, she has a busy schedule here, with ballet classes and swim classes and school, and she loves her cousin, Serena. I wouldn't want to interrupt any of that or take her away from those things. This is where her life is. It's better if I come here."

I smiled at him. "That sounds very generous, Luke. I like how this is sounding. Thank you."

He nodded. "So, if you think it's a good idea, I'll call a real estate agent today while you're catching some shuteye."

"I approve of that plan," I replied.

A moment later, we pulled into my driveway. Luke picked up his things from inside the house, told me to sleep well, and I let him borrow my car for the day.

Twenty-one

Luke

I had never minded a flight home to Victoria from the eastern provinces, but that particular flight across the country seemed to last forever. I resented every westward mile in the sky because it took me farther and farther away from my daughter.

It killed me to leave her behind in Halifax. She had cried at the airport when she hugged me good-bye and asked when I would return. I promised it would be soon, but in truth, I wasn't sure.

It crushed my heart when I started to walk away and she cried even harder. I think Bev was shell shocked. Going through security was pure agony for me.

When I finally touched down at the airport in Victoria and picked up my suitcase at the baggage claim, my head was in a fog, and it had nothing to do with jet lag. I had to apologize to my driver for not wanting to engage in conversation on the short trip home to my house. I blamed it on the length of the flight.

After he dropped me off, I wheeled my suitcase to the bottom of my steps, but before I entered the house, I decided to check out my garage. I walked over and keyed in the entry code. The heavy door lifted noisily to reveal an empty space where Emma's furniture had been, barely a week before.

I stood in a daze, staring at the emptiness. Someone had swept the floor clean.

Strangely, I felt liberated. I was glad she'd hired the movers to come while I was gone. Now she was no longer a part of my life, and under these new circumstances, that was quite all right with me. Sure, maybe I still held some bitterness toward her for the way things ended, but for the most part, I understood why she had to leave me and I was okay with it. This was how it was meant to be and I wished her well. I didn't want her back. It was Louise that I missed.

And Bev.

I hit a button on the key pad and the garage door lowered in front of my face.

From there, I returned to collect my suitcase, carried it up the stairs, and entered my house.

Leaving my suitcase at the door, I wandered from room to room, feeling an emptiness like never before. This was far too big a house for just one person. It was meant to be a family home. I'd always known that. I don't know why I bought it. Wishful thinking, I suppose. It certainly didn't help that my dogs weren't here to greet me, though I'd pick them up soon. Then, God willing, it wouldn't feel so lonesome here.

But still… What the devil was I going to do now? I thought of Louise at the airport—her heart-wrenching wails, how she had clung to my neck and refused to let go. Bev physically peeled her off me. I hadn't wanted to let go either.

Looking around at this big, vacant house, I felt entirely forlorn and utterly displaced.

~ C

An hour later, my laptop chimed as I connected with Bev through a video call. Her image on the screen appeared like magic, and my mood instantly lifted.

"Hey there." I leaned forward in my chair.

Bev pulled Louise onto her lap so I could see them both through the webcam. The sight of them thrilled me. They were so beautiful. Mother and daughter. I wanted to be where they were.

"How was your flight?" Bev asked.

"Long," I replied. "I miss you guys already."

"We miss you, too!" Louise shouted. I loved the sound of her sweet voice.

"Do you want to meet my dogs?" I cheerfully asked.

"Yes, we do!" Louise cried out.

I raised my laptop to capture Max and Toby in the webcam lens. They were lying on the floor behind me, sleeping.

"They're gorgeous," Bev said. "They must have been very happy to see you when you got home."

"Yeah, it was quite a reunion. I nearly got licked to death."

Louise laughed hysterically. "That's so funny!"

I threw my head back and laughed along with her. "Yes, it was pretty fun. How was school today?"

She launched into an animated account of the science project she'd worked on during class where they had to paste pictures of all the different types of clouds into a collage, with labels.

"I love clouds," she said.

"You love everything," Bev added, kissing her on the cheek.

"I do." She spread her arms wide. "I love the whole wide world!"

I felt another rush of euphoria, and started to wonder if I was being touched by something miraculous here, or if this was just what regular parenthood was like. Because this child had some sort of power over me. It was as if, whenever I was in her presence, she waved a magic wand and drenched me with happiness.

Or inconceivable agony—like at the airport when I left.

I resigned myself to the fact that parenthood must be a state of emotional extremes. There was nothing lackluster about it. Everything was vivid and amazing.

We chatted for a while about french fries and *Frozen*, and Leo's new frisbee. Louise laughed about all the "F" words and soon we were in hysterics.

Later, Bev sent Louise to brush her teeth because it was past her bedtime. As soon as we were alone, Bev asked, "Did you decide about the condo on Spring Garden Road? Are you going to make an offer?"

"I don't think so," I replied. "Something doesn't feel right about it."

"Really? I thought it was so nice. It was close to Public Gardens, and not that far from our house."

"Yes, but I can't imagine not having a yard for Toby and Max to run around in. They'd have to be on leashes all the time."

Bev inclined her head. "But you wouldn't bring them back and forth with you from Victoria, would you? They'd have to travel in the cargo hold. I think that would be stressful for them."

I steepled my hands together in front of my face. "Yes, it definitely would, which is why I'm starting to think that a secondary residence might not be the way to go."

"I don't understand."

"I don't want to be away from them half the time, and away from you guys the other half."

Bev narrowed her eyes with keen interest. "What do you have in mind?"

I sat back, took a breath and folded my arms across my chest. "Now that I'm back here on my own, this house feels way too big for just me. I think I should sell it. That would free me up to buy a principal residence in Halifax— something with a yard. Maybe on the water."

Bev's eyebrows lifted. "A house. So…" She paused. "Would you settle here full-time?"

"Yes. I can run my consulting business from anywhere, as long as I can fly to Toronto when I need to."

"There are flights from here every day," she replied. "That wouldn't be a problem."

I studied her expression and strove to get a read on how she truly felt about this. "Are you sure you'd be okay with that, Bev? You wouldn't feel like I was encroaching on your territory?"

She laughed as if I were crazy. "Not a bit. And Louise would love it. You and I could be co-parents. You could be with her fifty percent of the time if you wanted to be. Although, we'd probably have to get lawyers involved to work out the details, just so there's no confusion or misunderstandings about how this is going to work."

I sat forward. "I haven't called a lawyer yet. Have you?"

"Not yet," she replied. "I've been waiting to see how the cards might fall before I started paying someone three hundred dollars an hour to figure out where to place those cards."

I nodded. "You are a wise and frugal woman, and I like it. At least now we know that the cards are falling in Halifax."

She gave me a dazzling smile, and it nearly knocked me out of my chair. I felt like I was back in that crowded, noisy dance club five years ago, seeing her for the first time and thinking she was the most beautiful woman I ever laid eyes on.

I realized that without me really knowing it, my anger toward her had subsided over the past week. She was just so darn reasonable, and I appreciated how open and honest she had been with me. She was apologetic and empathetic. But more than anything else, I loved the way she loved Louise. She was a perfect mother. That's what really wore me down.

"So, what happens now?" Bev asked.

I leaned very close to the screen. "You should go and put our daughter to bed, and I'm going to go online and see if I can find some houses that might look promising."

Bev's face lit up. "Call me tomorrow and keep me posted?"

"I will. And can you give Louise a kiss goodnight for me?"

"I'll kiss her twice," Bev replied. "One for you and one for me."

I grinned. "I wish I was there."

"I wish you were here, too."

We stared at each other for a long moment, still smiling.

It was difficult to believe she was thousands of miles away. It felt like she was right there in the room with me.

If only she were. I couldn't guarantee I wouldn't want to kiss *her* good night too.

"Good night, Bev," I finally said.

"Good night." She blew me a kiss before she disappeared from my screen.

As soon as it went black, I had the distinct feeling that I was falling for her again, and I didn't mind one bit.

CHAPTER

Twenty-two

Bev

This was it. Today was the big day.

It had been three weeks since Luke left us at the airport. Louise had sobbed inconsolably in my arms and I had wanted to cry, too, because that was the moment I knew I loved him. I loved him with all my heart and wanted to chase after him and beg him to stay with us.

Why is it that we don't we appreciate the best things in life until they're gone?

But he wasn't truly gone. I kept telling myself that, and I focused on the promise of his return because I had confidence in the depth and sincerity of his love for Louise. And I prayed that one day, if I was fortunate, some of that love might spill over and flow in my direction.

Now, here we were. It was two o'clock on a Tuesday afternoon and Luke was in the air, flying across the country to take possession of a house he had purchased in Halifax. He hadn't even set foot in it. He told me that he'd made an offer based on the photographs and descriptions online because he simply knew, at first sight, that it was the right one. When I asked where it was located, he refused to divulge that information because he wanted to surprise us. He wanted the three of us to walk through the front door and see it for the first time together.

This left me waiting for his arrival with feverish anticipation and bated breath.

While Louise was at school that day, I ran a bubble bath and soaked for a long time. I closed my eyes, lay my head back on the rim of the tub, and relaxed while I thought about the future and what might be possible. Then I washed my hair and used the loofah with a coconut-scented body gel.

Luke's flight was due to arrive from his Toronto connection at 4:20 p.m. My plan was to pick Louise up at school at 3:00, then bring her home for a quick snack and drive to the airport to greet him when he stepped off the plane. I could hardly wait. I missed him desperately and had every intention of hugging him and telling him so.

I had just gotten out of the tub and was wrapping my hair in a towel when the telephone rang. It was 2:10 p.m. I quickly tied the belt on my terrycloth bathrobe and padded to the kitchen in my bare feet, leaving wet marks on the floor.

I picked up the phone and said hello.

It was my mother. She was at home, listening to the news.

"He's supposed to arrive at 4:20," I said as my heart began to race and my veins filled with fire. I hurried to the living room, hunted through the sofa cushions for the remote control, and finally found it. I turned on the TV and saw the coverage.

My stomach burned as I stared with wide eyes at an amateur video of a plane falling out of the sky and crashing to the ground somewhere outside of Chicago.

"No. That's not his flight," I said with relief. "He's not in the U.S. He's on a connecting flight from Toronto. But still, I'm going to call him." I ran to get my cell phone on the kitchen table and dialed his number. It rang and rang and rang. "He's not answering, but if he's still in the air, he'd have his phone on airplane mode anyway."

I ran back to the living room to watch the coverage. The newscasters were debating the possibility of a terrorist bomb, but they didn't know for sure. No one seemed to know anything at this stage.

All I could think about was the fact that it *could* have been Luke. What if it had been? I was desperate to hear his voice.

"Don't worry, he's fine," I said to my mom. "I'm sure of it." I continued to stare at images of a charred, smoking wreckage in the distance and emergency response vehicles in the foreground. A female reporter tried to describe the situation, but there was very little information. She kept repeating the same headline descriptors over and over.

"I think I need to hang up," I said to my mom. "I'll call you back."

Tossing the phone onto the coffee table, I strove to take deep, calming breaths, because I couldn't bear to think about how I'd be feeling right now if it *had* been his flight. What would I do?

I picked up my phone and tried to call him again, but still, there was no answer. My mind was reeling with *what ifs.*

Then my doorbell rang. I leaped to my feet, thinking it might be Claire or Scott. Leo followed me to the door and I unlocked it and pulled it wide open.

There—standing on my veranda with a big smile on his face—was Luke.

Luke!

I stared at him in openmouthed shock, wondering if this was a dream. He looked impossibly gorgeous in a brown leather jacket, black wool turtleneck and jeans. His hair was thick and wavy around his face. A few colorful autumn leaves had dropped from the oak tree and blown onto the veranda at his feet.

"Hi," he said, spreading his arms wide.

I could do nothing but burst into tears. Still wearing my bathrobe and a towel on my head, I pulled him inside my house, threw my arms around his neck, and pressed my cheek to his chest. "I'm so happy to see you. I didn't want to think about never seeing you again!"

"What do you mean?"

I drew back and looked up at him. "A plane just crashed outside Chicago. I knew it wasn't your flight, but it made me think…what if it was? But wait a second. What are you doing here? You're early. And why didn't you answer my calls just now?"

"I switched my flight to catch an earlier one," he replied. "And if I'd answered my phone, you would have known I wasn't on the plane, and it wouldn't have been a surprise." Then his brow puckered. "But there was a plane crash?"

"You didn't hear about it?"

"No. I've been driving from the airport, listening to music. What happened?"

I took him by the hand, led him into the living room, and pointed at the TV. "They're talking about it now."

We stood holding hands while we watched the coverage.

"That's awful," Luke said, frowning.

I nodded. "But what made you come early?"

"I was impatient to get here," he explained. "I didn't want to wait any longer."

My heart nearly burst open with love and relief that he was here and he was safe. I was so thankful—just like I was that day in the helicopter when Louise had begun to breathe again.

"It made me think about losing you," I said. "I don't know what I would have done if…"

Operating on pure adrenaline, I tore the towel from my head, rose up on my tiptoes and wrapped my arms around his neck. He smelled like leather and coffee. All my senses began to hum. A breathtaking warmth filled my body and I couldn't get enough of him.

Suddenly, his mouth caught mine. Holding me snug in his embrace, he backed me up against the wall and kissed me passionately. Desire heated my blood as his hands slid down the length of my back, then up under my damp hair, cupping my head until I was weak and trembling with need. His kiss was electrifying. I was so happy, big salty tears streamed down my face.

"I missed you so much," I said breathlessly as he dragged his lips across my cheek and down my neck while I clung to him, my arms tight about his shoulders. "I can't lose you again."

"I don't want to lose you either," he said.

"I know you came back here for Louise, but is there any chance that…?"

He drew back and looked me in the eye while he stroked my cheek with the pad of his thumb, rubbing away my tears. "Bev. I'm here for you, too. I want to be with you."

I started laughing and crying at the same time. "Why didn't we call each other five years ago? Why did we just let it all go?" I glanced at the television. "When you see something like that…" I sucked in a breath. "It makes you realize how precious life is. We were so stupid, wasting all that time."

He nodded. "But we're smarter now, and I'm not going to walk away again. Not this time. I want to be where you are."

I rested my cheek on his shoulder. "Thank God you weren't on that flight, Luke. For a minute, I imagined all of this ending like a Nicholas Sparks novel."

He laughed softly in my ear. "Not a chance."

Eventually I realized I was still wearing my bathrobe and no makeup, and I needed to put clothes on.

"I should go and get dressed," I said, backing away and giving him a flirtatious look before I glanced at the clock. "We'll need to get Louise soon. She'll be so excited to see you."

"I can't wait to see her, too," he said, taking a few steps forward, his eyes full of desire. He looked as if he wanted to follow me.

"You stay right there," I said with a grin, wagging a finger at him, "or we'll be late."

"All right," he replied with amusement. "But after we get Louise…" He reached into his jacket pocket and pulled out a set of keys. "Would you like to come and see my new house?"

My eyebrows lifted and my whole being lit up with joy. "Yes."

~*O*

The home Luke had purchased was located five-minutes away from my house and was situated on a private wooded lot overlooking the Northwest Arm—a picturesque ocean inlet with yacht clubs and parks on either side.

The house itself was a brick mansion built during the Edwardian period. It boasted original hardwood floors and exquisite craftsmanship throughout. The staircase railing and antique fireplace mantel were show stoppers. At the same time, it had been recently renovated to include every possible modern convenience—a gourmet kitchen with granite countertops and high-end stainless steel appliances.

Upstairs, a luxurious ensuite off the master bedroom impressed us with a claw-foot tub and a large, separate shower enclosed in glass and marble.

Louise ran through all the empty rooms and called to us from the top of the stairs. "I picked out my bedroom!" Her voice echoed in the unfurnished house.

Luke and I smiled at each other. "You might need to arm wrestle her for the master," I said.

He held up his biceps and squeezed his left arm. "See these guns?"

I laughed. Then Luke opened the sliding glass doors off the kitchen. This took us outside to a stone patio that overlooked the Northwest Arm where the odd sailboat was tacking against the cool breeze.

It was late-afternoon, mid-October, and the sun was low

in the sky. The water was calm and gleaming, reflecting the rich and vibrant hues in the autumn forest.

Louise joined us at the rail and I slid my arm around her. "This looks almost as pretty as one of your paintings."

"That's because it's here," she said.

I looked down at her, my brow furrowed. "What do you mean?"

"Don't you see it?" she asked.

"See *what?*"

She grinned, as if I were teasing her because I must already know. But I didn't know what she was trying to say.

"How beautiful it is!" she replied. "And it's right here."

"What are you talking about?"

"Heaven! It's here. It's just different. You can't really see it because you're not *there*. You're *here*. But it's here, too. It's all around us."

It wasn't easy to make sense of how a five-year-old explained the unexplainable. "I thought heaven was above the clouds."

She shook her head. "No, it's everywhere."

"Like...a different dimension?" Luke asked.

"I don't know what that word means," Louise replied. "I just know that I walked across a bridge to get there and it wasn't very far. Just beyond what we can see. But you'll see it someday, and you'll be happy when you get there." She noticed a flower garden at the edge of the grassy lawn below. "Can I go down there?"

"Sure," I replied. "Just stay where we can see you."

We watched her walk down the stone steps and explore the yard. Then she waved up at us. "Look! There's a birdbath!"

Luke bent forward and rested his elbows on the railing.

"Can you believe we made a whole person? An amazing little person?"

I leaned forward as well. "We did all right." I turned to him. "What do you think we should do with her paintings? I feel like they're too beautiful not to share with the world. But I don't want to profit from them either. That wouldn't feel right."

"We should think about that," he said. "You could always donate them to an art gallery, or maybe offer some of them to be displayed in your church hall?"

"I'd hate to part with any of them," I replied. "I like looking at them. They make me feel happy." I turned to gaze back at the house. "You have a lot of empty spaces to fill in there. Would you like me to bring some of them over?"

"Absolutely. You know I'd love to have whatever you're willing to part with. The front hall would make a terrific gallery."

We faced the water again and I breathed in the salty scent of the sea mixed with the fragrance of fall leaves in piles on the ground. "It's incredible here, Luke. You found the perfect house. I'm so grateful that you're here."

He turned to me. "And I'm grateful that you were born, Bev. And that I met you in the bar that night. And that Emma dumped me, so that I could find you again and end up here, where I belong—with you and Louise. This feels like home already."

I laid my hand on his shoulder. "I'm so glad, because I want you to be happy here, Luke. I want you to know that you're surrounded by family now—me, my mom, Claire, Scott and Serena. It's going to be good for all of us."

He pulled me close and kissed my temple. I closed my

eyes, basking in the desire I felt for him, and opening myself to the possibility of more. In time.

"I'm not sure what the future holds for you and me," he whispered in my ear, "but I don't want to lose you again."

I laid my open hand on his chest and smiled up at him. "I don't want to lose you either."

"Then let's promise each other we won't."

Louise stood at the edge of the lawn, waving exuberantly at a sailboat as it passed by. All the passengers waved back at her, and the captain shouted across the water, "Ahoy there! It's a heavenly day!"

"It sure is!" Louise shouted in return, then she swung around and faced us. "Did you hear what he said?"

We both smiled and nodded, and went to join her in the lush and colorful garden over the water.

Epilogue

Emma

One year later

I t was one of those magical evenings at the playhouse in the forest, where the sun beamed down from behind the clouds after a heavy rainstorm. The air was still. Hazy rays of light reflected off raindrops that dripped from the ferns. Insects floated like fairy dust in the vapor, and the air smelled of fresh pine and damp earth beneath the moss.

"It's so peaceful," I said to Carter as we pushed the stroller over exposed tree roots on the forest floor. A squirrel darted across the path in front of us and raced up a tree trunk.

At last we arrived at the playhouse. Carter opened the door, bent forward and entered the cozy, miniature Tudor cottage where he poked around for a few seconds before sticking his head out the door. "No leaks," he said. "Dry as a bone in here."

"That's good news."

During the summer, we had laid flat stones on the walkway next to the hostas out front, so the stroller was easy to maneuver. I parked it at the front door, set the brake, and reached inside for our newborn daughter, Penelope—who was one week old today. I had bundled her in a snug fleece blanket before we left the house.

"Would you like to see your playhouse now?" I asked as I cradled her in my arms. Carter held the door open and I bent to pass through the child-sized entrance. I was able to stand upright once I was inside. "Here it is. What do you think? When you're bigger, we can have tea parties in here."

Carter swept a hand over the white painted mantel to wipe away any dust. "The place looks good." He gave the small rocking chair a gentle push with the toe of his boot.

I shifted Penelope in my arms. "Remember how Sammy used to love to rock so fast in that thing, he'd practically bounce across the floor."

Carter laughed. "He was fearless, that's for sure."

We heard the ticking tap of a woodpecker outside and stood quietly, looking around until Penelope began to fuss. "I think she's hungry again." I took a seat on the window bench and began to unbutton my blouse.

Carter sat on the opposite window bench, watching me. "Do you know how beautiful you are? You're the most beautiful woman I've ever known. And somehow, you get prettier every day."

My eyes lifted and I smiled. "Maybe that's because I'm happier than I've ever been."

"I'm happy, too."

While he looked at me with tenderness and love, the

little chair slowly stopped rocking and a luminous ray of sunshine entered the playhouse through the window over my shoulder.

~*C*

Later, after we'd returned to the main house and I'd settled Penelope in her bassinet, I found Carter in the kitchen, scooping pistachio ice cream into two bowls.

"Yum." I moved closer to kiss him on the cheek.

The doorbell rang just then, and he looked at me. "Are you expecting anyone?"

"No."

He set down the plastic scoop, and while he left the kitchen to answer it, I continued filling the second bowl. Just as I was placing the carton back in the freezer, Carter returned with a large package.

"This came by courier. It's addressed to both of us, but you should probably be the one to open it."

He set the box on the counter and fetched the scissors out of the junk drawer. I read the return address on the label.

"It's from Luke." I met Carter's gaze with a look of surprise and uncertainty.

"Well," he said, handing me the scissors. "Go ahead and open it. See what's inside."

I sliced through the packing tape and pulled back the cardboard tabs. Under a double layer of plastic bubble wrap, I found a gift-wrapped box with a card. Sliding the pink envelope out from under the ribbon, I tore at the seal.

"It says: 'Congratulations on the little miracle that just came into your lives.'" I opened it and read the verse inside.

"'Don't you just love new beginnings? Love Luke.'"

My eyes filled with tears and Carter put his arm around me.

"There's a letter, too." As I unfolded a sheet of stationery with a lengthy, handwritten message that began with *Dear Emma*, a picture fell to the floor. Carter bent to pick it up.

"My goodness." I took it in my hands. "She's pregnant. How wonderful."

Although Luke and I had occasionally 'liked' each other's Facebook posts, we had spoken only twice since the day I ended our relationship. The first time, I'd called his cell phone to let him know about the movers coming to clear out his garage.

The second time happened a few weeks later after he emailed me to let me know he'd sold his house. He told me he was moving to the East Coast to be with the daughter he'd just found out about. Naturally, I was floored by this, so I called him.

When we spoke on the phone, he explained who she was—the little girl who had gone to heaven—and I nearly fell over. He then described how he had learned about her: because he'd seen a picture of her and her mother on my laptop the day after I left him.

For some unknown reason, I'd left that website page open on my computer constantly. I simply liked looking at it, and I was considering contacting the mother to try and talk to her about her daughter's experience, but never found the courage. Then Luke stumbled upon it and recognized her as the woman he'd slept with many years ago. What were the odds?

After I hung up, I became convinced that we'd all been

fated to find each other in this miraculous way. Luke was destined to meet me, and I was destined to unwittingly lead him to his true family—although a part of me wonders if there was some kind of unconscious recognition of Louise on my part. I suppose I'll never know for sure, but even Carter hasn't tried to convince me that it was mere coincidence. Not after our experience with Maria, the psychic, and his dream about Sammy. These days, he believes anything is possible. Maybe angels or spirit guides whisper in our ears. Who knows?

"Let's open the gift before I read the letter," I said, wanting to save the best for last.

As I unwrapped the box, I found a darling little pink sleeper with a fairy and magic wand embroidered on the front. "How sweet. I love it." There was also a pair of white leather baby shoes resembling the ones that belonged to Sammy—the ones I'd kept and had shown to Luke on the day Carter and I cleared out Sammy's room.

That room now belonged to Penelope, and the antique box Luke and I had purchased to hold these keepsakes resided on a shelf by the window.

Leaving my ice cream on the counter, I moved to the kitchen table and sat down to read the letter.

Dear Emma,

Please find enclosed a gift for you and Carter and your new baby girl. Congratulations. I'm so happy for you both.

It's been a while since we spoke, but I occasionally check your Facebook page to see how you're doing. I saw pictures of your renovations to the playhouse recently, and now I understand why you didn't want to part with it. It's amazing. I'm thinking about building something like that here.

Bev and I are doing well. We were married last June and Louise was a flower girl. We now live in the home I purchased when I first moved here, and it's in the same school zone for Louise, so it was an easy transition for her. And it's only five minutes away from Bev's sister, Claire, and her daughter Serena who is like a sister to Louise. The little girls are here all the time, playing together, and I've become good friends with Claire's husband, Scott. It's been good.

I'm sure you can see from the photograph that Bev is expecting a child. She's due to deliver in about three weeks and we are excited and looking forward to bringing our new baby home. Louise can't wait to have a baby brother or sister.

So I guess that's all our news, but I wanted to write for another reason, too.

I hope you know that I wish you and Carter the best, and I harbor no ill will toward you. I now believe that you and I were meant to spend that brief time together so that we could discover where we were truly meant to be. It might have been painful at the time, and I'm sorry if I seemed angry. I was, at first. But they say every cloud has a silver lining. I think we've both found that to be true, and I'm grateful for it.

Take care of yourself and your family.

Best wishes,

Luke

Tears filled my eyes again, and I looked up to see Carter pulling more bubble wrap out of the box. "There's something else in here," he said.

Feeling too choked up to speak, I rose from my chair and approached him.

He withdrew a flat object wrapped in plain brown paper.

"What is it?" I asked.

He removed the paper and held up a stunning

impressionist-style canvas painting of a green meadow with colorful wildflowers and snowcapped mountains in the distance. I could almost hear the wind rustling through the grass. There were children playing, birds and butterflies, and an incredible sky with spectacular clouds and glowing rays of light. Everything was so beautiful, I nearly lost my breath. A tear of joy rolled down my cheek.

"This is unbelievable," Carter said. "I've never seen anything like it."

"Me neither." He passed it to me and I looked at the artist's signature. I ran the tip of my finger over the name. "It says *Louise*."

Carter's wide eyes met mine. "Isn't that Luke's daughter? But she's only what…six years old? How could she have painted this?"

"I don't know."

He turned the canvas over and there was a small card tucked into the wood frame. I pulled it out and recognized Luke's handwriting.

This is how Louise saw heaven. Please take comfort in the knowledge that it's a place of beauty, and Sammy is safe and happy in loving arms.

I turned to Carter and we smiled at each other. Then he took me into his embrace and all seemed right with the world.

Dear Reader,

Thank you for taking the time to read *The Color of a Silver Lining*. I hope you enjoyed reading it as much as I enjoyed writing it. Some books are easier than others, and this one was pure bliss the entire way through. I loved writing about these characters and I found myself not wanting to type The End.

If you're interested in reading about Bev's sister Claire, and learning how she found happiness with Scott, you can find their emotional story in *The Color of a Christmas Miracle*, which is available now. Bev is a significant character in that novel as well.

For those of you who have been following this series from start to finish, I promise this isn't the end. I still want to write more *Color of Heaven* novels, and I plan to start another soon. I don't have any info to share with you yet regarding a title or release date, so if you'd like to know when the next one will be available, please sign up for my mailing list and I'll send you an email when I know more.

In the meantime, I am working on a standalone novel, and I've included the first three chapters on the following pages. This isn't part of my *Color of Heaven* series, but it's a similar type of story—women's fiction with an uplifting ending that I hope will leave you feeling happy and satisfied.

The working title for this novel is *Fear of Falling*, but that may change in the coming weeks, and I don't have cover art to show you yet, so again, if you want to know when it's coming out, please sign up for my mailing list. Or you can follow me on Bookbub, where you'll receive new release emails as well as an alert whenever one of my backlist title ebooks goes on sale for 99 cents.

Read on for more information about the *Color of Heaven Series*, as well as a complete booklist which includes my historical romances. Most of my historical novels have love scenes (especially the Highlander romances!), but *Adam's Promise* is a sweet romance. That one holds a special place in my heart as it's set in Colonial Nova Scotia and was inspired by true events. I loved doing all the research about an area so close to my home. That novel was a Romance Writers of America Rita finalist for Best Short Historical Romance in 2003. I hope you'll check it out.

Lastly, I invite you to visit my website for all the latest news, and while you're there, be sure to enter my monthly giveaway where one lucky winner receives an autographed print edition of one of my backlist titles.

I guess that's all for now. As always, Happy Reading!

Sincerely,
Julianne

FEAR *of* FALLING
BY JULIANNE MACLEAN

*How easy is it to forgive the man you love
when he has destroyed everything you ever held dear?*

Successful surgeon Abbie MacIntyre is living a picture-perfect life with her handsome cardiologist husband and bright teenage son, until on a cold winter's night, she is run off the road by a drunk driver. After being pulled from the wreck, she is rushed to the local hospital, where shocking details about the other driver lead her down a path of troubling and unexpected discoveries. Soon, she learns that her husband has been keeping secrets from her, and her perfect marriage is not so perfect after all.

In the aftermath of the accident, nightmares haunt her to the point where she begins to question her own grip on reality. Is she merely traumatized, or is something medically wrong with her? And how can she possibly move forward when she can't even accept what her life has become?

Devastated by all that she lost on the night of the accident, and wounded by a betrayal she never saw coming, Abbie must find a way to move forward through her grief, put her shattered life back together, and learn not only how to forgive, but how to eventually trust in love again.

From the *USA Today* bestselling author of *The Color of Heaven Series* comes another emotionally gripping tale about love, loss and one woman's strength to come to terms with a future very different from the one she imagined.

EXCERPT FROM

FEAR
of
FALLING

CHAPTER

One

Intuition is a funny thing. Sometimes it's a gut feeling, and you look around and just *know* something bad is about to happen. Other times, it's elusive, and later you find yourself looking back on certain events and wondering why in the world you missed all the signals.

Tonight, I am on my way home to Halifax after Sunday dinner with my mother. As I turn the key in the ignition and shift into reverse, she comes running out her front door, waving her hand through the air.

"Wait! Abbie! Wait!"

It's dark and foggy outside, but the porch lights give her kinky silver hair a luminous sheen. I see a look of panic on her face and my hands clench around the steering wheel. I wish she'd slow down instead of descending the concrete steps as if the house were burning down behind her.

Be careful, Mom...

While she dashes down the driveway, I shift into park and lower the car window.

My golden retriever, Winston, rises in the back seat and wags his tail. Mom reaches us and passes an enormous Tupperware container through the open window. It's full of leftovers from the chicken dinner she just cooked for me—

enough to carry us through the next two days. A much-appreciated gift.

"You forgot this," she says, out of breath.

I reach out with both hands, take it from her, and set it on the passenger seat beside me. Winston sniffs and paws my shoulder, wanting to know what's under the blue plastic lid. I give him a pat on his silky head.

"Settle down, mister. This isn't for you." Then I turn to smile at my mom who is bent forward, her arms folded across her chest to keep warm because it's late November and getting colder by the second.

"Thanks, Mom," I say. "The guys would never forgive me if I came home empty-handed."

By "guys," I am referring to my husband Alan—a cardiologist I've been married to for nineteen years—and my seventeen-year-old son Zack, who stayed behind this afternoon because he had hockey practice and a game tonight.

"Are you sure you don't want to take some of that pie with you?" Mom asks, speaking to me through the open window and trying not to shiver.

I know it's not a conscious thing, but it's obvious that she wants to keep me here a little longer. She's never enjoyed being home alone in that big empty house—especially on cold, dark nights like this. You would think, after twenty years of widowhood, she'd be ready to downsize, but I can't fault her for anything. I love her too much. It's why I drive over an hour from the city every Sunday afternoon to spend time with her in the house where I grew up.

"No thanks," I reply. "Alan's trying to cut calories again."

Truthfully, he isn't, but I don't have time to wait

because I'm hoping to make it back to the city in time for Zack's game. Then I have an early morning case in the OR—a gallbladder surgery scheduled for eight.

Mom gives my hand a squeeze. "Okay, dear. Wish our boy luck on the ice tonight, and say hi to Alan for me. Tell them I missed them today. And please drive safely."

"I will. Now get back inside, Mom. It's freezing out here."

She nods and hurries back up the stairs, while I feel that familiar twinge of guilt about leaving her alone. I tell myself not to worry. She's independent and self-sufficient, and I know she'll be fine as soon as she turns on the television and gets caught up in a smart documentary or a Charlie Rose interview.

Winston turns in circles on the back seat, then finally settles down to sleep for the next hour. That he'll rest helps me relax and focus on getting home. I shift into reverse and back out of the driveway.

~⊖

Despite the heavy fog, the roads are dry as I make my way out of my beloved hometown. Lunenburg is a picturesque fishing and shipbuilding community, also a bourgeoning center for the arts, and it's designated a UNESCO World Heritage Site to preserve its historic architecture. As you'd expect, it has a robust tourism trade in the summer. As I pass by the brightly lit restaurants along the waterfront, I can't help but glance wistfully at the sparkling reflection of the moon on the harbor that is casting undulating shadows from a tall ship's masts over the dockyard.

I feel a twinge of sadness and I'm not sure why.

Something just feels off. Maybe it's because Mom seems so much older these past few months. She never used to refer to herself as a "senior citizen," not even when she turned sixty-five, but lately she's been making jokes about it, saying things like "Old age ain't for sissies!" and "If only I could remember what it is I'm forgetting to remember." Today, when she couldn't figure out how to get the messages off her phone, she said, "Look out nursing home. Here I come."

I love that she has a sense of humor about growing old, but it reminds me that she won't be around forever, and eventually our Sunday dinners will be a thing of the past.

Suddenly, I find myself imagining, somewhat morbidly, what I'm going to do with the house when she's gone. Will I keep it? And will that just be a desperate attempt to hang onto the past? I remind myself that I have my own life now, and I've never been happier. I love my career, I make boatloads of money, and I have a handsome, devoted husband at home, along with a smart, responsible son who is a superstar in every way.

Zack is just like his father—intelligent, sensible and respectful. He's also captain of the hockey team and president of the student council. Alan and I couldn't be more proud of him.

Although it surprises me, Zack has never had a steady girlfriend—at least not yet. I'm biased, of course, because I'm his mother, but seriously… He's an amazing catch. He's extremely good looking—again, just like his father—and there's nothing biased about that. I see the way girls look at Zack. They discreetly check him out in the grocery store, or chat him up at hockey games and other school events. But my son seems totally oblivious to it all.

A few weeks ago, while Alan and I were cooking dinner together, I asked quietly, "Do you ever wonder if he might be gay?"

Alan, who was chopping cucumbers for the salad, froze on the spot. "No. Do you?"

Facing the stove, I dropped a handful of uncooked spaghetti noodles into a pot of boiling water. "Would it bother you if he was?" I carefully asked.

For a few seconds, Alan didn't speak. He just stood there, motionless, the knife paused on the cutting board.

"Of course it wouldn't," he said with a frown, his gaze moving sharply to meet mine. He stared at me for a moment, his brow furrowed with annoyance. Then he lowered his gaze and resumed chopping the carrots.

I inclined my head. "You can't blame me for asking. You know what your father's like. He's not exactly tolerant."

He nodded, but there was an unmistakable note of impatience in his voice and he began to chop more quickly. "Yes, but I'm not my father."

I had touched a nerve and I knew it, because Alan hadn't spoken to his homophobic, bigoted father in more than ten years. He despised the man who had been emotionally abusive to his wife and children. We rarely ever mentioned his name.

I lay my hand on Alan's shoulder. "Of course you're not. I'm sorry. I shouldn't have said that."

Alan simply nodded while I moved back to the stove to break the pasta noodles apart with a fork.

"As far as Zack is concerned," I carefully continued, "even if he was gay, it wouldn't matter to me. I just want him to be happy."

"Me, too," Alan replied.

Before I knew it, he was standing behind me, massaging my neck and shoulders and apologizing for his chippy tone.

I turned and wrapped my arms around his neck and hugged him. "I'm sorry, too. I shouldn't have mentioned your dad. You're his opposite in every way, and that's one of the reasons I love you."

"I love you, too," he replied, squeezing me tight. "More than anything."

Winston's heavy sigh in the back seat of my car pulls me out of the past and back to the present. I glance over my shoulder and he's curled up on his wooly blanket with his eyes closed, which makes me feel sleepy because I'd worked late in the OR the night before.

I turn on the radio to help keep me awake, then I flick my blinker and turn onto the on-ramp. I check the dashboard clock. It's only seven o'clock, so I have time to make it home, drop Winston off at the house, and reach the hockey rink before they start the game at 8:15.

Within seconds, I am merging onto the main highway. I switch to cruise control once I hit a speed that works in the fog, and tune in to a classic rock music station.

CHAPTER

Two

It all happens in an instant, so fast I don't have time to think.

An oncoming vehicle crosses the center line and I'm blinded by headlights. Adrenaline burns through my veins. Instinctively, I wrench the steering wheel to the right to swerve around the oncoming car, but it's too late. It clips my back end with a thunderous crash of steel against steel and sends my SUV spinning like a top, as if I'm on a sheet of ice.

My head snaps to the left. I shut my eyes and hang on for dear life as the car whirls around in dizzying circles. Winston yelps as he's tossed about in the back seat. Suddenly, we catapult into the air. The vehicle flips over at the edge of the highway, then we bounce like a ball—crashing, smashing—tumbling down the embankment.

Something strikes me in the side of the head and I feel multiple slashes cutting the flesh on my cheeks. I realize it's Winston, who yelps as he's thrown toward the rear.

I want to hold on to him, to keep him safe in my arms, but there's nothing I can do. It's all happening so fast. All I can do is clutch the steering wheel with both hands while the world spins in circles and glass shatters all around me.

We crash hard against something... The bottom of a

ravine? Then everything is quiet, except for the pounding of my heart hammering against my ribcage.

Panic overtakes me. My eyes fly open. It's pitch dark outside, but my headlights are shining two steady beams into the mist, and the dashboard is brightly lit. I blink repeatedly and realize blood has pooled on my eyelashes. I swipe it away with the back of my hand.

Think, Abbie. What do you need to do?

The vehicle has been beeping an alarm since we came to a halt, as if it's confused by what just happened and wants me to fasten my seatbelt. Or is there some other urgent problem? Is the engine about to explode? I quickly shut off the ignition. The interior is overcome by darkness.

With an altogether new rush of anxiety, I fumble for the red button on my seatbelt, desperate to escape, but my hands shake so severely, I can't release it. I shut my eyes and pause, take a few breaths, then try a second time.

Click.

The seatbelt comes loose and I think—for one precious second—that I am free to move, but I'm not. My legs are stuck. I'm trapped.

I fight to break loose but I'm pinned under the dash. The roof is pressing down on top of my head and I can't free myself. I try to open the door but it's dented and won't budge. There is broken glass everywhere.

My heart pounds faster and faster. I feel lightheaded, and am certain I'm about to pass out from shock and fear.

I shut my eyes again and try to remain calm. *Breathe… One thousand one, one thousand two…*

"Help…" I whisper in a trembling voice.

Then I turn my head to the side. "Winston? Are you okay?"

No response. I twist uncomfortably, trying to see into the back. There's no sign of him anywhere and the rear window is completely blown out.

"Winston!" I shout. *"Winston!"*

I can't make out anything in the darkness, and I worry that he's injured or dead, lying somewhere outside the vehicle. I fight wildly to free myself but it's hopeless. The dash is pressing down on my legs and I can't move.

I reach frantically to find my purse on the seat beside me, to locate my cell phone and call for help, but the seat is empty. Everything's been tossed out the windows.

Then I hear sirens in the distance, and I exhale sharply with relief. *Thank God, someone's coming.*

Knowing help is on the way, I let my head fall back on the headrest, and try to calm my racing heart.

If only I had my phone. All I want to do is call Alan. It's all I can think about as I swipe at the blood from my forehead and struggle to free my legs from under the crushing weight of the dashboard.

CHAPTER

Three

"Try and stay calm," a young firefighter says as he removes a glove and takes hold of my hand through the driver's side window. It has no glass left in it.

"Have you seen my dog?" I ask. "He was with me in the car but he must have been thrown out the back window."

"What kind of dog is it?"

"A golden retriever."

Troy directs one of the other first responders to use his walkie-talkie to report my missing dog, then search the area.

I hear the wail of more sirens and vehicles arriving—fire trucks and cop cars and ambulances. Colored lights are flashing, but they're swallowed up by the fog.

"We're gonna get you out of here," the firefighter says. "What's your name?"

"Abbie. Abbie MacIntyre."

"Hi Abbie," he says. "I'm Troy. Everything's going to be fine now."

I shake my head, fearing I might be sick. "I don't feel so good."

"No wonder. You just took a nasty tumble, but don't worry. Help's on the way."

Two other firefights do a 360 around the vehicle,

shining flashlights everywhere. I watch the beams sweep across the dark ravine.

One of them speaks on a walkie-talkie to someone above us. He says something about the patient appearing to be stable. It takes me a few seconds to realize he's talking about me.

"If I could just get my legs free…" I say with a grunt, trying to move them, but it's hopeless, and any movement makes my head hurt.

Troy pats my forearm. "Don't strain yourself. Just relax and leave it to us to get you out. We have all the right tools. It'll just take a few minutes to get the equipment down here."

I nod my head. "Can someone please call my husband? I don't know where my phone is."

"Of course. What's his name?"

"Alan."

Troy whistles and waves to the police officer who is skidding down the steep embankment. "Can you call the husband?"

"Sure." The cop arrives and peers in at me. "How are we doing in there, ma'am?"

"I'm okay," I reply. "Just pretty shaken up, and I can't move my legs." I don't know why I'm telling him I'm okay when I'm nothing of the sort. "Can you please call my husband?"

"Of course." He pulls out a cell phone and dials the number as I recite it. I watch as he waits for a reply, then shakes his head. "I'm sorry, there's no answer. Should I leave a message?"

"Yes," I say without hesitation, frustrated that Alan isn't answering his phone when I need him most.

The officer explains the situation to Alan's voicemail service and leaves a message that his wife has been in an accident. He leaves a number for Alan to call and tells him that I'll be taken to the Fishermen's Memorial Hospital in Lunenburg, only five minutes away.

The cop ends the call. "I'll try again in a few minutes."

I thank him, then realize I'm shivering uncontrollably. I concentrate and try to relax my body, but not even my fiercest, most focused willpower can stop the shaking.

"Just try to stay calm," Troy says. "You're in good hands and we'll have you out of there before you know it. Here they come."

I nod my head and try to be patient, wishing this nightmare would hurry up and be over. *Just get me out of here...*

A team of five firefighters arrives with some heavy equipment they set up around my vehicle. This includes a noisy generator, a giant steel cutter, and a powerful spreader.

I turn to Troy, who is still at my side. He looks so young... Not much older than my son, Zack.

"Any sign of my dog yet?" I ask.

Troy turns to look toward the cluster of flashing lights and emergency vehicles on the road above. "I don't think so."

"Can you please find out?" I ask desperately, while one of the other firefighters proceeds to let the air out of my tires and places blocks under the wheels to stabilize the vehicle. "I'm worried about him."

Still holding my hand, Troy turns to call out to the cop who stands at the base of the embankment talking on his phone. "Hey. Can you check on Abbie's dog? He's a golden retriever and he was thrown from the vehicle. His name's Winston and he can't have gone far."

With every passing second, I grow increasingly worried, because Winston is deeply attached to me and extremely protective. If he ran off, he must be injured or in shock.

The cop trudges up the hill and I fight not to become hysterical while Troy tells me he's going to cover me with a blanket that looks more like a canvas tarp.

"They're going to use the Jaws of Life to cut the vehicle apart and lift the dash upward to free your legs," he explains. "This will shield you from bits of flying glass and metal."

I nod my head in agreement because I want to be calm, but I'm terrified, and he knows it.

"I'll be right here with you the whole time," Troy says as he covers me, then he slides into the seat behind me to move out of the team's way.

The noise of the cutter is deafening. All I hear is the roar of machines, the crunching of metal, the shattering of glass. I'm afraid it's all going to collapse on top of me, but the feel of Troy's hand squeezing my shoulder and the sound of his voice in my ear, explaining everything along the way, helps me stay grounded.

"They're making a series of relief cuts in the frame," he says. "I know it's loud…"

My stomach turns over as I recall the horror of the crash, and the rapid, tumbling descent…

"Okay…" Troy says when the cutter shuts off, "you're doing great, Abbie. Now they're going to use a spreader to lift the dash, which should ease the pressure on your legs. Just hang in there. We're almost done."

I try not to think about the potential damage to my legs. It's not easy to assume everything will be fine. I'm a surgeon. I know there are certain things that simply aren't fixable.

Instead, I focus my thoughts on Alan and pray that he's gotten the message, and I think of Zack at the rink, who has no idea his mother is trapped in a car wreck at the bottom of a ravine. Then Winston... Where is he? *Please God*, let him be safe.

I wish the police officer would try calling Alan again, but I can't ask him because I'm secured under a tarp and surrounded by rescue workers who are ripping my car apart at the seams.

The spreader begins to slowly lift the dash, and I feel a weight come off my legs. Suddenly, my thighs ache with a bone-deep pain, but I can wiggle my toes. A good sign.

As soon as there's an opportunity, while the spreader is still raising the dash, I reach down to run my hands over my knees and calves. My jeans are ripped and there are a few surface abrasions, but I'm able to bend my legs at the knee joints.

Another good sign.

Troy removes the tarp, but I barely have time to look down and get a visual on my legs before a brace is fastened around my neck and I'm gently lifted out of the vehicle and onto a backboard laid on a gurney. All this is carried out by two paramedics, one male and one female, who must have scrambled down the slope with their equipment while the firefighters were cutting my vehicle apart.

"I'm a doctor," I tell them. "What are your names?"

"I'm Carrie and this is Bubba."

I can't move my neck, but I can shift my gaze to Bubba, who looks like a bouncer with a brush cut. The name suits him.

Carrie, on the other hand, is a pretty, petite blond who

appears extremely focused and capable as she wraps a blood pressure cuff around my arm. I give her a few seconds until she releases the air in the cuff.

"What's my BP?" I ask.

"It's excellent. One-twenty-six over eighty-five."

"That's a bit high for me, but given the situation, I'll take it."

Others gather around to transport me up the hill.

"How's your pain?" she asks.

"Manageable. My legs are sore, and these abrasions on my face are stinging a bit, but it's no big deal. Let's just get me out of here."

I'm aware of Troy still at my side, helping to carry me up the steep slope, which is no easy task because the rocks and debris are unsteady.

As luck would have it, it begins to rain. Soon I'm feeling ice pellets on my cheeks and I'm forced to close my eyes.

A moment later, we are up on the road, and again I ask, "Has anyone seen my dog?"

Carrie is busy pushing my gurney toward the ambulance. She slips and slides on the ice. "You had a dog with you?"

"Winston. He's a golden retriever," Troy adds. Then he leans over me. "Don't worry, Abbie. We're looking for him, and I promise, we'll find him."

"Can you check about it now? I need to know he's okay."

Troy nods and leaves my side.

I wish I could sit up and look around, but I'm strapped to the gurney and wearing a neck collar. There's even a strap across my forehead, and two red foam blocks press against my ears so I can't turn left or right. All I can see is the cloudy night sky over the paramedics' heads, and the glistening freezing rain coming down as they slide me into the back of the ambulance.

"Wait. Please… I don't want to leave without my dog. *Winston!*" I shout, hoping he'll hear me and come running.

My heart rate accelerates.

Carrie speaks reassuringly while she secures the gurney in the ambulance. "Don't worry, Abbie. Troy is a dog lover. He'll do everything he can to find Winston. But we really have to go."

Bubba closes the ambulance doors and I feel a lump form in my throat. I want to cry because I can't bear for Winston to believe for one single second that I've abandoned him.

And what about Alan? Does he even know yet? I ask Carrie to try calling him again, but there's still no answer. Then I ask her to call Zack, but he must be on the ice by now. He doesn't answer either.

At last, I ask Carrie to call my mother. Only then—as she's dialing the number—does it occur to me to ask about the people in the other vehicle. "Was anyone else hurt?"

Carrie is hesitant, but honest. "Yes. The other car was totaled. The driver collided with an eighteen-wheeler that was behind you. It was the trucker who called 911. He said the guy was weaving all over the road just before he hit you."

"And the driver of the car?"

She lets out a heavy sigh. "He's alive, but I think he was drunk. At least that's what they're saying. They found an open bottle of vodka in the front seat."

I feel an explosion of rage in my belly as I recall how the driver had drifted across the center line, directly into my path.

He was drinking in the vehicle?

I don't have time for anger, because Carrie gets through to my mother. She holds the phone to my ear so I can speak to her and reassure her that I'm okay. Mom begins to cry, but I tell her not to worry.

She pulls herself together and agrees to meet me at the hospital. Carrie ends the call and we speed toward Lunenburg, sirens blaring.

It's hard not to think about the drunk driver and how badly I want to shake him and shout at him for being so irresponsible, but my anger won't change anything. At least not now.

And what about Winston? It's killing me to imagine where he might be. What if he's lost and alone in the woods? Traumatized by what happened? Fearful of the noisy rescue vehicles? He's terrified of fireworks in the sky. He always darts into a corner and shakes.

Please, Troy... Please find him.

━◎

For more information about when this novel will be available for purchase, please visit Julianne's website at www.juliannemaclean.com and sign up for her mailing list.

The COLOR *of* HEAVEN

Book One

A deeply emotional tale about Sophie Duncan, a successful columnist whose world falls apart after her daughter's unexpected illness and her husband's shocking affair. When it seems nothing else could possibly go wrong, her car skids off an icy road and plunges into a frozen lake. There, in the cold dark depths of the water, a profound and extraordinary experience unlocks the surprising secrets from Sophie's past, and teaches her what it means to truly live…and love.

Full of surprising twists and turns and a near-death experience that will leave you breathless, this story is not to be missed.

"A gripping, emotional tale you'll want to read in one sitting."
—*New York Times* bestselling author, Julia London

"Brilliantly poignant mainstream tale."
—4 ½ starred review, *Romantic Times*

Includes Bonus Content: A Bookclub Discussion Guide

The COLOR of DESTINY

Book Two

Eighteen years ago a teenage pregnancy changed Kate Worthington's life forever. Faced with many difficult decisions, she chose to follow her heart and embrace an uncertain future with the father of her baby—her devoted first love.

At the same time, in another part of the world, sixteen-year-old Ryan Hamilton makes his own share of mistakes, but learns important lessons along the way. Twenty years later, Kate's and Ryan's paths cross in a way they could never expect, which makes them question the possibility of destiny. Even when all seems hopeless, could it be that everything happens for a reason, and we end up exactly where we are meant to be?

Includes Bonus Content: A Bookclub Discussion Guide

The COLOR *of* HOPE

Book Three

Diana Moore has led a charmed life. She is the daughter of a wealthy senator and lives a glamorous city life, confident that her handsome live-in boyfriend Rick is about to propose. But everything is turned upside down when she learns of a mysterious woman who works nearby—a woman who is her identical mirror image.

Diana is compelled to discover the truth about this woman's identity, but the truth leads her down a path of secrets, betrayals, and shocking discoveries about her past. These discoveries follow her like a shadow.

Then she meets Dr. Jacob Peterson—a brilliant cardiac surgeon with an uncanny ability to heal those who are broken. With his help, Diana embarks upon a journey to restore her belief in the human spirit, and recover a sense of hope—that happiness, and love, may still be within reach for those willing to believe in second chances.

Includes Bonus Content: A Bookclub Discussion Guide

The COLOR of A DREAM

Book Four

Nadia Carmichael has had a lifelong run of bad luck. It begins on the day she is born, when she is separated from her identical twin sister and put up for adoption. Twenty-seven years later, not long after she is finally reunited with her twin and is expecting her first child, Nadia falls victim to a mysterious virus and requires a heart transplant.

Now recovering from the surgery with a new heart, Nadia is haunted by a recurring dream that sets her on a path to discover the identity of her donor. Her efforts are thwarted, however, when the father of her baby returns to sue for custody of their child. It's not until Nadia learns of his estranged brother Jesse that she begins to explore the true nature of her dreams, and discover what her new heart truly needs and desires…

The COLOR of A MEMORY

Book Five

Audrey Fitzgerald believed she was married to the perfect man—a heroic firefighter who saved lives, even beyond his own death. But a year later she meets a mysterious woman who has some unexplained connection to her husband...

Soon Audrey discovers that her husband was keeping secrets and she is compelled to dig into his past. Little does she know...this journey of self-discovery will lead her down a path to a new and different future—a future she never could have imagined.

The COLOR *of* LOVE

Book Six

Carla Matthews is a single mother struggling to make ends meet and give her daughter Kaleigh a decent upbringing. When Kaleigh's absent father Seth—a famous alpine climber who never wanted to be tied down—begs for a second chance at fatherhood, Carla is hesitant because she doesn't want to pin her hopes on a man who is always seeking another mountain to scale. A man who was never willing to stay put in one place and raise a family.

But when Seth's plane goes missing after a crash landing in the harsh Canadian wilderness, Carla must wait for news… Is he dead or alive? Will the wreckage ever be found?

One year later, after having given up all hope, Carla receives a phone call that shocks her to her core. A man has been found, half-dead, floating on an iceberg in the North Atlantic, uttering her name. Is this Seth? And is it possible that he will come home to her and Kaleigh at last, and be the man she always dreamed he would be?

Includes Bonus Content: A Bookclub Discussion Guide

The COLOR *of* THE SEASON

Book Seven

From *USA Today* bestselling author Julianne MacLean comes the next installment in her popular Color of Heaven series—a gripping, emotional tale about real life magic that touches us all during the holiday season...

Boston cop, Josh Wallace, is having the worst day of his life. First, he's dumped by the woman he was about to propose to, then everything goes downhill from there when he is shot in the line of duty. While recovering in the hospital, he can't seem to forget the woman he wanted to marry, nor can he make sense of the vivid images that flashed before his eyes when he was wounded on the job. Soon, everything he once believed about his life begins to shift when he meets Leah James, an enigmatic resident doctor who somehow holds the key to both his past and his future...

The COLOR of JOY

Book Eight

After rushing to the hospital for the birth of their third child, Riley and Lois James anticipate one of the most joyful days of their lives. But things take a dark turn when their newborn daughter vanishes from the hospital. Is this payback for something in Riley's troubled past? Or is it something even more mysterious?

As the search intensifies and the police close in, strange and unbelievable clues about the whereabouts of the newborn begin to emerge, and Riley soon finds himself at the center of a surprising turn of events that will challenge everything he once believed about life, love, and the existence of miracles.

The COLOR *of* TIME

Book Nine

They say it's impossible to change the past…

Since her magical summer romance at the age of sixteen, Sylvie Nichols has never been able to forget her first love.

Years later, when she returns to the seaside town where she lost her heart to Ethan Foster, she is determined to lay the past to rest once and for all. But letting go becomes a challenge when Sylvie finds herself transported back to that long ago summer of love…and the turbulent events that followed. Soon, past and present begin to collide in strange and mystifying ways, and Sylvie can't help but wonder if a true belief in miracles is powerful enough to change both her past and her future….

The COLOR *of* FOREVER

Book Ten

Recently divorced television reporter Katelyn Roberts has stopped believing in relationships that last forever, until a near-death experience during a cycling accident changes everything. When she miraculously survives unscathed, a long-buried mystery leads her to the quaint, seaside town of Cape Elizabeth, Maine.

There, on the rugged, windswept coast of the Atlantic, she finds herself caught up in the secrets of a historic inn that somehow calls to her from the past. Is it possible that the key to her true destiny lies beneath all that she knows, as she explores the grand mansion and property? Or that the great love she's always dreamed of is hidden in the alcoves of its past?

"I never know what to say about a Julianne MacLean book, except to say YOU HAVE TO READ IT." – *AllRomanceReader.ca*

The COLOR *of a* PROMISE

Book Eleven

Having spent a lifetime in competition with his older brother Aaron—who always seemed to get the girl—Jack Peterson leaves the U.S. to become a foreign correspondent in the Middle East. When a roadside bomb forces him to return home to recover from his wounds, he quickly becomes the most celebrated journalist on television, and is awarded his own prime time news program. Now, wealthy and successful beyond his wildest dreams, Jack believes he has finally found where he is meant to be. But when a 747 explodes in the sky over his summer house in Cape Elizabeth, all hell breaks loose as the wreckage crashes to the ground. He has no idea that his life is about to take another astonishing turn…

Meg Andrews grew up with a fear of flying, but when it meant she wouldn't be able to visit her boyfriend on the opposite side of the country, she confronted her fear head-on and earned her pilot's license. Now, a decade later, she is a respected airline crash investigator, passionate about her work, to the point of obsession. When she arrives in the picturesque seaside community of Cape Elizabeth to investigate a massive airline disaster, she meets the famous and charismatic Jack Peterson, who has his own personal fascination with plane crashes.

As the investigation intensifies, Meg and Jack feel a powerful, inexplicable connection to each other. Soon, they realize that the truth behind the crash—and the mystery of their connection—can only be discovered through the strength of the human spirit, the timeless bonds of family, and the gift of second chances.

The COLOR
of a
CHRISTMAS
MIRACLE

Book Twelve

Claire Radcliffe has been blessed with a wonderful life—a loving husband, a fulfilling career, and a perfect house in a charming historic neighborhood. But with each Christmas that passes, the one thing she longs for most of all continues to elude her, and before long, her life doesn't seem so perfect anymore.

When yet another holiday season approaches and she finds herself facing the fact that all her dreams have flown out the window, Claire must learn to have faith in destiny, and allow herself to believe that miracles can happen to anyone—especially at Christmastime.

Heartwarming and inspiring, The Color of a Christmas Miracle is the tale of one woman's journey to find happiness, and to learn the power of forgiveness and redemption on the path to true love.

About the Author

Julianne MacLean is a *USA Today* bestselling author of many historical romances, including The Highlander Series with St. Martin's Press and her popular American Heiress Series with Avon/Harper Collins. She also writes contemporary mainstream fiction, and The Color of Heaven was a *USA Today* bestseller. She is a three-time RITA finalist, and has won numerous awards, including the Booksellers' Best Award, the Book Buyer's Best Award, and a Reviewers' Choice Award from Romantic Times for Best Regency Historical of 2005. She lives in Nova Scotia with her husband and daughter, and is a dedicated member of Romance Writers of Atlantic Canada. Please visit Julianne's website for more information and to subscribe to her mailing list to stay informed about upcoming releases.

www.juliannemaclean.com

OTHER BOOKS BY
JULIANNE MACLEAN

The American Heiress Series
To Marry the Duke
An Affair Most Wicked
My Own Private Hero
Love According to Lily
Portrait of a Lover
Surrender to a Scoundrel

The Pembroke Palace Series
In My Wildest Fantasies
The Mistress Diaries
When a Stranger Loves Me
Married By Midnight
A Kiss Before the Wedding – A Pembroke Palace Short Story
Seduced at Sunset

The Highlander Trilogy
The Rebel – A Highland Short Story
Captured by the Highlander
Claimed by the Highlander
Seduced by the Highlander
Return of the Highlander
Taken by the Highlander

The Royal Trilogy

Be My Prince
Princess in Love
The Prince's Bride

Dodge City Brides Trilogy

Mail Order Prairie Bride
Tempting the Marshal
Taken by the Cowboy – a Time Travel Romance

Colonial Romance

Adam's Promise

Contemporary Fiction

The Color of Heaven
The Color of Destiny
The Color of Hope
The Color of a Dream
The Color of a Memory
The Color of Love
The Color of the Season
The Color of Joy
The Color of Time
The Color of Forever
The Color of a Promise
The Color of a Christmas Miracle
The Color of a Silver Lining

CPSIA information can be obtained
at www.ICGtesting.com
Printed in the USA
FFOW02n1254090418
46216985-47528FF